Madam X

Madam X

NIOBIA BRYANT

KENSINGTON PUBLISHING CORP.
www.kensingtonbooks.com

DAFINA BOOKS are published by

Kensington Publishing Corp.
119 West 40th Street
New York, NY 10018

All Kensington titles, imprints, and distributed lines are available at special quantity discounts for bulk purchases for sales promotion, premiums, fundraising, and educational or institutional use.

Special book excerpts or customized printings can also be created to fit specific needs. For details, write or phone the office of the Kensington Sales Manager: Kensington Publishing Corp., 119 West 40th Street, New York, NY 10018. Attn. Sales Department. Phone: 1-800-221-2647.

The Dafina logo is a trademark of Kensington Publishing Corp.

ISBN: 978-1-4967-3072-5
First Trade Paperback Printing: May 2023

ISBN: 978-1-4967-3074-9 (e-book)
First Electronic Edition: May 2023

10 9 8 7 6 5 4 3 2 1

Printed in the United States of America

For my ancestors.

"Rather than love, than money, than fame, give me truth."
—Henry David Thoreau

Madam X

Prologue

January

"*Hello, everyone. I am Maria Vargas, your new host of* Celebrity Spotlight, *and let's get right to our explosive top story.* NBA *superstar Marquis "MQ" Sanders, considered one of the greatest basketball players of all time, has revealed in his autobiography* My Game, My Way *that his success on the court is due in part to his lengthy dealings with a top madam who made sure his every sexual need was met.*

"*Sanders goes into intimate details of a few of his encounters with high-priced courtesans, including a threesome just before the NBA finals last year. It's important to note that although Sanders is currently unwed, he has been involved in a year-long relationship with social media influencer Chai. Here's the couple leaving Catch LA last night as paparazzi unsuccessfully attempt to get a statement.*

"Celebrity Spotlight *reached out to Sanders's rep about revealing the identity of the madam and they issued the following statement: 'Mr. Sanders used his autobiography to reveal his truth. Everything he wanted to say has been said within the pages of his book. Concerning his personal life, there is nothing more to add.'*

"Interesting indeed. *Stay tuned as we continue to investigate this story and perhaps one day reveal the identity of the person we are calling Madam X . . . for now."*

Chapter One

Loyalty should beget loyalty.

Desdemona Dean picked up the pace of her run on the treadmill as she focused on the splendid view of the early winter morning in New York. Anger led to her picking up the pace to a grueling run for the last mile of her daily five-mile goal. The modern and spacious gym was one of the amenities she enjoyed in the prewar, sixteen-story luxury building in the Murray Hill section of Midtown Manhattan—still, it did not compare to the routine she enjoyed during her stay in the Tribeca eighty-two-story high-rise building that was part five-star hotel, part luxury residences. There, when she was done with cardio, she would've enjoyed a session in the sauna and a deep massage in the spa before ordering delicious French cuisine from room service.

It had been a sweet lifestyle, but by selling that condo and downsizing to another two months ago, Desdemona had made a fiscally sound move—along with being careful with her savings, lessening jewelry splurges, and relying heavily on the success of her evening wear boutique.

The type of freedom I'm enjoying at thirty-five was worth any cost.

Desdemona slowed the treadmill to a stop and pressed her eyes closed in a weak attempt to leave her past in the past.

And for the last year and a half, I did just that. My goal was to enjoy life to the fullest.

With deep breaths meant to calm, she picked up the burner flip phone that cost less than a hot dog and a drink. Her hand gripped the phone tight enough to snap the cheap plastic. There was nothing she wanted more than the right number to call. But she didn't have it. The last one she knew was deactivated.

"Shit," she swore, snatching her towel from the handle-bar of the treadmill to pat down her sweat in the white running unitard that clung to her curves.

"Can you believe he admitted that?" a woman said.

"OMG! A threesome. Too juicy," another chimed in.

"I'm buying his book."

"With all the secrets he dropping, me too!"

Desdemona shifted her gaze to the two women standing near the treadmill. They both were looking down at a touch screen phone.

Motherfucker. Mo-ther-fuck-ah!

She took long strides away from the gossip to cross the gym, feeling her waist-length hair fall from its loose topknot to float around her shoulders and down her back.

"Hello, beautiful," a male voice called over to her.

She was used to that and gave him a polite but distant smile as she pushed against the frosted glass door. She barely noted the elegant décor of the wide hall as she pressed the button for the wrought-iron elevator. Once she stepped on the lift it couldn't rise fast enough for her. Time had been moving at a slower pace lately.

Desdemona's heart pounded with ferocity as the doors opened to the floor of her condo. Then she admitted to the fear that was blended with her anger She stepped off onto the polished floors but paused for a moment, feeling weakness in her legs and a tightness in her belly.

Is this the beginning of the end?

But she remembered who she was and stiffened her spine as she locked her legs. She had overcome far too much in her life to crumble now. Especially because of the actions of someone else.

"This too shall pass," she whispered. "Best believe *that* shit."

Desdemona made her way down the brightly lit hall to the condo. Although there were just four apartments on each of the dozen floors, the move had also led to a loss of nearly six hundred square feet. She unlocked the double front doors and entered, pausing in the foyer to take in the beauty. Sixteen hundred square feet. Open floor plan. Floor-to-ceiling windows. Eleven-foot ceilings. Five-inch-wide solid wood flooring. Modern fireplace. Beautiful décor. Stunning views. It was pure luxury. Hard-earned. Well deserved.

And so very far from the fifteen-year-old girl who ran away from home straight into homelessness.

And worse.

She rushed across the great room to stand before the windows. Her emotions held her captive. Betrayal had a way of doing that—evoking fear, bitterness, and sadness—especially after years of being the keeper of secrets that could have quadrupled her worth. She had offered nothing but loyalty and protection. In return, she expected nothing less.

And with that thought, the anger clawed its way with a vengeance on top of the other emotions.

"Son of a bitch!" she snapped, looking down at the phone still clutched in her grasp.

Now she did turn and fling it into her unlit fireplace to crash and shatter.

Fuck it.

That morning when she purchased that one, she had gone to three other places to buy three more. Each hard for the authorities to directly trace back to her.

And this too shall pass.

Desdemona's life had been a series of overcoming challenges, and so far, she had taken down each one by one.

Losing my mother at five.

And then my father at ten.

She turned to lean back against the window as she opened the locket that hung around her neck from a long, thin diamond chain. It held a picture of her at the age of one with her parents, Daniel and Portia—a gift from her father when her mother passed. Recently, she had the gold encrusted with diamonds to match all of her other expensive trinkets.

If only our life had been as perfect as it seemed in this photo.

Her mother had been her father's mistress, and when she passed away, he presented his kindergarten-age daughter to his wife, Zena, and begged not only for her forgiveness but for her help in raising her. That would be a bitter pill for any woman to swallow. But Zena's façade of love and acceptance of Desdemona faded to cruelty upon his death—particularly when she learned he had left the bulk of his estate to his daughter and she would benefit only from Desdemona being her ward.

The next five years had burst with hurt and a unique hell of open scorn from her stepmother until Desdemona ran away at fifteen, when she felt her stepmother would kill her to get her hands on the inheritance.

And then the shit really hit the fan . . .

Desdemona released a heavy breath and crossed the living room to the large, L-shaped chef's kitchen to remove a bottle of her favorite wine, a French 2001 Château Rieussec, from the custom refrigerated wine cabinet. She opened it and poured only a little of the sweet drink into a crystal goblet before turning to lean against the marble countertop that matched the backsplash and island. She finished the pour in one deep sip. Just enough to take off the edge but still leave her clearheaded.

It's not the time to be off my game.

She set the glass on the counter. As she crossed the distance from the kitchen to the foyer, she gathered her hair up into a tight topknot. From the hall closet, she pulled out a full-length, chevron-quilted, puffy down jacket with a fur-lined hood and the monogrammed designer tote she'd carried the day before. By the time she made it out of the condo and back down on the elevator to the underground garage, she longed for the days at her old building, when she used a tablet to alert the valet that she wanted her vehicle. Her metallic-black Maserati Levante GranLusso would have been awaiting her in front of the building with the heat on and the seats ready to warm her bottom. Instead, she used the key fob from across the garage to automatically start the engine as she took long, quick strides to reach her assigned parking spot.

The music on her SiriusXM station was playing when she opened the door and slid onto the leather seat.

"Okay, let's get back into this bombshell autobiography that dropped yesterday because MQ is straight wildin' right now," the *male radio host said, his voice filled with the bravado of a New York accent. "Yo, Marquis, I need Madam X's number. Yo, he's the plug. Shit. Hook us up because page 238 is goals."*

"I'll pass," the woman announcer chimed in.

"Let's take it to the audience. If you have read the book call 1-888-555-HEAT. We want to know if there is any amount of money that would make you get down with Marquis Sanders like

page 238. If you don't have the book, go buy it. Shit wild yo. Mad wild!"

Desdemona eyed the dashboard—hard—before she reached over to turn off the radio.

Her iPhone vibrated inside her bag, but she ignored it. She was in no mood for pleasantries of any kind from anyone. Desdemona made the drive to the large, national chain bookstore on the corner. She snagged a tight parking spot around the corner and strode up the street to enter the two-story building. She came to a stop at the large display of hardcover books right near the front of the store. There was a life-size cutout of him in all-black basketball gear, with his tattoo-covered, muscled arms exposed as he wore the sneakers named after him. Numerous championship rings on his fingers, a cocky smile on his lean and angular, handsome face.

Her heart hammered as she moved through the crowd surrounding the display to grab a copy of the book.

"Listen to this part, Madge," an elderly woman's voice said. "'When Angel saw me naked for the first time, her eyes were big and she—'"

"She what?" Madge asked. "What did *she* do?"

I looked at his dick and told him it was too big.

Desdemona clutched the book and eased through the crowd to reach the long line. Nearly everyone had a copy of the book—and some had numerous copies. Like all of his endeavors, the book would be a roaring success. *Damn*, she mouthed, raising her hand to pinch the bridge of her nose.

It had been a long time since she'd been called Angel—an alias known only by her tricks and johns.

Things she had long since forgotten came rushing back to her. Causing anxiety. Racing pulse. Nervous stomach. Old pains felt searing. Buried secrets fighting to the surface.

She winced as she thought of Majig, her brutal pimp, lying on the floor of his bedroom with a syringe in his arm as his life faded from an overdose.

I let him die.

After running away from a home that felt more like an emotional prison, the coming of the night had called for finding new places to seek shelter. It was in a twenty-four-hour laundromat that she met Majig. He seduced her with his smile and pampered her with his money...before telling her she owed him back for every cent and would repay him by selling herself to men of his choosing.

His physical and mental abuse of her and the other young girls he lured into his trap had no limit.

Saving him would've meant choosing captivity for myself.

After three years she had had more than enough of his shit.

"Turn to page 236," a woman said with urgency.

"You sure that's what they said on the radio?" another woman asked.

Desdemona stiffened at the whispered voices behind her. There was no escape.

His mouth is as big as his dick.

"Oh wow, MQ get down like *that?*"

Desdemona was tempted but fought the urge to see just what freaky frolicking had been revealed. She knew his every delectation very well and so it could be any number of things, including anilingus.

"The butt, though?"

So, it was about the rim jobs.

"He wouldn't have to pay me," one of the women said.

"You'd be on call?" the other asked.

"Whenever. Wherever. And *whatever.*"

Desdemona opened the first page of the book, hoping to

tune the chatty women out. "*'For my true love. I have nothing to hide,'*" she mouthed as she read the dedication. "*'This is the last hoorah for my past so that* we *can focus on* our *future.'*"

She rolled her eyes, unable to deny herself the immature act.

Feeling her anger and annoyance quickly rise, Desdemona dug her wallet out of her tote and pulled out several crisp hundred-dollar bills as she stepped out of line and walked to the nearest open register. People behind her immediately began to protest and complain—New Yorkers would have it no other way.

She held up the money. "I'm paying for my book and the books of the eleven people that *were* in front of me," she said loudly, setting the book and the cash on the counter as the noise ceased and the people rushed to stand in line behind her.

A few offered thanks, most did not. Desdemona didn't care either way. She just wanted out of the bookstore ASAP.

The cashier rang her up quickly and slid the book into a paper bag. "And keep any change," Desdemona told the young woman before taking the bag and taking long strides to leave the store.

The winter winds whipped around her and she stood still, seeking calm as anxiety rose again. And for a brief moment, she was able to block out the familiar noises of the city, thoughts of Marquis "MQ" Sanders's tell-all book and her desire to wring his fucking neck.

"Hey, Desi."

Desdemona opened her eyes and turned on the street with a smile for her friend and neighbor. Melissa Colbert was crossing the street with her fawn-colored French bulldog trotting at her feet. The petite, thirtysomething Samoan beauty was the first friend Desdemona had dared to have. Ever.

"Hello. You off today?" Desdemona asked, knowing the

advertising executive was dedicated to her profession and had been rewarded with a quick ascension up the ranks to vice president at the Manhattan firm where she worked.

"I wish. My dog walker couldn't make it today so I came home for an early lunch to walk Frenchie," Melissa said, holding up the leash. "What about you? What are you up to today? You going to your showroom for your online boutique?"

"Classes start tomorrow, so I'm just relaxing," she said, thankful as she realized Melissa was the first person she'd encountered who wasn't enthralled by Marquis's autobiography.

"Annnnnnd?" Melissa said as Frenchie trotted around her feet.

Desdemona arched a brow. "And?"

"Your major? Where are you with that?" Melissa asked before stooping to stroke Frenchie's shiny coat.

Desdemona released a breath. "Nothing yet," she admitted, knowing it was a choice she would have to make, and soon, to ensure none of her time, credits, or money were wasted on classes that might not count toward her major.

"Not even a business degree?" Melissa asked. "It could help you grow your boutique."

Desdemona gave her a soft smile and shook her head. "I thought about it, but that's not my purpose, and I want to align my education with my purpose," she said. "That's the *only* thing I do know."

"Meet with your academic adviser," Melissa suggested before letting Frenchie lead her by the leash down the street toward the dog park. She looked back over her shoulder. "Let's plan dinner for the weekend. Benji will be back in town tonight."

"Will do," Desdemona agreed before making her way down the snow-lined street to her vehicle.

After starting the ignition, Desdemona sat and stared off into the distance, remembering being teased in high school when rumors of her being a prostitute had reached her last safe place. And she had wanted so badly to graduate one day. Shame and ridicule had snatched that from her.

"I heard you selling ass at night. Can I get a freebie?"

She closed her eyes and fought off tears as the memory of her sneakered feet beating against the floor of the hall as she ran from school echoed. Finding a price list of tricks she would turn on the school board had been the final insult.

"Fuck you, Marquis," she said.

His trip down memory lane in his book had shoved her back into things she hadn't thought about in a long time.

Like becoming Angel.

Her days as a streetwalker were a trauma she was still fighting to overcome. Late nights and hours of walking in heat, snow, and rain. Johns and tricks. Hand jobs. Blow jobs. Rim jobs. And much more. Much worse. Roughness. Hits and punches. Thefts. Rapes. Perversions. Abuses. Of all kinds.

Jesus. Thank God I made it. Some did not.

Murder, drug use, or jail had claimed many a soul.

Desdemona checked for oncoming traffic before she exited her parking spot to make the short trip back to her building. Soon she parked and gripped the book encased by the paper bag as she rode one of the elevators up to her floor. She was thankful to be alone. Her thoughts were full.

The ramifications of Marquis's actions could be irrevocable.

How could he do it?

She had asked herself that question a thousand times and never come up with an answer that settled well on her shoulders. This felt like a betrayal—another to add to her long list.

Reaching her front door, she used her key to unlock it.

She closed the door and leaned back against it as she pulled the book from the paper bag. She had to see just how much Marquis had revealed and if any of it could lead back to her or any of the other prostitutes who had serviced him during those five years.

Although she thought about taking a shower, like she normally did after her workout, she dropped her coat and tote on the sofa and claimed one of the club chairs flanking the fireplace on the far wall. She tucked her feet beneath her bottom and opened the book.

Briefly, she remembered that two years ago she'd struggled to read. Those days were over and now she got lost in the words, flying through the pages, no longer needing to look up the definition or pronunciation of words. When she finally closed it, she looked up to realize that day had turned to night and there was more of a chill in the air. She rose and used the tablet to ignite the fireplace and raise the lighting throughout the condo.

The book was well-written and Marquis's story of climbing from poverty to prominence was inspiring. Thankfully, his mention of sexual dalliances were few, no major details revealed. For that, she was thankful.

She tossed the book into the fireplace and stared into the flames as she stroked her bottom lip with her thumbnail. She lost count of the moments that passed.

With a heavy breath, she rose and made her way across the living room and down the hall past two bedrooms to the owner's suite. She made a trail behind her with her clothes as she undressed before stepping into the marbled shower to cleanse herself with her favorite Jo Malone London Nectarine Blossom and Honey shower gel. She inhaled deeply of the scent as she fought to remain calm. To think. Strategize. Scheme.

The balls are back.

Foolishly, she'd thought her days of juggling were over. *Think. Think. Think.*

Always plotting five steps or more ahead. Maintaining alliances. Keeping secrets. Covering steps.

Constantly.

Desdemona stood naked before the mirror as she pulled her hair back from her face and let raw vulnerability fill her eyes. All her life she had been told she was pretty—and at times she was disliked because of it. She once wore her hair with blond streaks but now settled for ebony to frame her heart-shaped face and doe-shaped eyes, surrounded by thick lashes and a pouty mouth above her small, dimpled chin.

Beauty had not shielded her from a world that could be ugly and brutal.

For twenty years of her life, she had been in the sex trade.

She had successfully avoided arrest by being savvy and strategic. She had always thought five steps ahead. Every move was well thought out. Like warfare. Tell this. Keep that. Do this. Don't do that. Juggling each and every ball. Trusting no one and nothing.

Twenty years.

It was a long time to live with your guard up.

A very long time.

Desdemona stepped inside her walk-in closet. There, atop the center island, all her diamonds were on display. She preferred them that way instead of hidden away in her safe. She wanted to see them. Touch them. The trappings of wealth. And her armor. Wearing them was a show of her success, from poverty to prosperity.

But during her climb from the gutter, she had lost *so* much.

She trailed her fingers across the bracelets, watches, rings, and necklaces nestled atop the black velvet. Needing her armor, she adorned herself with all of it before she walked out into the hall in front of the seven-foot mirror leaning against the wall. The glitter of the jewels against her brown nudity was nearly blinding. Fifty pieces or more. Millions of dollars.

She kissed her palm before pressing it to the portrait tattoo of her mother on her right shoulder. *What would she think of my life?*

Angel was the name she used as a streetwalker and Marquis had been her first celebrity trick—in fact, he had introduced her to the world of wealthy and prominent clients.

From streetwalker to high-end call girl to...

"Hey, baby."

With her heart still pounding with fear of her secret being exposed, she turned to find the love of her life, Dr. Loren Marc Palmer. Or Lo, as she called him. And he was a handsome man. Today he wore his wild mane of shoulder-length, jet-black curls in two neat braids. With his medium brown complexion, his dark, slanted eyes seemed even more intense. His tall frame was slender but well defined and fit. He was a sneakerhead who preferred casual clothing, but he was versatile and looked sexy in his suit and tie—his normal wear when he was an English professor at the university she attended.

They now lived together. She had given her body to many when she prostituted herself for survival, but he was the first—and only—man she had given her heart. The last six months had conquered all fears she had about the differences between them working against them. She had truly begun to believe their love would last forever.

Until now.

"I know you like being naked, but the diamonds are a bit much, babe," he teased in his deep voice before crossing the closet to pull her close.

Desdemona's eyes searched his as she pressed her hands to

his back and enjoyed the feel of his touch against her body. The heat between them always came in a rush. Simply undeniable.

They'd gone from tutor and tutee as she prepared to take her GED test, to friends and then lovers when she agreed to teach him to be a better sexual partner.

She smiled up at him.

Loren returned the gesture. As his eyes studied hers, his face filled with concern. "What's wrong?" he asked.

Oh, Lo. My sweet Lo.

He was always so in tune with her. He missed nothing. He neglected not one thing.

Desdemona raised up on her toes to press a kiss to both corners of his mouth before wrapping her arms around his neck. "Nothing, Lo," she lied with softness before pressing her face against his neck.

The pounding of his pulse beat against her lips. She kissed him there and his hold tightened.

Tell him.

Panic seized at her heart.

He'll leave.

And now Desdemona held him tighter.

This amazing man, scholar, artist, and forever optimist who was ten years her junior had entered her life and swelled it with laughter, happiness, a belief in goodness, and adventures. Great—*amazing*—sex. Love. So much love.

And trust, most of all. The one thing she had given him that she'd rarely doled out before. In him, she had found a place to fall and be vulnerable and be loved. It was losing Loren that scared her more than losing her freedom or her wealth. In the last six months, he had become the most important person in her life.

She held his face with her hands. "I love your kisses," she said to him softly.

He smiled and the pockets of his dimples deepened. "I know," he admitted.

Their first lesson in his becoming a great lover had been the art of kissing. "Do you?" she asked as she took his hand in hers and led him to their bedroom.

"Your body is *amazing*," he said from behind her.

She glanced back over her shoulder to find his eyes watching the movement of her buttocks. "I know," she said.

"Do you?" he countered.

He undressed as they continued down the hall, and when they reached the side of their king-size bed, Loren sat on the side and pulled her down to straddle his thighs. "Honestly, the diamonds and your nudity are like some queen shit," he said in wonder with a shake of his head as he cupped her breasts in his hands.

The warmth of his touch caused her to shiver as her nipples hardened.

She undid each of his braids to run her fingers through his deep curls. Their eyes locked and they both smiled as they leaned in to share a kiss. She moaned and shivered at the feel of his mouth before he deepened it with his tongue.

And it was just as delicious as the first time. Their fiery chemistry was undeniable.

She had been celibate for five years before meeting Lo. He was the first man to entice her enough to welcome him into her bed. And the attraction had been on all levels: physical and mental. Each and every time they made love it was intense and electric.

There was no other man who could compare.

No one.

At times, that truth completely blew my mind.

The inches of his dick lengthened with hardness and stood up tall. She embraced his hard heat with both hands and stroked him from root to tip, following the wicked curve. She rose on her knees to ease her throbbing core to sheath him.

They both cried out and they mingled in the air.

Loren pressed his face to her cleavage, kissing each swell, as Desdemona rode him. Slow and easy, with a tight circle of her hips at the tip before gliding back down his length. "Desi, Desi, Desi," he moaned, holding her with one hand splayed on the middle of her back and the other gripping one fleshy buttock.

She closed her eyes and quickened the pace, riding him like it was the last time and fueled by a fear that it just might be. And when Loren turned her over onto her back and delivered one deep and delicious stroke after the other like a well-oiled piston, she looked up into his face and got lost in his dark, intense eyes.

"I love you. I love you *so* much," she whispered up to him.

His eyes studied hers just before he dipped his head to taste her lips. Over and over again. Like tiny blessings. "You are the love of my life," he said against her mouth in between heated kisses.

Tears rose as she was overcome with one explosive climax and then another.

Please don't let us end.

Never had she felt so afraid and desperate.

Thankfully, Marquis had not revealed that Angel had gone on to become Mademoiselle via the powerful connections made through him. In his book, he had put her at risk, yanking her from the privacy she'd carefully crafted over the last seventeen years of her life. No one knew the real name or identity of Mademoiselle—she had made sure of that by putting many safeguards in place. Still, she had always known it might not be her own crimes that would lead to her arrest. The possibility had always existed that a consort would expose her or trade her in to save themself.

Long after their explosive climaxes left them spent and clinging to each other in the middle of their bed, Desdemona thought of her secret. She felt some of the light dim in her eyes. At the start of their relationship, Loren agreed to accept that there were things about her life she could *never* reveal to him; she knew he would never—could never—accept her truth.

I am Madam X.

Chapter Two

One week later

Marquis Sanders hitched the strap of his duffel bag over his head to cross his body as he walked up the tunnel of the coliseum. He wore a black do-rag and a hoodie with AirPods in his ears as he moved toward the waiting SUV with long strides. Twice he stopped to shoot imaginary free throws before opening the rear door and swinging the duffel inside in front of him.

"Hello, Number 1," Desdemona said to him, removing the shades she wore from her place on the rear seat.

Marquis froze as his eyes widened at the surprising sight of her. "Angel," he said, his voice as deep as the sharp angles of his face.

"Mademoiselle," she corrected him.

None of her johns, tricks, or consorts knew her real name. For a long time she yearned to be called by her given name of Desdemona—but understood the extra layer of protection it offered her. As a madam, she assigned each consort a number to maintain their privacy and assigned them each a burner phone to be used exclusively to contact her. As her first consort of wealth and prominence, Marquis Sanders had been Number 1. At one point she'd had as many as a hundred consorts on her client list and had successfully memorized each like, dislike, and sexual preference, and had held their secrets. Protected them.

His eyes searched the vicinity.

"We're alone," Desdemona told him with a forced smile while waving a hand for him to join her inside *his* vehicle.

He paused.

"Loyalty deserves loyalty," Desdemona said as he folded his six-foot-nine frame into the seat and closed the door.

"Still beautiful as ever," he said with a toothy smile that raised his high cheekbones as he took in the fluffy mink she wore over a formfitting black leather dress and ankle boots.

Desdemona only wore dresses. As a streetwalker, dresses and skirts meant easy access and easy cleanup. Perfection for a whore on the go. Over time, what started as a function became more about fashion.

"Cut the bullshit. You put me in jeopardy, motherfucker," she said, her voice hard and unrelenting as she pierced him with a hard stare.

"No. I told my truth, and my days using your services is a part of *my* truth," Marquis said.

"Fuck *that* and fuck *you*. You wanted to sell books. Be number one. I guess the championship wasn't enough. Huh?" she asked, fighting the urge to reach inside her crocodile Birkin for her Taser.

She hadn't needed to carry any type of weapon since she let the pussy game go.

Marquis wiped his face with his hand and shook his head.

"How long after I retired did you get the book deal?" Desdemona asked.

"You trippin', Angel—"

"Don't call me that," she snapped.

Angel used to sell herself. Mademoiselle never did.

"A year ago," he admitted.

"Six months after I retired," she corrected him, after counting back the months on the tips of her fingers in the leather gloves she wore to ensure she left no fingerprints behind. She reached over to grip his chin tightly. "One of the things I offered clients like you, outside of women I trained to fuck each of you *properly*—to be whatever you all needed them to be for the hour, night, weekend, or longer—was my protection. I am the keeper of secrets. There was no amount I could be paid to reveal any of you in any way. And you all paid a high fee for the coverage."

"Ang—"

She growled as she gripped his lips into her fist. "Shut the fuck up," she snapped with fiery eyes. "Play *any* role in revealing my identity further and I cannot offer you my protection any longer. We both know there are things I could reveal to *destroy* you."

Desdemona had risked a face-to-face confrontation with Marquis to make sure he knew how serious she was. The desire for a second bestseller might lead to him exposing the sought-after identity of the notorious Madam X.

The press was still ravenous for the identity of the un-known madam. The speculation about the madam's identity ran the gamut from Z-list celebrities, a group of sexy reality TV stars, Hollywood movie producers, and even members of a sorority. Feeling angry with him, she released a noise of frustration, and nudged his head backward before releasing his mouth.

Any hope of the frenzy dying down was futile.

Just fucking ridiculous.

He had peeled back the veil shielding the secrets of the wealthy and influential like blood dropped into a cesspool of sharks.

"I deserved better from you, Marquis," she said, using his

name for the first time in a long time before sliding on her shades.

"There was not one inch of pussy you gave me for free, Mademoiselle," he reminded her.

Her hand paused on the door handle. "And if I knew your mouth was as loose as your asshole, I would have charged more," she said, demanding—and receiving—his silence in return.

Desdemona left the vehicle and raised her shoulders to adjust her fur as she walked up the length of the tunnel. Marquis's longtime driver, Carlisle—dressed in all black—leaned against the wall while he gave them privacy. He pushed off the wall at her approach.

"I told him he fucked up," he said to her as they passed each other.

"Big damn time," she returned before continuing to walk away.

As both MQ's chauffeur and security, Carlisle was paid well, and with a recommendation from Marquis, he'd made it onto her client list. Once a year he'd splurged for a weekend ménage à trois.

It was one of the major keys to her success as a multi-millionaire madam. New consorts needed a recommendation from another consort in good standing and then had to pass a deep vetting and provide proof of a clean physical. She had required the same of any of her courtesans. Violence and drug use were prohibited from both. None of the women were forced to work for her and she had always encouraged them to use it as means to an end, not a lifelong goal. Among her ex-courtesans, Mademoiselle counted attorneys, doctors, lawyers, models, and business owners.

She had never been to her courtesans what Majig had been to her—violent, demeaning, and cruel. She offered them the same privacy and protection as the consorts.

So much that I lost myself in the process.

Desdemona released a deep sigh as she retraced her steps to reach her vehicle, left in a parking garage several blocks from the arena. Making contact with Marquis had been a risk, but she had implemented a lot of her old tricks of the trade to avoid leaving a trace.

Bzzzzzz.

She pulled the vibrating iPhone from the pocket of her coat. It was Lo. She was constantly amazed that just a call or text from him sent her heart pounding faster. "Hello," she said after answering, turning down the radio and placing the call on Speaker.

"Hey, baby," Loren said, his voice deep.

"Hey, you."

"I'm home. What you up to?" he asked.

She thought he would be on campus all day, teaching classes and in a faculty meeting. "I–I–I had to go into my showroom today," she lied, her grip on the steering wheel tightening.

"Cool. How about I cook dinner and when you get here you let me eat my Desi dessert?"

Loren's sexual appetite was voracious—a benefit of a younger man who, thankfully, couldn't get enough of her.

"That sounds good," she said, eyeing the time on the dashboard. "Let me finish up here for the day and then I'm headed straight to you."

"Sounds like a plan. Be careful; the snow is getting heavy, so the roads might not be safe."

Desdemona lightly bit down on her bottom lip to keep from releasing a sigh heavy with guilt. This was the first time she had lied to Loren during their relationship and he was a solid man with passion and vision who always had her back. He loved her and loved on her. In every way possible.

"I'll be careful, Lo," she said softly before ending the call as she started her drive toward the interstate.

The six-hour trip back to New York gave Desdemona time for reflection. With the soft hint of a smile, she remembered the pure joy of cutting ties with everything and everyone—including Lo—and traveling the world for a year, focused on discovering herself and enjoying being addressed by her real name for the first time since before she ran away from Zena's home.

Desdemona Dean.

Not Angel. Not Mademoiselle. And not Alisha Smith— an alias complete with credentials thanks to a hefty price tag.

It was as Ms. Smith she was first introduced to Loren as her GED tutor, and he was none the wiser about her moniker until the day she discovered he was the professor of her college English class. Afterward, she had approached him, feeling as if nothing but fate had brought them back into each other's lives, and saw the same surprise she'd felt at the start of the class.

Desdemona pressed her free hand to her chest as her heart pounded and raced just like it had that day six months before.

"Great class, Dr. Palmer," she said before coming down the steps to the front of the lecture hall.

"Were you in this class the whole time?" he asked, after clearing his throat and removing his glasses.

She nodded.

"Your name isn't on the register," he said, looking down at a paper on his desk.

"It is. You just don't know my real name," she admitted before she extended her hand. "Desdemona Dean."

Loren took a step back in surprise. "Oh, so when you said there was so much I didn't know . . . that was an understatement."

After a year it had felt good to be near him again. To see the love he had for her in his eyes. Their differences—age and viewpoints—no longer mattered. With Loren, she wanted to dream of forever.

"Madam, may I love you?"

"With all you have."

Desdemona tensed at the memory, that he had no clue she was indeed a madam at the time. No idea at all.

The truth will destroy us.

Once before they had happened upon a conversation about prostitution and sex trafficking.

"You don't feel a woman has the right to do what she wants with her body?" she asked him after he'd shown such disdain for a madam—who he'd called a female pimp, selling souls for the sake of money.

"Of course I do, but there are a lot of women who believe their only worth is between their thighs and many who are forced into prostitution via sex trafficking. Not to mention the kids in the middle, who think they're in control of their bodies and foolishly don't realize they are being used and demeaned. No one should be paid for sex. It's revolting."

His scorn and judgment were burned into her memory.

"You do understand that the ones who agree to prostitute themselves and give off this ridiculous notion of empowerment help to create a culture in which men think all women and gay men want to be sexualized?" Loren had asked with an incredulous expression. "Thus leading to assholes willing to trick, kidnap, or brutalize someone else into selling themselves. One begets the other."

Desdemona had begged off any further debates and arguments because she couldn't properly defend herself—her actions—without revealing her secret to him. Instead, she brought their tutoring sessions to an end—both for her GED test and schooling him on being a great lover.

Loren discovering she was Madam X would be about more than how many dicks she had fucked and sucked. She halfway believed he could forgive her prostituting herself— *maybe.* It was her role as a madam that he could not swallow.

He would hate me.

She gnawed a bit at her bottom lip. And sometimes she hated herself. Was what Loren thought true?

"One begets the other."

Looking for a diversion, she turned on the radio with the volume loud, forcing herself to sing along with R&B slow songs as she finished the rest of the ride home. As she pulled into the underground parking garage, she found a space next to Loren's twenty-year-old Chevy Tahoe. The only things of value on it were the expensive rims and updated audio system. It had close to two hundred thousand miles on it, with cracked leather seats, and a lot of the features no longer worked properly.

But Loren loved it.

She had offered to help him purchase a new luxury vehicle but he declined, just like he insisted on paying some bills—mostly the utilities because the condo was paid for. Still, she loved his independence and that he did not want to feel *kept.*

"I have more to offer you than just hard dick."

Desdemona smiled as she left her vehicle and crossed the space to the elevator. Thankfully, there were no stops, and she rode up to her floor alone. When she reached the double doors and unlocked them, she was excited to see him. Be near him. Have him.

The scent of his spicy chili swelled in the air. It was the first meal he'd cooked for her in his little studio apartment when he was still a doctoral student. She removed her fur and hung it in the closet on a wood hanger with wide shoulders, remembering that was also the first time she'd braided his hair and he offered to eat her out. Slowly. With intensity. And heat.

Her climax had been explosive.

"Grade, please?" he had asked with his slanted eyes twinkling.

"B-b-b-b-b-b-b-b plus," she'd said with effort, in between harsh breaths and trembling thighs.

He chuckled. "I'll get that A the next time," he promised.

And he had worked at it until he was that skillful.

She taught him to be the *very* best.

Her clit throbbed to life, wanting to feel his tongue and mouth.

"Lo," she called as she unzipped her boots and began to undress, leaving the black garments on the floor as she searched for him.

"In the bathroom," he called back from the owner's suite.

Barefoot and naked, she paused.

Wait.

Every bathroom moment wasn't meant for sharing…

"Come here, babe," he called to her.

Desdemona arched a brow before continuing down the hall past the guest bedroom and to the open double doors of the suite. She ignored Loren's suit and shoes piled at the foot of the bed and moved to lean against the frame of the bathroom door. Her sultry smile turned into a frown.

Loren was in the tub, filled with steaming water, reading a book. *That* book.

Marquis's photo on the cover seemed to wink at her. Mockingly.

"Join me?" Loren asked as he closed the book and set it down on the heated floor next to the double-size soaking tub.

She forced a smile and tried to forget that her man—the love of her life—was a huge Marquis Sanders fan. *Huge.* Wore-the-official-jersey, watched-every-game, knew-all-the-stats, and was-just-short-of-buying-a-poster-to-put-on-the-wall level fan of "MQ."

Buy-his-favorite-sports-star's-autobiography type fan? Yes.

Loren slipped down beneath the clear water for a quick

dip before emerging with his wild hair now wet and plastered to his head.

Would he be a happy-to-fuck-the-same-woman-MQ-had-banged level fan?

She shook her head as if to clear it of her thoughts as she walked over to him, loving the way his slanted eyes took in her body like a hawk—as if seeing it for the first time. With awe and desire. When she reached the side of the tub, she used her foot to kick the book away. It spun across the floor to land behind the commode.

Just where the bullshit belongs.

"Where are the bubbles?" she asked as she stepped in the tub, soon releasing a soft moan at the feel of the hot water against her body as she sank beneath the depths until it gently teased the tip of her chin.

"I want to be able to see every bit of you," Loren said, raising his strong legs to bend one over each side of the freestanding tub.

"Same," she said softly, wrapping a hand around his dick to stroke him from thick root to smooth tip.

He draped his sinewy, tattooed arms over the sides as well and let his head fall back, exposing the length of his throat and his newest ink—her name in cursive from one pulse point to the other.

Love for him flooded her until she was overwhelmed with emotion.

Never had she thought she would love or be loved like this.

He hardened in her hands with ease, letting her know he was aroused and ready to please. Built for it. Built for her. "I don't know which will be better." She sighed as she eyed him. "This bath, the chili, or the lovemaking."

Loren chuckled, causing his Adam's apple to bob a bit. "Definitely the chili," he said with his eyes closed.

"It is *really* good chili," she agreed.

That caused him to open one eye to look at her.

She laughed.

He raised his head with a jerk, as if something had just occurred to him. "Babe, MQ's book is wild," he said, his eyes wide and bright.

Desdemona could only hope she covered her sudden unease well enough. "Oh yeah?" she asked, keeping her tone light and casual as she continued to stroke him, hoping the heat of hot sex would make him forget MQ.

Fuck him. The M and the Q.

Loren glanced back over his shoulder at the book, still wedged against the commode.

"Focus on us, Lo," Desdemona urged.

He shifted his gaze back to her. "Sorry. The writing is good. Really good. And the story of his path to basketball and the people who influenced him is clutch," he said, even as his handsome face became lined with annoyance. "But giving such credence to buying pussy to celebrate wins or relax pregame is just some bullshit. He brags about it. Like a badge of honor."

Desdemona rolled her eyes and released a heavy breath as she freed his hardness and leaned back to rest her head against the tub's edge.

Here the fuck we go.

"What?" he asked.

"I'd rather fuck than worry about who Marquis Sanders is fucking and how much it cost him," she said, locking eyes with him.

Again, Loren looked back to glance at the book, as if he desired it more than her at that moment. "It's not lining up with the clean-cut image he had," he said. "How much of it all is bullshit when he out here promoting prostitution and applauding this Madam X like she helped his career. Like, what the fuck?"

I am Madam X.

"Sex with a grown, consenting woman hardly makes him a pervert, Lo," she snapped, lashing out at feeling judged, insulted, and triggered.

It was Loren who had first introduced her to the idea that prostitution and pornography were two of the causes of the rampant sex trafficking of young women—particularly women of color.

Like I was when Majig tricked me into prostitution, taking advantage of a teenage homeless girl hungry for any kind of stability.

In her mind, the brutality, misogyny, and cruelty she faced with Majig was everything she fought not to be to those who freely chose to work for her.

The consorts she removed from her exclusive list if they were disrespectful or violated one of the courtesans.

The men she handled with the thick end of her retractable baton if she received a call letting her know one of the courtesans was in fear.

She'd gladly lost count of how many courtesans she had helped pay off school loans, medical bills, and other large debts if they no longer wished to work in the pussy game.

Or those she put in rehab and offered a three-month stipend upon completion of the program, even though their use of drugs meant they were off her roster.

There were countless more stories of her trying to help one of her courtesans—male, female, or nonbinary—trying to get ahead. Offering far more than had ever been offered to her.

No, I'm no Majig.

Bottom line, they both sold sex—and for Loren that was all that would ever matter.

One begets the other.

"What I do know is a man doesn't get to *dick*-tate what a grown woman does with her pussy," she said, tired of his high-handed opinions and plagued by guilt that she had been a victim who became a predator.

Shit.

"Come on, Desdemona, think," Loren stressed as he tapped his finger against his temple, his eyes hot with annoyance.

"Think?" she flared with a hard stare. "Just because we don't share the same opinion doesn't make me incapable of using my brain. I am not a dumbass, Loren! Don't do that."

Loren looked taken aback. "Now you're trippin'. This ain't about us."

Desdemona released a bitter laugh. "And the insults continue," she said. "Careful, Professor," she said with coldness as she stood up in the tub and looked down at him. "Even a GED-earning high school dropout like me knows *ain't* isn't proper English, Mr. Perfect."

Water splashed over the side as she stepped out of the tub.

"Wait. What the fuck is goin' on right now?" Loren asked, his face showing his shock.

Desdemona opened the frosted glass door of the shower. "Instead of using the free time, that history degree, and your PhD in creative writing to finish the book you've been working on for a year and a half, you're reading someone else's," she said, grasping at straws, knowing her anger was the fuel for throwing anything and everything at him to injure him the way she felt wounded by him.

Just childish, and I know it.

Loren rose to his feet in the tub.

She eyed the sight of his tall, chiseled frame, now glistening wet with droplets of bathwater racing down the hard contours of his body. She turned her back to him to enter the tiled stall to deny the temptation.

Sexy motherfucker.

Before she started the rainfall shower, she heard him follow, with the water splashing and his wet feet slapping against the tiled floor. Moments later, the door flung open.

"Where'd you pull that from?" Loren asked. "You have a problem with me not working on *my* book?"

Stop it, Desi. Just stop it.

"No, not at all," she admitted as she let the water pelt down on her body before putting on her shower gloves and reaching for her favorite body gel. "I'm pissed because you low-key called me stupid, Lo."

"That's bullshit. Not once did I call you that," he spouted.

She eyed the water dripping from his nude body and pooling around him onto the tiled floor. He released a short, exasperated breath and stepped inside with her beneath the water. "You implied it," she said. "I don't have a bunch of degrees or teach college courses, but I am not stupid, Lo. I am *far* from stupid. Clever, in fact. Street smart. Bursting with common sense. Not to be taken lightly. Okay?"

His eyes studied hers as the water beat against them. She could tell he saw something in the depths that made him take her very seriously. "I know that, Desi," he assured her, his voice deep and filled with reassurances that she didn't need from him because she meant—and believed—what she said.

"I wish I knew more about you," he added, reaching to take the soap from her hand.

No, you don't.

She took it back from him, knowing all too well what him lathering her body would lead to. "You finish your bath," she said.

His body stiffened. "Dammmmmmn," he said, drawing it out. "Like *that*?"

In the world they created together, they agreed that nothing messed with their sex. No-thing. Not even if they were annoyed or angry. It was a deal they had—and now it was being tested.

"Desi," he moaned in regret as he looked pointedly down at his dick.

She continued to lather her gloves and rub circles across her body. Breasts, belly, upper thighs, and then the clean-shaven vee she knew he was *hungry* to get into. "Sorry, Lo," she said, gently swiping away his hands when he reached for her. "I thought about it and you're right. It kinda feels like fucking a dude when you're not in the mood to fuck is all sorts of wrong. Kinda like those women needing to feed children or pay their bills or survive and truly feeling they have nothing else of worth so push through and fuck a dude they don't want to fuck. With your high ideals, I'm sure you would understand that whether for money or to keep someone happy in a relationship, you wouldn't want a woman to push through and fuck someone she wasn't in the mood to fuck. *Right?*"

His eyes hardened as he stepped back from her. "Something we agreed on—as a matter of fact, something you suggested—you now twisting into the same as somebody selling they ass. Really, Desi?" he asked, his tone cold. Brutally so.

"Really. It's still transactional...like you tutoring me for my GED in exchange for me teaching you how to make love to a woman," she shot back. "Now I know you believe I have difficulty in *thinking*, but wasn't that transactional?"

"Don't compare yourself to a hoe just to prove a point, Desi," he said heatedly.

A hoe? Motherfucker, I was the top hoe.

She fell silent, realizing she was walking a very thin line that could land her into revealing far more than she was ready to do.

"Fuck it," he said. "No sex, then. Just like everything else, it's all up to you," he muttered before opening the door and escaping the shower, along with the steam.

Arching a brow, she leaned outward to eye him stepping back into the tub. "What's all up to me? Like what?" she asked.

Loren sank into the water. "Where we live, where we go, what we do, keeping secrets," he shot off like a bullet list—ready, loaded, and about to be aimed right at her.

And it succeeded in rocking her. She was stunned. It was the first time he had voiced discontent.

She leaned back in to turn off the shower before stepping out to walk over to him. Naked and shivering—but not from cold. It was from fear. The kind that could evoke a rampage to protect oneself. That deep and visceral terror.

He looked up and locked gazes with her.

Whatever words she had thought to say to defend herself and to fix the wrong between them faded like a fine mist. There, in the dark depths of his eyes, was something akin to the pain of a wounding. "And whether we have a baby, Desi," he added, his voice matching the raw emotion in his eyes.

The words she'd said—the words that obviously wounded him—came back to her. Quickly. As if sitting nearby and waiting to be called upon.

"I don't think I want to have children, Lo."

Before that very moment, he had so very well hidden his true feelings about it. But there it was like a stain—old and faded but still present—marring a perfect piece of linen.

She bent down beside the tub and grabbed his forearm with both hands. His eyes stayed locked on her. Searching. Hoping. She closed her eyes to break the connection. "I thought you understood how I felt," she said softly, also hoping.

"And I thought you would change your mind," Loren countered.

She dared to look at him and his optimism remained—steady and unrelenting. She shook her head, denying him before she could find the strength to say the words to do so. "Lo, we discussed kids in the beginning and I thought we agreed. I thought we felt the same," she said, hating how *everything* seemed to be unraveling. "If I knew I wouldn't have—"

Loren sat up straight. "Wouldn't have what?" he asked.

"Let things get so deep," she admitted, in a voice barely above a whisper.

Loren eyed her for long and countless moments before he nodded and looked away as he shifted his arms to free them of her touch.

Her throat felt tight with emotion. "Lo, I love you so much," she stressed, reaching to stroke the side of his face.

He leaned away from her. "Not too deep, remember," he said with a tinge of sarcasm.

"Lo, we're in it. We love each other. We are building a life together and I couldn't imagine me without you," she admitted unabashedly as she spoke her truth.

He eyed her. "Why?" he asked.

He wasn't clear, but she knew what he asked: why didn't she want children?

For years, as Mademoiselle, she had held up the world, the safety, the well-being, and the protection of so many people, that it wasn't until she retired and traveled that she came to grips with the knowledge that she no longer wanted to be held responsible for someone else's well-being or safety—especially not a child.

But she couldn't say that. It was a revelation she could not make.

"Lo, I have my reasons," she said. "In a perfect world a baby with you would be amazing... if things were different."

The intensity of his stare made her shift with discomfort.

"You won't share your past with me, but it keeps fucking with our future, Desi," he said.

Desdemona pressed her eyes closed. A tear rose and raced down her cheek, and Loren, being her Loren, used his thumb to wipe it away before pressing his hand to the side of her face. She leaned into it. Into him.

Tell him the truth. Win, lose, or draw.

Her body caved under the weight of it all. She dropped down onto her bare bottom and covered her face with her hands. The irony of losing her greatest love because of a horrible past was clawing. A raw and guttural scream escaped and she flung her head back, opened her mind, and gave it life.

Loren rushed from the tub and gathered her trembling body into his arms, pressing kisses along her cheek as he carried her damp body to their bed and lay her down. She curled into the fetal position, wishing in a way that she was a baby in the womb, ready to be birthed into a world where her life was different. Where decisions like having children were effortless. Where having Loren in her life for forever and a day was possible. No secrets. No past. No fear of the loss of freedom. No judgment.

When he started to move away after covering her body with a warm blanket, she blindly reached for him and felt his wrist. With a tight grip, she pulled him down onto the bed beside her. Soon he was spooning her—somehow being both her rock and her cushion.

Chapter Three

Two months later

Desdemona's walk across the university campus was slow as she enjoyed the thaw of snow and a little less chill in the air as spring claimed its turn. She had just left her history class, and although her stomach rumbled and called for a trip to the student center to grab lunch, she had another appointment. Besides, she preferred a stop at a true restaurant with high cuisine rather than burgers or pizza.

Although she was deeply entrenched in her classes, she had no desire for the camaraderie of campus culture. She even chose to forgo casual wear. She liked standing out, even if she did look to be fifteen years or better older than the majority of her classmates. She couldn't care less how well the sports teams were doing. Owned not one piece of paraphernalia with the school logo and generally only spent time on campus for classes before she kept it moving. At thirty-five, hanging around the twenty and under crowd was a hard no. She had lived a dozen lives in comparison to the young ones just leaving home for the first time after graduating high school.

What should we discuss? The highs and lows of prostitution?
That made Desdemona chuckle as she jogged up the stairs into the sleek and broad glass-fronted building. She paused a step in her movement toward the automatic doors when she spotted a brilliantly colorful butterfly resting on the glass. As she neared and the doors slid open, the butterfly fluttered its wing and then briefly landed on her arm before rising into the air.

She looked and turned to watch it until it disappeared from her view. Her heart pounded a bit and she felt a nervous energy.

"Excuse me."

Startled, she lowered her head to see a tall white man with blond hair and green eyes dressed in a sweatshirt and khaki shorts. She was blocking his entrance to the building.

"Sorry," she said, stepping out of his path.

"No worries," he said before entering the building with a look back over his broad shoulders that was filled with appreciation and a bit of flirtation.

The look she gave him said: *Little boy, I would destroy your life. Don't play.*

He gave her a broad smile before continuing across the lobby to jog up the stairs with ease.

And for a moment, Mademoiselle resurfaced. Over the years she had acquired an instinct on studying a new consort and knowing just what he needed to be pleased. It had become a little game of sorts she played, always testing whether her instincts were right. Most times they were.

A plus-size woman of color to fuck, dominate, and comfort him would have made him a loyal customer.

I wonder if I would have been right.

With one last look up at the sky to hopefully catch sight of the butterfly's ascent, she finally turned and entered the building. Were the butterflies just signaling the return of spring...or something more?

When she began to tire of her life as a wealthy madam and fought the boredom seeping in, Desdemona had felt drawn to butterflies—even purchasing a diamond bracelet of 3D butterflies. And then she began to notice them floating near her in all colorful varieties. In time, she had learned the beautiful insects symbolized change and transformation.

Like leaving behind a thriving business.

Earning her GED after dropping out of high school fifteen years ago.

Deciding that her handsome tutor, who had taught her about hope and optimism, was just the man for her to set aside five years of celibacy.

Burning the journals she had kept during the entirety of her life after running away from Zena's home.

Making her first friend ever in Melissa.

Traveling around the world.

Using her real name. Desdemona Dean.

Enrolling in college.

Falling for Lo.

And a million more minuscule things.

It was one butterfly, Desi. Just one.

She hitched the strap of her leather book satchel higher up on her shoulder before deciding to skip the elevator and tackle the flight of stairs in the navy, pointed-toe crocodile flats she wore with a floral-embroidered A-line skirt and a crisp, striped button-up shirt with her hair pulled back in a low ponytail.

She made her way down the hall past the glass doors of the offices to come to a stop before the one on the corner. Inside was a woman in her early sixties, with silver, waist-length locs and skin that was a deep brown that evoked hunger for decadent chocolates—especially with the crimson red she wore. The woman's style was exotic mixed with trendy, with a statement piece from different cultures, prints, and embroidery matched with simple pieces and bold jewelry.

Dr. Ophelia Toussaint.

Force. Wonder. Shero.

And director of the university's academic advisement department.

Currently, her head was down as she traced with her finger a report she was reading.

Desdemona bit her bottom lip as she lightly rapped her knuckles against the glass.

Dr. Ophelia looked up through her large, round, red tortoise glasses. She smiled and rose to her petite height to wave Desdemona inside the large office. She seemed to be engulfed by her large wooden desk, which was covered with stacks of papers, books, and framed photos revealing a life well lived. Family. Travels. Accolades. Prestige.

"Hello, Dr. Ophelia," Desdemona said, crossing the space to take the small hand offered to her.

"Ms. Desdemona. How's your journey?" she asked, her voice far more formidable than her slight stature.

My journey through life.

Desdemona took one of the seats before the desk. "Unsure," she said.

"Still?" Dr. Ophelia asked as she came around her desk, revealing that her coat was knee length and paired with a simple white T-shirt and jeans skirt with heels.

Desdemona loved it. And her. She could not explain the comfort she felt in the woman's presence. A kinship. Like they had known each other before. Like they were meant to know each other now.

She felt lucky to have her assigned as her academic adviser last semester.

"The wonderful thing about this journey we each are traveling is that we have the power to decide what that journey looks and feels like," the woman began, leaning against the edge of the desk. "The wonderful thing about college is the help it can provide in reaching a goal in your journey."

Desdemona nodded in agreement. "But can't it be a deterrent if it doesn't steer you in the right decision?" she asked.

Dr. Ophelia flung her head back and laughed from her belly. "Absolutely not," she said when she was done. "The journey will have highs and lows. Up and downs. And all of it, my dear, every last bit, is part of the plan. Even the bad things—the unjust, the corruption, the hurt—all of it serves a purpose in forward motion."

Desdemona felt confused. It must have shown on her face.

The doctor reached to take each of Desi's hands in one of her own. She raised the left. "In the highs are blessings," she said, her eyes twinkling behind her spectacles as she lowered the right. "In the depths are lessons—things we now know never to do again. And during life there's balance."

Dr. Ophelia brought both hands to be equal with each other in the middle. With a chuckle, she settled Desdemona's hands back on her lap before turning to walk around her desk.

Desdemona's eyes widened at the beautiful brocade embroidery of flowers and butterflies on the woman's jacket. *Wait. What? The hell?* she thought as her adviser reclaimed her seat.

The butterflies are just a coincidence. Right?

"Ms. Dean?"

She looked over at the older woman. "Yes?"

"I asked you a question," Dr. Ophelia said, her tone a little sharp.

"Yes, ma'am," Desdemona said, not sure if she'd ever given such deference to someone before. "I'm sorry. I didn't hear it."

Dr. Ophelia gave her a look that was chastising but still amused. "Who are you?" she asked again.

I am Madam X.

"Uh... I'm an undecided student attending college at thirty-five after dropping out of school at fifteen and getting my GED just two years ago," she said. "I—"

Dr. Ophelia shook her head, almost woefully. "No, child. If someone asked me that question, I wouldn't bring up this job or my degrees or even my husband or my children," she said, splaying her hands before pressing them together. "Not anything I owned or anything I acquired."

"Okay, then, Dr. Ophelia. Who are you?" Desdemona asked.

The woman's smile was toothy and brilliant. "I am light. Love. Determination. Integrity. Joy unbound. Fairness. Leadership. Veracity. Toughness. Criticism. Peace. Intelligence. Wisdom. I am everything I was meant to be from birth and determined to be even more," she said, with her face bursting with the confidence of a woman who knew herself.

"All of those things I am at my core were there, born in me, like seeds to be discovered, explored, watered, and magnified," the woman continued. "Before I was a daughter, a sister, a wife, or a mother, I was *me*. And what aligned with me and my purpose was to advise, guide, lead, and love. See?"

Desdemona did, but she also knew that she was not that in tune with her qualities. Her being. Who she was at her core.

"Who are you, Desdemona?" Dr. Ophelia asked her again.

She blinked away tears that welled as she remembered never having the freedom for that discovery. "I don't know," she whispered before shifting her eyes to the window to look at the sunlight seeming to burst inside. She gave in to the urge to rise and walk over to step inside the warm rays.

And Dr. Ophelia let her have the moment.

Desdemona didn't know how much time passed as she stood there with her eyes closed, living in the sun. She knew she had to outrace her past. Put it behind her and release all the regrets—like living in survival mode, ready for war, and never relaxing—since the death of her mother.

She pressed her fingertips to the tattoo on her inner wrist: "No regrets." Loren had taught her that.

I'm still exhausted.

A small hand was pressed to her shoulder. "All is well. I promise you that," her adviser said. "The advantage you have over these teenagers possibly choosing far too early what they want to do for the rest of their life cannot be ignored."

Desdemona opened her eyes and looked down at the woman standing beside her. She towered over her by nearly a foot, but it was Dr. Ophelia who gave her strength. "Yes," she said.

"And you don't have to create who you are. It's there in your everyday decisions and actions. Your motivations. I promise you, it's not a puzzle. It's just giving credence to those things about yourself that make you individually Desdemona Dean," she said with one last reassuring pat. "Now, do that. Learn that. Then come back to me and we'll try to home in on a major. Let's get some focus on this journey, and no, there is no wrong. Just correction and lessons learned. Okay?"

Desdemona nodded in agreement before moving over to pick up her satchel. "Thank you," she said, before moving to the door.

"Blessings upon your journey, Ms. Dean."

She closed the door and released a heavy breath as she checked the time on her phone. It was just after three in the afternoon. Loren's class was over. They were traveling to an all-inclusive resort in upstate New York for spring break. She started to call him, but an alert caught her attention.

IDENTITY OF MADAM X REVEALED!

Desdemona's hand trembled so badly she almost dropped her phone. She felt light-headed and nauseated. Was that what the white boy's smile was truly about? Was her secret let loose?

"Shit, shit, shit, shit," she swore as she rushed to open the article. "Shit. Shit. Shit."

"Everything okay, Ms. Dean?"

She whirled to find Dr. Ophelia standing in her now-open doorway.

No, definitely not.

"Yes," she lied, before rushing over to the elevator.

Her heart was near ready to burst as she pressed the button for the elevator and then stepped inside before turning to find her adviser still standing there, watching her in open curiosity.

Does she know?

Does he know?

"Lo," she said as the door closed.

Her cell phone signal was lost inside the lift. She was anxious to read just how much of her life had been exposed. Was her freedom gone along with her privacy?

Had Marquis finally caved in to the pressure and revealed her identity?

She gripped her phone, wishing she had taken the stairs. "Get your shit together, Desi. Chill the fuck out," she muttered.

The talk of Madam X and Marquis's book had finally begun to die down. Foolishly, she had begun to relax. Life began to almost feel normal again.

As soon as the doors opened, she stepped out and opened the link for the article from a popular celebrity gossip blog.

"Desi."

Lo.

She looked up at him walking toward her, handsome as ever in a crisp, black button-down shirt and denims, with a hint of his wild socks peeking from his Air Jordan 5 Retros. "Hey. Hey, Lo," she said, her voice breathless with trepidation.

Is this it?

He came to a stop before her and looked down through the spectacles he rarely wore anymore in favor of contacts. "What's wrong?" he asked.

Was he pretending? Clueless? What the fuck is going on right now?

"You surprised me," she said. "I was just gonna call you and let you know I was done with my meeting with my adviser."

"I got done a little early and decided to walk over and wait for you, so it worked out perfect," he said, before pulling her close with one arm and placing a kiss on her temple.

Desdemona pressed her arms to his back and clung to him as she looked over his broad shoulder at a dozen different focal points. She hated feeling so lost and unsure.

No. Lo played no games. Covertness wasn't in his DNA. If he knew, I would know he knew.

"Let's ride, then," Loren said.

Desdemona leaned back to look up at him. "Yeah. Yeah. Of course," she said.

He doesn't know. But for how long?

They fell in step together to walk across the lobby and out of the building.

Freshmen were not allowed to park on campus, but Loren had faculty permits for both of their vehicles. It was supposed to be solely for his use, but Desdemona used that permit like she was on staff and gave not one care.

"I can't wait to relax and do absolutely nothing," she said.

Loren frowned. "I was planning on working on my book. There's an agent interested in reading the full manuscript when I'm done," he said as they neared the Maserati.

He opened the passenger door for her, but Desdemona paused in claiming the seat. "You sent out proposals?" she asked, feeling her surprise and confusion wrinkle her brows.

Loren had talked to her about his book, a sweeping historical novel set in pre-slavery Africa that allowed him to combine his two loves—history and creative writing. He had given her an in-depth look at the publishing proposal. She knew more about the proposal, hook, and submission guidelines than any nonwriter would. Step-by-step, he had filled her in on his road to being published. Daily word count. Revisions to his detailed outline. Days where he found his writing profound or flawed.

Loren glanced at her over the hood of the car before shrugging nonchalantly. "Yeah, about six weeks ago," he admitted before climbing into the vehicle without meeting her gaze again.

That stung.

Unfortunately, it was becoming familiar. They were not the same. *He* was not the same. The man she once knew to be wise, fun, good-natured, affectionate, and hopeful was fading before her very eyes. They made love and went through the motions of trying to feel the same, but it was becoming clear that sex was the only part of their relationship where they were still of one accord.

As Desdemona climbed into the SUV, she thought of the sudden return of the butterflies around her and fell quiet. Not quite sure what to say. Or how to feel.

She tilted her phone to avoid him seeing the screen and finally opened the gossip article.

March 12 | by Nicole
After months of speculation, bets taken, and guesses
made, the identification of the high-priced Madam
first revealed in the blockbuster autobiography of
basketball phenom Marquis Sanders is believed to be
none other than the infamous former madam, Liona
Paxier, also known as the Midtown Madam, who
went into seclusion after serving three years in New
York State Prison for procurement—

The tension faded from Desdemona's body and she released a long stream of air through gloss-covered, pouted lips. Her relief was palpable. Quickly she read the rest of the article, which turned out to be nothing more than speculation that was wholly incorrect, with both MQ and Paxier offering no comments.

As Loren drove them through the New York streets toward Interstate 80 to begin the four-hour drive to Seneca Lake, she stared out the window and thought of different scenarios that could occur because of the article. And with each, she formulated a plan in her head to keep herself protected. For the moment—for at least the day—she would accept that the true identity of Madam X was safe.

To break their silence, Desdemona leaned forward to turn on the satellite radio. Adele's "All I Ask" filled the interior. It was a song about heartbreak. Love lost. And just one last night to say goodbye.

"It matters how this ends 'cause what if I never love again—"

Desdemona reached forward to turn the radio off, feeling as if the lyrics hit too close to home. She hated her emotions stinging the back of her throat and the tears that threatened to rise and fall. Blinking rapidly and feeling foolish, Desdemona kicked off her shoes and pulled her knees to her chest as she rested her head against the tinted glass of the passenger window.

The touch of Loren's hand squeezing her thigh surprised her. She didn't glance at him, though, not wanting him to see the sadness etched on her face and swimming in her eyes. "Stop, Lo," she said softly, shifting her leg away from his warm grasp.

He withdrew his hand.

As Desdemona looked out at towering trees and long stretches of wildflowers just beginning to bloom, the song of a relationship's reckoning played in her head, seeming to mock her. She closed her eyes and hungered for the feel of happiness again, wishing she recognized herself from the weepy and worrying soul she had become.

When the car eventually slowed, Desdemona opened her eyes to look out the window. Loren drove the Maserati with ease down a long and curving road with the late-afternoon sun beaming down as they soon caught their first sight of the boutique resort hotel styled as an Italian villa. Lush green landscaping and spring florals gave it more decadence.

It exceeded the photos on the website.

"You told me my share for this trip was three hundred dollars and that *clearly* wasn't fifty percent of the total bill. Right?" Loren asked as he drove the SUV up the paved driveway and through open bronze gates with an intricate scroll design.

"I thought we really needed this," she said. "No. No.

Nope. We needed something—*anything*—because things are not the same between us. *Maybe* a luxury weekend wasn't it, and maybe I was wrong to upgrade our mini-vacay without you knowing because I didn't want to have another debate about how much something costs. I don't know if you don't know or don't give a fuck, but this right here"—she used her finger to motion between their bodies—"is not working anymore."

"Agreed," Loren said, his tone and the look on his face so very solemn.

He slowed the SUV to a stop.

Even as the grand double doors of the villa opened and a squad of uniformed staff descended the stairs, they remained sitting there.

"I'm trying, Desi."

"So am I, Lo."

She was the first to grab her things and exit the vehicle. With her feet firmly planted atop the paved courtyard, she looked around at the lush grounds and inhaled deeply of the decidedly fresher air. Across the distance was an elaborate garden, already beginning to add color to the greenery.

When she finally turned, the bellhop was headed up the stairs with their luggage in each hand, the valet was driving off in the SUV to park, the butler held a tray of filled crystal flutes balanced on one hand, and the concierge awaited them with a broad smile.

"Welcome to Bellissimo Posto," the tall, thin mustached man said. "Mr. and Mrs. Dean, I assume? I am the concierge, Anastasio Aloia. We've been expecting you."

Loren chuckled.

"Mr. Palmer and Ms. Dean," Desdemona corrected the concierge with a warm smile as she accepted a flute. "It was an honest mistake. I made the reservations."

He gave them a brief nod that served as an apology as the butler swiveled a bit to offer the flute on the tray for Loren to take. "Your lakeview suite is right this way."

As they followed the man up the stairs and into the villa, Desdemona ignored the look Loren gave her and focused on the decadent décor and towering ceilings, adorned with Old World painted murals.

"Your home for the next five days and four nights," Anastasio said with relish before opening the double doors and stepping aside for them to get a full view of the luxurious, all-white suite and their luggage awaiting them.

Desdemona stepped inside and instantly kicked off her shoes as Loren allowed the concierge to give him a tour of the suite. Over the rim of her flute, she kept her eyes locked on the view of the lake through the open terrace doors as she crossed the foyer and living room to reach it. The air was light and the water tranquil in the distance. Her eyes dropped down to the garden and found it even more beautiful from that angle.

She shook her head and chuckled as a bevy of butterflies flew up from the gardens. "Here we go again, then," she whispered into the glass before taking a deep sip of the prosecco.

She turned in the doorway to eye Loren setting their key cards on the desk in the foyer.

Their eyes locked across the grandeur.

He closed the distance to join her on the terrace. His eyes searched her face. "I am trying, Desi," he said. "I know shit is fucked up between us. I know. I feel it. But I'm *trying*. I swear."

"Trying to what, Lo? Love me? Stay with me? Stop punishing me for not being sure about wanting to be a mother? What?" she asked, unable to keep a tinge of bitterness from her tone.

Loren licked his soft mouth. "I will *always* love you, Desdemona," he said.

"But?" she asked with a softness that was telling.

"I want kids. Grandbabies for my parents. Hell, grandbabies for us. Legacy. Our family to be there to hold our hands when we're old and about to leave this world," he stressed. "To have you means I might not have that. I'm not perfect, Desi. That shit is hard. It's a lot to give up."

"Fuck!" she swore in a gasp as she pressed her eyes closed and hated the tears that fell despite that. She swiped them away. "I am not some evil, coldhearted bitch too selfish to have children. It's not about *that*, Lo."

Loren leaned against the side of the terrace and watched her. "Then what is it about?" he asked, his deep voice seeming to echo among the grass-covered hills.

I am Madam X.

"Is it about the past you won't tell me about?" Loren asked.

"You knew there were things I could never share with you," she insisted, willing him to remember that day in the classroom when he accepted that caveat and welcomed her into his life. As is.

"Why?" he countered. "Why can't you tell me? For a damn year I didn't know your real name. Why do you need a fucking alias? What have you done that you can't tell me? And where did all the money come from?"

Loren stalked inside the suite and splayed his hand to wave around at their luxury accommodations. "The condo. The car. The jewelry. The trips," he said, before crossing the space to rejoin her on the terrace. "It can't be the showroom because you barely go there. What the hell is going on, Desi? How did you make so much money? Are you a widow? On the run? In a drug cartel?"

Desdemona felt foolish for believing the rubber would

never meet the road on the issue of her past. And just as foolish to believe he would be okay with not having children.

Love was blinding.

"Desdemona, *say* something," he insisted, gripping her upper arms as he looked down into her eyes.

"Don't force me to lie to you," she said, her voice hollow.

Loren was shocked by that. His face showed it. He turned from her with his hand clutching his mouth before he turned back. "Do you trust me?" he asked.

Her success in avoiding arrest was built upon trusting absolutely no one with her truth. So she remained silent. She had seen far too much while helping spouses betray their marriage to believe in a complete happily ever after. And it was in the embers of a fiery breakup that anger led to retribution. She refused to deliver the knife with which to stab her in the back.

Trust no one.

As much as she loved Loren and believed that no one had her back the way he did, she couldn't pull him into her confidence. Especially now. Not when the end of their relationship now seemed inevitable.

"So, I should trust you hiding such a huge part of your life from me, but *you* don't trust *me*?" he asked. "Not to tell me the whole truth. Not to have my children."

"I *love* you," she said, hating how he lowered his head at that. "I love you so much. I am so thankful for everything you added to my life. Everything. You taught me how to see the good. How to *find* the good. And I am so sorry because I never intended to hurt or disappoint you. Or make you feel unworthy of everything you want in life. I really and truly thought—I hoped—this was my forever."

He turned but kept his head down, with his eyes to the floor of the terrace.

"I don't know what made me think I could have something good. That something good would be just for me," she admitted, hating how the brokenness of her childhood, her parents' death, and years of abuse at the hands of her pimps and johns refused to heal.

What kind of mother would I be?

They locked eyes.

"You would hate me," she admitted with a woeful shake of her head, unable to deny him that small bit of her truth.

They were not going to make it. What other choice did she have but to end it and give him the freedom to find the woman who could be everything he needed without question?

"Give me a memory I can use..."

The lyric from Adele's song was so fitting.

Loren swiftly crossed the terrace and pulled her body against his. Tightly. He ran his hands up her back and then under the layers of her hair. Tightly. "I could never hate you. There is nothing you could do to make me hate you, Desdemona," he whispered with passion in between kisses against her temple as he massaged her scalp. "Nothing."

I am Madam X.

He tilted her head back and studied her face. Missing nothing. "Never," he said as he lowered his head and pressed a kiss to each corner of her mouth. "Never."

The first feel of his lips upon hers made her shiver down deep. It was sexy and sweet. It hinted at a hunger unbridled.

Loren swooped her up into his strong arms with ease and carried her inside the suite and stood her atop the bed to undress her. Slowly. With each garment removed and dropped to the floor, Desdemona stroked the side of his face as she reveled in his heated touch. Committing it all to memory.

He nuzzled his face against her clean-shaven, V-shaped mound of temptation. "Always so fresh," he moaned, as if it was torn from him.

She smiled as he stepped back to undress, rushing through the task. When he came close again she raised her leg over one of his broad shoulders as he offered her stability atop the bed with his hands clutching her buttocks. Heated kisses were pressed to her inner thigh, and she released a gasp of deep pleasure as she let her head tilt until the tips of her hair lightly breezed against her lower back. "Yes, Lo," she sighed as he nestled his mouth between the lips of her plump core and licked at the throbbing bud hidden there.

First a deep stroke, then featherlight flickers.

Desdemona cried out, not caring if it carried from the suite through the open terrace doors. There was no care or shame to be found as he tasted her and excited the nerve endings that made her feel hot in her arousal.

Her nipples hard.

Her body trembling.

Her knees weak.

Passion was its own drug and she craved it. In the best way.

Feeling naughty, Desdemona lowered her leg and turned around while looking back over her shoulder as she bent over with her legs spread wide.

"Damn!" Loren swore before dipping his head to taste her from behind.

She grabbed her ankles and wiggled her bottom against his face the way he liked. His hard inches hung from his body and above the edge of the bed. So tempting. With a deep lick of her lips, she used her storied flexibility to ease her upper body back between her legs as much as she could, making her mouth able to suck the smooth tip of his dick.

Loren released a deep, guttural moan even as he suckled her. Slowly. With intensity. As he gripped her thighs.

I taught my lover so very well.

She had to fight not to be too engulfed by the pleasure he gave her to remember what she was doing to him. He brought his hand up to slap her buttocks before spreading her cheeks. She could tell he leaned back to study her. With his thick tip still in her mouth, she smiled and worked the inner walls of her core.

"I love you *so* much," he said in awe.

She felt his dick harden even more against her lips.

Loren was twenty-six and it was such a good year. Good and stiff.

Desdemona lay down on her stomach with an arch to her back that rose her buttocks before turning over. "You ready?" she asked.

"Damn, your body is beautiful," he moaned, bending to press kisses from her ankles and up her body as he climbed on the bed to lay on his side next to her. He eased a middle finger inside her as he continued to eye her body before locking his gaze on hers.

She didn't keep her pleasure from showing on her face and knew he was driven to satisfy her. "Oh, Lo," she whispered.

He closed his eyes and lowered his head to kiss her as he stroked her clit with his thumb. "I don't want this to end," he said, low in his throat before the first touch of his mouth down on hers. Desdemona said nothing, knowing her love for him would not fade easily—maybe never at all.

She lost count of how long they shared deep and heated kisses. Who cared? Those touches of their lips and tongues stoked their fever for each other. He withdrew his finger for them both to suck away her juices in between more kisses as he pressed his body down atop hers. His hard inches were sandwiched in between them and, at times, throbbed against

her belly. She ached in longing in places above and below.
The need to have him inside her battled with her hunger for
more kisses. And touches. And sweet anticipation.
His seduction could be just as addictive as his thrusts.
And when she could barely deny them their pleasure any
longer, she spread her legs wide and drew his tongue into her
mouth as he worked his strong hips to guide his dick to her
opening.
The first feel of him was electric, and every inch after
that, intoxicating. Each thrust dizzying. Every slow circle of
his hips maddening.
Damn.
She clung to him and matched the wicked back-and-
forth motion of his hips with her own. Passion was their fuel.
Chemistry held them spellbound. At times, their lovemaking
was slow and sensual. Sometimes fast and furious. Sweat and
tears. Moans and whimpers. Thrust after thrust.
It was the type of madness where you weren't quite sure
you'd remember everything you said, did, or had done to
you. And they didn't care one bit. Nothing else mattered
except the white-hot moments they cried out and clung to
each other—almost desperately—as they climaxed together.
If this weekend was all they had, she wanted memories
she would never forget.

Desdemona rose from the king-size bed, nude and a bit
sore from four days of sex with Lo. They'd feasted upon each
other, savoring every moment, and never left their suite. She
was sure their bill at checkout would be sizable because of
room service. She hadn't wanted the weekend to end
because it was also the finale of her love story with Lo.
She pulled on a silk robe and closed it loosely before
leaning in the door frame to look out at the spectacular view.

The sun was just beginning to break, the darkness fading to a deep blue. She got lost in it, looking for a distraction as her life as she knew it with Loren was ending. She lost track of time, but it was clear that it moved forward as the sun reigned and daybreak became clear.

Who are you?

Dr. Ophelia's voice seemed to whisper to her at that moment.

Thoughtful. Emotional. Fair. Protective. Intuitive.

She glanced back over her shoulder, surprised to find Loren sitting up in bed, sketching on his pad atop a portable light board. He was so focused and the strokes of his pencil just as fast and furious as the strokes of his dick just hours before. He was so busy with teaching and writing his book that he rarely took time to draw anymore. And he was so talented. She had a case of nearly two dozen sketches he had done of her—mostly nudes.

Loving.

She smiled, enjoying the sight of him—a beautiful man with a beautiful soul. "I wouldn't trade the last eight months for anything, Lo," she said.

"I'm not ready to let you go," he said without looking up as he continued to capture something from his memory.

She let her robe fall open as she crossed the bedroom to stand beside the bed. "Lo, we don't agree on some really major things," she said, letting the silk fall to the floor before climbing back on the bed. "The end is inevitable."

"I know," he said before tearing off the sheet of paper from the pad to hand it to her.

Her eyes locked with his as she took it and then looked down at the sketch.

On it was her profile as she gazed out at the lake with the wind blowing her waist-length, ebony hair back from her face and body. Desdemona knew without him saying so that there was love in every line of the drawing. Never had she felt more adored and beautiful.

Loren pulled her body close to his with his sculpted, tattooed arms tightly. So tightly. "But not yet," he said. Or maybe asked.

Desdemona nodded and pressed a kiss to his hard chest. "Okay," she simply agreed.

Chapter Four

Saturday, March 20

Welcome back, old friend. I need you...

Desdemona scratched her scalp with the capped end of her pen as she looked around the Harlem hair salon from her seat in the waiting area. The small shop was bustling with activity as women of all ages in varying shades of brown treated themselves to a new hairdo. Hairstylists and customers chatted away and the television on the wall blared in a battle with music pumping through the speakers. Old school curling irons clanged as they were roughly slid inside heating elements and the smell of the food people ate as they awaited their turn in their hairstylist's chair blended in the air with hair products.

All of that combined with the bright décor reminiscent of the 1990s made it chaos. A beautiful one to Desdemona. MiMi had been doing her hair since she started earning some money tricking for Majig. Keeping up with her hygiene, using condoms, and keeping her hair fixed had provided normalcy as she succumbed to a life of sex work and strange men.

Even once she became wealthy and could afford a luxury lifestyle as a top madam, Desdemona had continued her weekly appointments in the small, chaotic salon. In a way, it felt more like home than any other place since her mother's death. Now it kept her grounded in her rich Black culture—everything from music and fashion to politics and socioeconomic issues.

Sometimes wealth had a way of removing those things for people of color.

Desdemona crossed one leg over the other in the olive leggings she wore with a matching, long-sleeved silk tee and suede booties. She rubbed the empty lines of the journal's page. It was smooth and cool to the touch—and begging to be fed her words, thoughts, and feelings.

She went to the page where she listed who she was at her core. She added two more.

Loyal.

And vain.

The good and the bad. The truth.

In the days since their return from the trip to upstate New York, there had been yet another shift between her and Lo. To her anyway. She drew a small butterfly on the corner of the page before writing her entry—a confession...

Lo is constantly assuring me that he loves me, but one day he will finally walk away to have his dream life that I'm not sure I can give him. His love will eventually fade and I will be left to pick up the pieces without him.

Having him for just a little while longer was its own kind of sweet torture.

"You ready?" MiMi asked with her ever-present smile in place as she motioned with her hand for Desdemona to follow her to the shampoo station.

Desdemona tucked her pen inside the leather-bound journal before sliding it inside the designer crossbody bag she wore as the tall, full-figured woman patiently awaited her.

"You make me want to grow my hair back," MiMi said, rubbing her hand over her close-shaven head, colored a bright cherry red.

"And you make me want to cut mine," Desdemona returned as she settled onto the chair and raised her chin as the cape was placed around her.

MiMi reclined the chair and looked down into her face to study her. "You *would* slay," she surmised.

Desdemona closed her eyes and enjoyed the feel of her scalp being massaged as she was shampooed and given conditioner. She hated for it to end as MiMi wrapped a towel around her damp hair and led her back to her station.

"Soft curls or bone straight?" MiMi asked, knowing Desdemona wore both styles.

"Straight with a middle part," she answered, reaching for a glossy gossip magazine in the chair next to her. On the cover was a photo of Marquis, looking angry as he left a hot spot with several silhouettes floating around his head as inner thoughts with a bold headline: WHO IS MADAM X...AND WHAT SECRETS DOES SHE HOLD?

Allowing a moment of spite, she felt gleeful that Marquis's peace was still being interrupted by his salacious tell-all. *Good for his ass.*

With a roll of her eyes, she tossed the mag back to where she found it.

She wondered just how many of his fellow consorts had reached out to him. When she cut ties with the sex procurement business, she had called each consort and instructed them to destroy the prepaid phones she'd assigned each one to be used exclusively to contact her. Her last act of freedom had been destroying her own. She had no way to contact them and vice versa—even if she saw many of them in the headlines on the regular.

Would one of the courtesans step from the shadows in search of money or notoriety? That she doubted. Desdemona had ensured that each woman was carefully screened and had plans in life for careers. Goals. Dreams. No, if her instincts had been correct, none of them would risk their freedom and respectability to join in with MQ's mess.

But never say never.

Trust no one.

Desdemona closed her eyes as MiMi dried her hair. When she felt light pressure atop her thigh, she opened one eye to look down at the adorable face of a little girl of about six or seven with her hair in two Afro puffs as she licked a red teddy bear–shaped lollipop.

Desdemona tried not to cringe at the idea of the sticky candy ruining her pants.

"You getting rid of your curls?" the child asked, confusion twisting her face.

"For now," she said, instead of telling her to beat it.

She's adorable. MiMi raked her long nails through the portion of Desdemona's hair that she had already given a silk press. "This is the work of my hair growth oil," she boasted with pride. "I sent bottles of it all over the world that year you wore braids while you traveled. She came back with most of *this*."

"Fact," Desdemona agreed as the hairstylist held the inches up from her scalp.

"I like my curls," the little girl said with *lots* of attitude.

"Me too," Desdemona agreed.

MiMi stiffened behind the chair. "Ain't somebody missing a child?" she asked with a snap to it.

"Joie!" a voice exclaimed from the shampoo station. "Go and sit your little nosy self down and get out that lady's face like that!"

The imp made a face filled with spunk and Desdemona had to fight not to laugh—and to imagine the little spitfire with so much character was her daughter. Laughing with her. Filling her life with youthful energy. Dressed in designer gear and posed as if she knew it.

Or wearing glasses and having a constant smile filled with charm like Loren.

Agreeing to have children would make Loren happy, but what she wanted mattered as well, and motherhood had never been a part of her plan before. Joie looked to be about the same age as Desdemona was when her mother died.

Perhaps if my mother had lived, I would make her a grandmother. A baby to experience the deep love I was shown every day before her death.

Joie twisted her lollipop around in her mouth and gave her mother a quick glance over her shoulder. "I'm just using my words like you said, *Mama*," she called back.

"Oh, hell no," MiMi muttered under her breath.

Desdemona chuckled.

Moments later, a tall, thin woman wearing a cape with dripping hair grabbed little Miss Joie's wrist. "Excuse her. She is a character," she said.

The little girl held up a free hand. "I hear that *all* the time," she said as her mother led her away.

I bet you do.

Desdemona winced at the sticky, cherry-scented spittle on her knee and then thought about a little one around her, chattering away all day, and what little urge she had to be a mother faded fast.

Labor? Breastfeeding? Crying? Potty-training? Tantrums?

Finding babysitters? Cooking meals? Rising every morning to get them off to school? Homework? Extracurricular activities? Teenage attitudes? College tuition?

And with all that, plus more trying to instill morality and fairness so he or she wasn't a horrible human being?

Failure could mean a child addicted to drugs or being lost to the streets.

She was proof of that, and the last thing she wanted was to set a life down the wrong path the way she had been.

"Now *this* some wild shit right here," another customer said as she eyed the large television on the wall.

MiMi paused to look over at the screen. "What's going on?" she asked.

Desdemona focused on checking the website of her on-line boutique to ensure Patrice, her partner and the manager of her showroom, was on top of the job with which she was entrusted. The business had once mostly served as the front for her prostitution ring but was now completely legitimate—just not a priority any longer. Thankfully, the fashionable style Desdemona inherited from her mother had also helped to develop the boutique as a valuable resource for the wealthy and fabulous. A lot of the wives of her former consorts continued to shop from the boutique, keeping it profitable.

"Something else about Madam X coming up on *Celebrity Spotlight*," the customer said.

That got Desdemona's attention.

"They still worrying about Madam X?" MiMi asked. "MQ know he done started some shit. Turn it up."

Desdemona stiffened and her stomach muscles tightened. *Now what?* she thought as she looked over at the screen with nearly everyone else in the salon.

"Now back to our lead story about the elusive Madam X.

Celebrity Spotlight *has exclusively learned the publishers of Marquis Sanders's explosive autobiography plan to release an open letter to Madam X, offering a one-million-dollar advance to write a book of her—or his—own. . . ."*

Desdemona didn't fight the eye roll as her hand gripped her phone tightly. It was nothing but more trouble on the horizon.

"A milli?" someone exclaimed. "Sheeeit. I'm Madam X!"

The women all laughed, and many jokingly agreed.

"Nah. I am."

"It's me. It's me."

If only you all knew.

"Yeah, but why step forward and risk jail time?" someone else asked.

"For a million dollars, I'd do that bid!"

Right then, Desdemona would gladly pay a million dollars to be locked in a room with Marquis Sanders and a baton. *I'd wear his big ass out,* she thought.

"We reached out to Marquis Sanders for an official comment on the offer, but he declined to give one."

"Damn, they trying to flush that pussy peddler out like baby roaches!"

More laughter.

Desdemona only mustered a smile.

A million dollars. Desdemona wasn't in the least bit tempted, and not just because she had far more than that stowed away. Above all, her privacy and that of her clients were not for sale for *any* amount. She could only hope that none of her former consorts or courtesans believed otherwise and panicked.

She pondered if it was time to locate them all and make calls to reassure them. Calm them.

Or risk exposing myself.

"Maria Vargas be on it," a woman with auburn locs said. "She don't play about somebody else's business."

"O-kay," MiMi agreed as she parted Desdemona's hair. "I don't miss her show. It is good and juicy."

Desdemona needed quiet to think through her options, but none was to be found in her Harlem paradise. She used her phone's camera view to see that MiMi was nearly done silk pressing her hair.

Thank God.

"Yes! She's been in these gossip telling streets since that heifer who screwed her friend's husband and then he turned around and tried to kill her lowlife, scheming, backstabbing ass," another customer said. "Remember *that* mess?"

Desdemona looked around for Joie and was thankful her mother had her ears covered with bright red headphones as she watched something on her tablet.

"Who could forget when that heifer wrote a damn book and went on tour with her scandalous bullshit—"

"*And* opened a business to supposedly help women catch cheating husbands," a caramel cutie with half-done, floor-length knotless braids chimed in.

"What was her name again?" someone asked.

"Jessa Bell," Locs supplied.

"More like Jezebel," MiMi added.

"Tomato-tomatah!"

Desdemona was just pleased they had moved on from Madam X.

"Whatever happened to her?" MiMi asked.

"Sheeee-it. Somebody played target practice with dat ass but missed and shot the secret daughter nobody knew about."

"Well damn!" MiMi exclaimed.

"How do y'all know all of this?' Desdemona asked in wonder, unable to stop herself.

"Maria Vargas!" they said in resounding unison.

"And she seems determined to get Madam X," Knotless Braids said with a shake of her head, as if she felt sorry for the faceless madam.

Don't count me out yet. . . .

Desdemona was naturally apprehensive—and at times she forgot who she was and let her fears win—but then she remembered she hadn't survived that long in the business without being caught for nothing.

"All done," MiMi said, removing the cape and swiveling the chair so Desdemona now faced the large, round mirror over her cluttered workstation.

Desdemona eased the sides back with her stiletto-shaped nails to reveal her laid edges a bit more. "Thank you," she said.

"You ever miss the blond?" MiMi asked. "You wore that for years."

"No," Desdemona said without hesitation as she removed crisp bills from her billfold to hand the hairstylist. "Not one bit."

The blond hair had been all about rebellion and a cry for attention as she lived her life in the shadows for protection.

I have way more shit to worry about than hair. Long or short. Black or blond. Fuck it. Who cares? My life is tangled enough.

"See you next week," MiMi said as she motioned for her next client to sit in her chair.

As Desdemona slid on her olive suede jacket and took her leave, she gave the image of Maria Vargas on the television screen a look. This trip to the salon had revealed the woman was her nemesis, and it was time for Desdemona to pay the journalist a bit more attention.

"And if she dies?"

Desdemona would never forget the words she overheard

her stepmother ask about her. It was the moment she knew she had to run away from home or risk her stepmother harming her to ensure the daughter of her husband and his mistress was no longer her responsibility. And the hefty sum left to Desdemona by her father would be Zena's all alone.

After nearly five years of neglect and being treated like a bother in what was supposed to be her home, those words had scared—and scarred—Desdemona to her core. She wished she could forget the scene and it didn't live rent-free in her head....

The pretty pink princess bedroom meant for a younger child had become Desdemona's prison. Within those four walls, she'd avoided her stepmother's unspoken disdain, but within them, she also felt so very alone. A reminder that she had no family and hungered for love.

And help.

She raked her fingers through her hair, frowning a little at the rough ends, thick roots, and haphazard curls as she did the best she could to do her hair.

And washed her own clothes.

And cooked her own food.

Thud-thud-thud-thud-thud-thud-thud...

Her eyes went to the closed door, frowning at the sudden noise.

Desdemona had already done her homework, taken her bath, microwaved a TV dinner, cleaned the kitchen, and closed herself up in her bedroom for the night to avoid Zena and her hateful stares once she got home from work.

Thud-thud-thud-thud-thud-thud-thud...

Curious, she crossed the room and opened the door, looking down the dark hall at Zena's bedroom door. It was slightly ajar, leaving a sliver of light against the base of the wall and floor. A feminine giggle and a masculine chuckle sounded off from the room.

Desdemona's eyes widened as she crept on tiptoes down the unlit hall, careful to miss the loose floorboard in the middle that always let out a loud, all-too-telling squeak.

"Ssssh, before you wake her up," Zena said in a harsh whisper.

Desdemona pressed her back to the wall before peeking through the opening in the door. She frowned at the sight of Zena bent over the side of her bed with her dress up around her waist and her panties down around her ankles and Hervey Grantham—her father's attorney and best friend—pumping her from behind with his pants down around his ankles as well.

Her eyes widened in shock and she covered her mouth with her hand and prayed the fast beating of her heart wasn't as loud as it seemed to her own ears. She turned to ease her way back down the hall.

Mr. Grantham and Zena?

That hurt. Desdemona knew her dad wouldn't like it.

"Hervie, it's been five years that I had to put up with her."

Desdemona paused in the darkness.

He grunted in agreement.

"Why can't I send her away to boarding school?" she asked.

Desdemona peeked into the room again, shaking her head at the bored expression on Zena's face while Mr. Grantham was sweating profusely and licking at his thick lips.

"You...can," he said, punctuating each word with a thrust. "But...the...money...will...go...toward...pay-ing...for...it."

Zena looked back at him over her shoulder. "So, no kid—"

"No money," he finished with a deep bite of his full bottom lip.

It was Mr. Grantham's job to ensure Zena lived up to

her obligations, and now Desdemona understood why her stepmother supplied the very minimum. She bought his complicity with sex.

Anger flamed inside Desdemona.

"I hate her. I hate her," Zena said.

I hate you, too.

"Just three more years," he said, his thrusts quickening in pace.

Three more years of this. I can't.

"What if she goes to jail or something? What happens to me?" Zena asked.

Jail?

Fear flooded Desdemona. What lengths was Zena willing to go to to keep the money without being bothered with caring for her stepchild?

"The stipend would be put on hold."

Desdemona felt relief. Zena would not want that money to stop, not even to get rid of her. That she knew.

"And if she dies?"

That caused Desdemona's heart to stop.

Would she? She wouldn't. Right?

It didn't matter.

She already killed my soul.

A tear rose and fell down her cheek. She didn't bother to wipe it away as she turned. I can't do this no more, *she mouthed.*

Being sure to avoid the squeaking floorboard, she walked to her room and quickly packed a bag. There wasn't much to take that was meant for a teenager, but she was sure to jam her journals in with her things. With one last look back at the room, Desdemona closed the door and hitched her backpack up onto her shoulders.

Thud-thud-thud-thud-thud—

She looked down the length of the hall. For years there

was so much she wanted to say to the woman who made her life hell. She licked her lips, squared her shoulders, and gripped the straps of her book bag as she walked straight up the middle of the hall with quick and determined strides.

The floorboard squealed when she stepped on it.

Moments later, she pushed the bedroom door open wide. It hit against the wall.

BAM!

Mr. Grantham stopped in midstroke and Zena looked at her with her eyes wide with shock.

"But my momma was the ho, right?" she asked with a sardonic shake of her head.

"Get out!" Zena roared, rising and pushing back against her lover.

"Hey!" he roared as he stumbled and fell backward onto the floor with his feet and moist erection pointed to the ceiling.

"You don't have to tell me twice. I'm gone," Desdemona said, turning to run down the length of the hall and across the living room to the front door.

An odd mix of fear and excitement was her adrenaline as she took off down the stairs and into the night.

And that had been the last she'd seen of Zena Dean.

Desdemona picked up her glass of champagne fraise and took a deep sip of the cocktail as she looked out the window of the fresh restaurant in the SoHo section of New York City. It did nothing to focus her attention away from the past. That moment was imprinted on her life. The cause for so much that came behind it.

To choose living on the street over staying with Zena spoke volumes. Many stories such as hers had a very different, more final ending. She was lucky to be alive. Many had not survived the brutalities of the street.

Marquis's book had awakened a lot of the sadness she had

about her upbringing. The joy and self-love she'd worked hard to find had been nearly erased in the weeks since the book's release. She hated the steps backward when she had finally gained so much more than wealth and a close link to the same wealthy elite as her clients. That all was so very insignificant to loving herself.

Finally.

I want my joy again.

"Beautiful as ever."

At the sound of a male voice above the chatter of the busy restaurant, Desdemona looked up to see Trevor King. She chuckled warmly and gave him a smile as he bent his tall frame to press a kiss on her cheek. "It is nice to see you, Trevor," she said.

"May I?" he asked, gesturing to the empty seat at the small table.

She paused, thinking of Loren, but set aside any misgivings. The tall, slender, brown-skinned man with low-cut salt-and-pepper hair and goatee was in his midforties and fine. Stylish. Wealthy. Accomplished.

Just the type of man a woman of her age should want.

And they had dated after meeting at the Metropolitan Opera nearly three years ago.

He claimed the seat and they shared a bemused look at each other. "I stopped hearing from you," he said. "I think the kids call it ghosting."

"They do and I did. I apologize for not being more mature about it, Trevor," she said as she traced the edge of the flute with her index finger.

He pressed a hand to his chest and feigned being wounded.

Desdemona gave him mock applause for his performance.

He chuckled. "Alisha, can I assume someone else garnered your attention?" he asked.

Desdemona lowered her head.

Alisha Smith. Yes, that's how he knows me.

They'd met before her year-long trip, where she had finally welcomed being addressed by her real name, setting aside the moniker. She found no need to bother correcting him. "Yes," she admitted. "Someone very special to me who I'd known before I met you."

Trevor played with his silk tie. "The young dude I saw you with a few months ago at dinner?" he asked with a twinkle in his eyes. "Or was that your younger brother?"

Desdemona pouted and gave him a consoling look. "Trevor, don't be that way. It's clear since you didn't approach us—the way you've felt free to approach me now—that you knew we were a couple," she said. "Still are, as a matter of fact."

At least for now...

Trevor nodded. "I was hoping I was wrong. He's pretty young," he said.

Desdemona matched his look. "Not *too* young," she countered, her tone still pleasant. "It's very...*invigorating.*"

Trevor made a pained expression and chuckled. "You never gave me the chance to display my *mature* skills," he countered.

"True," she said. "But I promise you—and I *guarantee* it—that young man has been well tutored."

He chuckled some more. He was very good-natured. She had always liked his charm.

"Listen. When I first spotted you in that dress at the Met, I wanted you," he declared with confidence in his deep tone. "We dated. You vacationed for a year. We spoke a little during that time. Upon your return, we dated some more."

She nodded in agreement. "You say all that to say..."

"I still want you and I will have you, Alisha Smith," he said, before rising to his feet. "I'm very patient."

The scenario of being with one man and still longing for another reminded her of a book she read recently by a favorite author of hers. She had no desire for *that* to be her story. "And I'm still in a relationship," she reminded him as she looked up at him.

"For now," Trevor said. "When things change, call me. My number's the same."

She looked up at him, surprised by the slight thrill his words gave him. "Mine is not," she told him—and as a reminder to herself.

"Then it's completely up to you," he said, as smoothly as melted chocolate, with another warm smile before turning and walking away.

Desdemona let her eyes follow him.

Bzzzzzz.

With reluctance, she looked away from him and down at her phone.

Loren.

The swell of her heart and the race of her pulse just from him calling was far beyond any thrill Trevor had evoked. There was nothing like it. "Hey, Lo," she said after answering the call.

"Hey, baby. You done with your hair appointment?" he asked.

"Yes," she said. "I was getting lunch at Balthazar."

Tap-tap.

She looked up at Trevor, outside the restaurant on the street. He gave her a wink and a head nod before striding away.

"You heard me?" Loren asked.

"Huh? No. No, I didn't. What did you say?"

"I need you to pick me up. My truck overheated," he said.

Desdemona arched a brow. At the moment, the differences between Trevor and Loren were stark. "Lo, why don't you get a new car?" she asked.

"I will one day, Desi," he said. "I already called for a tow to take it to my mechanic."

Desdemona motioned for her server to bring her check. "I'm on the way," she said.

The line went quiet.

She paid her bill and stood. "Lo, you still there?"

"We not eating meals together anymore?" he asked.

Desdemona made her way through the restaurant and onto the street. "Loren, to be honest, I don't know when you will be ready to up and leave me, so I'm just getting used to going through life alone again," she said. "There's no need to pretend when all we have now is sex."

"And love," he added.

I believe that.

"But no future," she reminded him as she began her walk to the parking garage two blocks away.

"I'll see you when you get here," he said before ending the call.

If only things could be different.

When she reached the multistory, covered garage, Desdemona gave her claim check to the valet. He gave her an appreciative look before walking away to retrieve her vehicle. She made sure not to give him any false hope.

Her thoughts were on Loren.

He'd gone to his parents' two-story home in Brooklyn. Normally, she would have joined him. She had come to like his mother, Bell, and father, Garee—the music teacher and poet laureate, respectively. And they appeared to enjoy her company as well. Being in the family's company had at first been a reminder of the stable childhood she'd lost, but in time, her unease faded and she enjoyed them and their playful banter with one another.

She hated the thought of losing them along with the end of her relationship with their only son.

"Take me with you."

Desdemona turned to find the valet exiting her vehicle. She gave him a playful look as she stepped past him to climb into the driver's seat. "I already have one young dude who wanna leave me but can't work up the nerve to live without me," she said. "This is a grown-man situation right here."

With that, she drove off with a brief press of the car horn.

During the entire thirty-minute drive, Desdemona considered sending Loren a rideshare instead. Maybe sense would prevail and he would be waiting outside on the curb for her to scoop him up and keep it moving.

I doubt it.

Loren was the lone child of his parents and they were close-knit—though not in a toxic, enmeshed way. The music teacher and the poet laureate had devoted their lives to their son and their crafts—and not always in that order. No, Loren would invite her up and they would sit and sip herbal tea and make her feel like family. Treat her like she belonged. Welcome her.

And this time it will all be pretend.

Soon Loren would be another loss from her life.

First her mother.

Next her father.

Then herself, when she ran away from the stereotypical evil stepmother and had to shift into survival mode—savage level.

And then herself again, when Majig's heroin overdose set her free from his grasp and left his valuable client list up for her to grab.

Then she thought of being Mademoiselle. Felt drained and lost.

So that was her next loss.

Then her clients. Some who had become friendly. Revealed secrets. Granted favors.

And her courtesans. She had seen so many leave the work to pursue their dreams—as doctors, attorneys, actresses, or mothers. Some had betrayed the rules of no drug abuse, no other criminal activity, and no private connections with clients, etc., and had to be dismissed. Most played by the rules.

At times, she missed them all.

Especially Denzin.

She smiled thinking of her "stud." Denzin Anderson was smart, well-read, and handsome, with a hard body and an even harder dick. His mother suffered from a rare disease and he insisted on being her caregiver—physically and financially. He needed both the free time and the fast money work as a courtesan afforded him. Any woman attempting to join her roster had to show and prove her sexual skills by sleeping with Denzin. Pleasure was paramount, and the clients paid a high fee to be pleased. A woman could be beautiful but a stiff lay. Watching via camera let her know just who was skilled enough to join the ranks.

Desdemona bit back a smile, remembering the time he scrolled through his phone as a woman hoping to become one of her courtesans gave him a perfunctory fuck. Needless to the say that woman had not made the cut.

When she operated the mansion in the Riverdale section of the Bronx, he had lived on the estate, and when she finally began to take time off, it was Denzin she trusted—as much as she could trust anyone—to monitor the women on duty to ensure their safety.

And he tried like crazy to fuck me.
Never had she relented. No mixing business with pleasure—and she knew firsthand that Denzin's ability to bring a woman to climax was legendary.

No. Only Loren and his young, strong appeal had created enough urges for her to set aside the celibacy she claimed as a madam. Only Lo. And he made it worth the wait.

She shifted a bit in her seat when her bud came to life at heated memories of their sex play. Their chemistry was enough to make her climax from just him sucking her nipples. Ba-na-nas.

And when they finally went their separate ways, what then?

Back into celibacy? Loneliness? Trevor waiting in the wings?

I couldn't imagine letting another man into my life.

As she turned the corner of a suburban, tree-lined street in Brooklyn, she saw a wrecker with flashing yellow lights loading Loren's beloved Tahoe. He stood on the sidewalk outside his parents' home on a corner lot. Bell and Garee were nowhere in sight and she felt relieved.

Loren looked in her direction before giving the side of his battered SUV a couple of taps as he headed over to where she was double-parked. He removed his ever-present leather book bag and opened the door to climb into the passenger seat.

His closeness made her feel so alive. Like renewed energy. So kinetic.

"Thanks," Loren said, looking cute in the bright yellow hoodie he wore with knee-length cargo shorts and colorful socks pulled up to his knees with matching Jordans. His mass of curly black hair was in two thick cornrows.

Desdemona loved that Loren's style fluctuated from casual streetwear to stylish menswear with ease.

"Your *mommy* did your hair?" she asked in a teasing voice as she reached to tug the curled end of one.

Loren gave her a wink. "She talked shit the whole time, but I got a shampoo, conditioner, and she greased my scalp," he boasted.

"Good. I won't have to do it," she teased.

Loren made a face of disbelief. "Yeah right. Like you don't enjoy what happens while I'm sitting on the floor between your legs," he balked.

Like the very first time she'd braided his hair for him, Loren would turn and press kisses to her inner thighs before tasting her. Each and every time.

"Where are your parents?" she asked as she drove away.

"They just went up to get ready for an arts festival," he said, turning his head to look back at his precious Tahoe. "They missed you. My mom sent you a loaf of her banana walnut bread."

Her life went from arranging high-end sexual encounters around the world for the wealthy and famous to looking forward to lazy Saturday brunches with her boyfriend's parents.

"I'll call to thank her," she told him.

As she drove, she felt his gaze still resting on her. A glance proved she was right. "What?" she asked, feeling breathless.

"Nothing," he said with a shake of his head before looking out the window.

The set of his jaw was a bit tense.

"What, Lo?" she asked.

"I just would really love a little girl that looked just like you," he admitted, his gaze still out the window.

She fell silent.

So did he.

They had reached Manhattan before the ring of his

phone broke the stillness. "Dr. Palmer speaking," he said in answer.

He listened intently, and with each passing moment, he looked concerned.

Something's wrong.

"Yes, I'm very sorry to hear that. Thank you for calling me, Dr. Reightley," Loren said before ending the call.

Reightley. The dean of the university's English department.

"Everything okay?" she asked.

"The president of the university passed away," he said.

Francis McAdams. Consort #3. Addressed by her as Mr. President. Referred by a prominent governor.

His wife of more than forty years, Kimber, had slipped into a coma after a burst aneurysm. Seeking release without the bond of the love he held only for his wife, Mademoiselle had provided him a physical escape from his grief weekly for more than a year, always sending him a less educated courtesan with a trashier look and strict orders to limit conversation. Just sex.

His grief for his wife was always so palpable and his guilt for cheating on her would accept nothing else.

But Loren didn't know of any of that side of Francis McAdams.

"Nice dude. He was really helpful to me at the university. My first campus job was as a student assistant in the president's office. He was very invested in me succeeding. He said he saw greatness in me," Loren said. "Helped me with scholarships and—"

She glanced over at him when he paused.

Loren smiled. "In fact, it was Francis who recommended me to be your tutor."

Desdemona nodded in agreement. Shielding her apprehension.

He gave her a curious look. "I never did ask how in the world you knew Francis," he said.

Smoothly, Desdemona gave him a soft smile and a half-truth. "He and his wife were clients of the boutique," she said.

Loren nodded in understanding. "Nice dude," he repeated.

Desdemona said nothing more, hating that she had just deceived him.

Chapter Five

Monday, March 29

The butterflies. Should I be afraid or ready to be trans-
formed? Again. I choose the latter. Come what may.

"You're journaling again?"

Desdemona paused the movement of her Montblanc pen
against the page and looked up at Loren, standing beside
where she sat on the living room sofa. He was already dressed
for work in a tailored blazer and jeans, with his wild hair
restrained into a low ponytail and his rarely used spectacles in
place. "A little something," she said with honesty because
she didn't feel comfortable putting down her full feelings and
thoughts in the diary quite the way she used to in her childhood days.

When she left behind her work as a madam, she method-
ically burned her many journals, created during her lengthy
career. In them were her raw feelings and, at times, details of
the wild requests and shenanigans of her consorts and
courtesans. The ones still locked in her safe were from the
harrowing days after the death of her father. Those she kept
close.

"About how much you hate me?" Loren asked.

"Never, Loren. That's impossible," she said. "Do you hate me?"

He shook his head. "Myself," he said.

"Why?"

"Because I can't find the strength to leave you," he admitted. "I know that I should, but I can't stand the idea of never seeing you, kissing you, fucking you, lying in bed beside you, or another man being able to do so. I want to leave and I can't, Desi. Shit makes me feel weak or obsessed with you or some shit."

"Then maybe I should put you out of your misery and end it for you?" she asked, resting the journal on her lap.

"That easy for you, huh?" he asked, his eyes searching hers.

Gone was the light and the twinkle of joy that had once lived in the brown depths of her forever optimist. "No, not at all," she confessed. "I am enjoying every moment with you until there are no more. Selfishly, I was putting it on you to decide when it's done because I will have as much of you in my life as you will allow, Loren Palmer."

He broke their gaze and freed them from the intensity of it. "What do we do?"

Tell him the truth. All of it. Trust him. Maybe he will understand why I'm hesitant to have children because of it all.

"I don't know," she said instead, setting her journal beside her on the sofa.

Her robe fell open, exposing her nudity beneath the fine silk. His eyes dipped to take in the sight of her breasts. Desdemona eased the edges closed, fighting off her own temptation.

Sex clouded things for them. It had become their main distraction.

When Loren just stroked her cheek before turning to walk to the foyer, she knew he was not in the mood for a morning tryst either. He shifted his gaze out the windows lining the front of the condominium. His expression was pensive. So very serious. And troubled.

"Lo," Desdemona said.

He looked over at her.

"I haven't seen that smile of yours a lot lately," she said with a soft grin of her own.

Briefly, he glanced away before his smile spread and his dimples deepened. "I'm good," he said.

You used to be.

His constant warmth and kindness were fading. It was Loren who taught her to love life and enjoy every moment without fear. Find the good in everything. Smile more. Travel more. Dream more, and then achieve more. View the world in a better light. Step out of her comfort zone.

"What are you getting into today?" Loren asked before walking over to the closet in the foyer.

"Patrice called this morning. There's an issue with a shipment at the showroom, so I'm going in to get that straight," she said, rising to her feet to go get dressed to start her day. "Then I have an afternoon class."

Loren nodded as he held the straps of his leather book bag in one hand and opened the front door with the other. "Be safe. See you later," he said with one last look at her before taking his leave.

Missing was a portion of his normal goodbye to her: Love you.

It was a ritual now broken.

Desdemona busied herself with getting dressed, having already taken her morning shower. She chose a black, ankle-length wrap dress with cap sleeves and paired it with lace booties. Simple makeup, her diamond jewelry, and her hair pulled back into a sleek, low ponytail completed her look.

The drive to her showroom was burdened by traffic and the fast pace of pedestrians crossing the streets—at times not waiting for the right of way. What should have taken ten minutes was instead close to twenty-five. She was happy to park her car in a nearby garage and take the brief walk to the large, modern eighteen-story building on the corner. Glass doors opened into a beautifully appointed lobby. She rode one of the four large elevators up to the tenth floor of the building of commercial and office spaces.

Opening the thousand-square-foot showroom for the online boutique had been costly and a risk, but Desdemona felt it necessary in maintaining the look of legitimacy. During her days as Mademoiselle, the showroom had been closed to the public and she'd seen some "clients" by appointment only to ensure privacy. Still, every consort had to purchase a dress as part of their payment for the services of her paramours, and every dress was delivered like any other purchase made. The remainder of her fee was paid in cash. Sadly, many of the wives did indeed enjoy an elegant evening gown without knowing its connection to their husband purchasing sex.

As Desdemona stepped off the elevator and walked down the polished hall toward her corner unit, she paused a bit. This time the butterflies were in her stomach. She frowned.

One of the double doors to her showroom opened and a short, round man with a patch of bright red hair slicked to the side stepped into the hall and showed her his badge. "Right this way, miss," he said, motioning her forward with his free hand.

I am Madam X.

And at that moment, Desdemona pulled herself together, gathering every bit of the calm and calculated mode she had lived in for more than fifteen years. With each step, she reminded herself that fear was a foe and what she needed was to be *that* B.I.T.C.H.—Being In Total Control of Herself. She stiffened her spine, relaxed her face with a smile, and notched her chin just a bit higher.

The detective held the door open for her, and Desdemona walked in like she owned the place because she did. Patrice, a tall, full-figured beauty with plenty of style, had her arms crossed over her chest as she talked to another detective.

"Good morning, boss. These gentlemen asked me to call the owner to come down," she said in a rush, her words nearly colliding and shaking with nerves.

Desdemona gave her a comforting smile even as she noted that Patrice never called her "boss" and had always addressed her as Ms. Smith. Quickly, she knew they were not aware of her alias and had asked Patrice who she was.

Here we go. This is the moment you prepared for.

Desdemona turned and extended her hand to the first detective. "I am Desdemona Dean, the owner of the online boutique *Glitz* and the accompanying showroom. How may I help you gentlemen?" she asked with calm, even as her heart pounded with ferocity.

That was the first time Patrice knew her true identity and covered it well.

Loyalty begets loyalty.

The woman knew nothing of Mademoiselle. Her knowledge only went as far as the boutique, and that her employer, Alisha Smith, had been very good to her over the years, even offering her an opportunity to become a partner once she built the capital to buy in.

"I'm Detective Wilson and that is my partner, Milligan," the first detective began. "We have received an anonymous tip that this business serves as the front for a prostitution ring run by the owner. Which means you, Ms. Dean."

Someone snitched. Shit just got real as fuck.

Desdemona feigned confusion. "Ridiculous," she said, sliding her tote onto the bend of her arm to then play with her diamond bracelets—especially the one with the sparkling butterfly trinkets. "As you can see, we sell evening wear online, and this showroom is to exhibit our inventory by appointment only and *nothing* more."

She waved her hand around at the loft-style space with twenty shiny black mannequins displaying some of the high-end dresses she carried.

"Bullshit, *Madam X*," Detective Milligan drawled with sarcasm.

She eyed him coolly. *You're right, you thick-neck motherfucker. Now prove it*, she thought.

"Artie," Detective Wilson said sternly.

The doors opened and a half-dozen uniformed police officers entered the showroom.

"We also have a warrant to search the premises," the detective added.

Desdemona deserved an Oscar for her performance. Inside she was shattered, but her façade showed nothing of that.

"We are taking you into custody for questioning about your involvement in promoting prostitution, Ms. Dean," Detective Wilson said.

Patrice gasped in horror and covered her face with her hands. "No," she cried. "I don't want to go to jail!"

Oh, Patrice, please don't.

"You're not under arrest, but we will need you to come down to the station to make a statement," Detective Milligan said. "Right this way."

Patrice rushed to get her bag before following a uniformed officer out of the showroom with a look of apology at Desdemona.

She hoped her smile at the woman was reassuring enough to calm her down.

"May I call my attorney?" Desdemona asked as she opened her bag and reached inside.

"FREEZE!"

Desdemona looked around with cold eyes at all the

barrels of guns pointed at her. She held up both hands. "Really? At this point, cruelly, this scenario has become a cliché. That's disappointing, demeaning, disheartening, and above all...dangerous," she said, giving each a hard, frigid look. "Will the lesson of appropriate response by police officers *ever* be learned? How much more blood on your hands do you all need?"

Detective Milligan motioned for a female officer to step forward.

Desdemona released a long breath as the woman took her bag and quickly patted her down as she Mirandized her. She stood and patiently waited as they continued to search and gather files and equipment. Nearly an hour passed, but Desdemona said nothing more.

And when they finally led her out of the showroom and onto the elevator, she knew from their demeanor what awaited. They were far too victorious at being the ones to catch the infamous Madam X.

Even as they walked toward the glass front doors, the throng of people and press were not a surprise. Cameras. Microphones. Flashing lights. Fame was so addictive, and some hungered to touch even the fringe of it—even a madam to the wealthy and famous. The officers all seemed to preen for the camera, seeking a tiny piece of the fame. It was all so pathetic.

Be that B.I.T.C.H.

She didn't cower as they led her out of the building. Camera phones and the shouts of questions from the press and people were deafening.

"Madam X!"

"Any comment, Madam X?"

"Have you spoken to MQ?"

"Madam X, tell MQ I love him."

"Will you accept the million-dollar offer to write a book?"

"Who else is on your client list?"

"Hell, how much for an hour with you, love?"

"Madam X."

"Madam X!"

"MADAM X!"

Still, she kept her composure. There would be no scene from her.

Even as they manhandled her into the back of an unmarked car, she kept it all together. Even as she briefly wondered if every foolproof step she made would keep her free. Even as she struggled not to think of Loren's reaction when he saw the news.

It was him she thought of and worried about.

He deserved better than this.

Regrets over not telling him the truth served no purpose. What was done was done.

"That couldn't have gone any better," Detective Milligan said, sounding smug as he drove away from the havoc they meant to create.

Ambition is a motherfucker.

Feeling their eyes on her in the rear and side mirrors, she kept her face free of any expression and just looked out the window at the fast-paced life of Manhattan.

Was this my last day of freedom?

"You won't need all those diamonds where you're going, sweetheart," Milligan said.

His tone was filled with resentment and anger she didn't understand.

As a madam, she had made it her business to assess people and her accuracy rate was high. That ability ensured she fulfilled more than a sexual need for her consorts. At times, by their demeanor, words said and unsaid, the background check she ran on each, and other cues, she could get at the root of who they were and what drove them. And pleased them.

For some? Kink.

For others? To be praised—or even mothered.

Detective Milligan?

Humph. He would pay a high price to unleash his cruelty and dominate, probably harkening back to a childhood of being teased and ridiculed—probably for being impoverished.

His insecurity lingering into adult years numbered beyond forty made her chuckle.

He swirled in his seat to glare at her. "Laugh now," he spat.

She gave him a brief look that judged him before glancing away.

Fuck him.

The old Desdemona, who had been tricked and forced into prostitution and had taken far too many hits from her pimp and johns, would have plotted a million different ways to expose and embarrass the man. Now she just pitied him, knowing he had emotionally broken places he needed to heal.

I know I've been changed.

Behind her back, she used her thumb to stroke the butterflies on her bracelet as she closed her eyes with the slow release of her breath.

Oh, Lo. I am so sorry.

At the police station, Desdemona was processed and stripped of her belongings before being allowed to call her attorney. Quickly, she dialed the private number, aware of the eyes on her in the crowded police station.

"Jynn Nkosi, this is Desdemona. Midtown Precinct North. No arrest. Yet," she said, skipping any niceties.

"Got it. I have court, but I'll try for an adjournment and then I'm headed straight to you. Say nothing," Jynn said, urgency in her tone.

"Got it," Desdemona said before ending the call.

It was time for the high-powered criminal attorney to earn the hefty retainer she had paid the woman for the last six years, and to use the million dollars in cash set aside for her bail if needed.

Desdemona was placed in an interview room with nothing more than a table and three chairs. She claimed one. The hours seemed endless before the door opened for Wilson and Milligan to enter, carrying cups and now free of the blazers of their suits.

"My attorney is Jynn Nkosi and I will not be answering any questions without her being present," she said before they could settle into their seats.

The men shared a look.

"Not the behavior of an innocent woman, Ms. Dean. Your cooperation is best," Detective Wilson said before taking a sip of what smelled like coffee.

Desdemona crossed her legs and rearranged her dress atop them.

At her continued silence, the men rose and left the room.

There was more of a wait. Time to think and mull over regrets. Worry about Lo. Yearn to be free.

When the door opened again and Jynn strode in, Desdemona was happy to see the tall, full-figured, dark-skinned woman whose age was hard to discern but had to be in her early fifties. "Don't worry, this foolishness will end soon," she said, before setting her briefcase atop the table as she claimed the empty seat next to her client.

The questioning began.

Desdemona stuck to her guns. "I'm not sure why this accusation has been leveled against me. I run a reputable business. Nothing more," she said.

Detective Wilson opened a folder and turned it before sliding it across the table to the women. "Why the need not to include your name or the name of any other members on your LLC—out of Delaware?" he asked.

Jynn reached for the folder and closed it. "I'm aware of these papers because I filed them as the agent of record on behalf of my client, who wished to file an anonymous LLC, which is allowable in several states *including* Delaware. Not the first nor the last time a business owner wanted their privacy maintained, Detective," she said with a curt tone.

Desdemona fought the urge to arch a brow and say *take that motherfucker.* Her name was nowhere on the ownership papers. The business bank account and income tax were filed under the LLC, making the boutique a legitimate source of income to file taxes and still have a verifiable reason to be in contact with every consort on her list. The profit she made from the sale of the dresses had been a bonus.

"What reason would someone have to lie about your participating in a prostitution ring?" Detective Milligan snapped.

"Who? Who is the person? Unlike an anonymous LLC, which is legally permissible, leveling legal accusations against someone while hiding in the shadows is not," Jynn interjected.

The detective cast Jynn a leer as he slammed his hand atop the table, jostling coffee that overflowed from his cup. "Again," he repeated. "Why would someone lie?"

"A lot of people cannot stand to see a Black woman rise higher than their expectations to be nothing more than a bed wench and a cotton picker. We's free now and have every right to run a business and spread plenty of Black girl joy all over the land *our* ancestors built. Get into it. Black lives absolutely matter."

"How dare you!" Detective Milligan raged, with spittle flying as he jumped to his feet to leer down at them.

"Yes," Desdemona said softly, breaking her silence. "How dare we."

The door opened and another man with silver hair

entered, motioning for the detectives to join him outside the room.

The women sat quietly and waited.

Twice Jynn checked the time on her gold watch. Once she made a noise of annoyance in the back of her throat.

The door opened. The men entered. Detective Milligan was nearly as red as his partner's shocking patch of hair.

Desdemona's curiosity at what was to come next was stoked.

"Ms. Dean is free to go, but we are far from done with this," Detective Wilson said.

"We are coming for you, Madam X," Detective Milligan said.

His partner dropped his head, as if completely done with his partner's temperament.

Jynn rose and motioned for Desdemona to do the same. "Just keep it legal and we all can get through this misunderstanding without additional complaints or lawsuits being brought against the NYPD," she said.

I'm going home.

Desdemona felt such sweet relief. She had prepared herself for jail—at least until her bail hearing. Jynn stayed by her side as she signed for her belongings.

"Keep your chin up. Back straight. It's bananas outside," she advised her.

Desdemona shook her head as they began to walk toward the front door of the precinct. "Again? This will be the third time," she informed her attorney.

"*What?*" Jynn snapped.

"Coming out of the showroom. When we got here," Desdemona said.

"Hold on," Jynn said.

The woman chuckled as she stopped and looked across the large office bustling with activity to point at Milligan and

Wilson. "Three perp walks? Three?" she asked. "Do y'all want to continue down this road, because at the end of it, like the rainbow, there will be a pot of gold. Speaking on behalf of taxpayers: We don't want to pay for that."

Desdemona absolutely loved this warrior she'd hired. She had the presence and energy to shift the mood of those around her. To make a man shake in his shoes. She was bold. Unapologetic. And hella smart.

Queen shit.

"Let's go," Jynn said to Desdemona. "I will make one quick statement. There's our security to help get us to the car. Cool? As always. Say nothing."

Two large male bodies flanked them as they left the building. Soon they stepped outside, and the massive crowd exploded. The bright, flashing lights were nearly blinding. The noise deafening. The bodies falling in to encircle them seemed to suck the air from Desdemona.

"My client is *not* Madam X and will soon be vindicated. That is all. No further comment. Excuse us," Jynn said with authority as the bodyguards made a path to the Mercedes Sprinter waiting for them.

Desdemona blocked out the rapid-fire questions being shouted at them until she was finally guided into the rear of the vehicle. She claimed a plush leather seat and kicked off her booties—her first show of weakness. Soon Jynn entered, and the door was shut on the ruckus.

"What a shit show," Jynn sighed, looking out the tinted window at the crowd as the driver eased the vehicle through the throng of paparazzi, journalists, entertainment reporters, and ravenous onlookers. "Expect more of this at your condo building."

Desdemona felt sick at that.

Lo.

"I would advise staying somewhere else."

Desdemona shook her head. "I can't. I have to go there. I have to face it," she said, meaning her reckoning with Loren.

The time had come—not of her choosing—but it was there nonetheless.

Come what may . . .

Desdemona entered the building using the rear stairwell and thankfully avoided the chaos now outside the building. As she unlocked the rear door to the condo, she knew she would be hearing from the condo board soon, very soon. She had passed a few neighbors on her climb up and their leers told a story of forced eviction.

She entered and closed the door to lean back against it.

It was at that moment that she lost her resolve and slid down into a squat. She rested her head inside the groove created by her knees and released all the emotions that raged inside her. Every last one. The tears came. Softly at first, before building into a crescendo that caused her body to heave as she released a strangled cry.

Fury and fear battled for control. For one moment she wondered if that was how the brink of madness felt.

"Ay yo I'm slippin' I'm fallin' I can't get up . . ."

DMX's rhymes spoke her feelings to life.

"Get up, Desi."

She froze at the sound of Loren's voice before raising her tearstained face to look at him standing by the island in the kitchen, looking down at her. Never had she seen his energy be so dark. The man before her was so clearly angry. And hurt.

Freeing her hair from its low ponytail, Desdemona released a jagged breath as she wiped her face with her hands.

"I guess now I know why you were so pro-prostitution,"

he said, with a bitterness she had never heard in his voice before.

Desdemona longed for the strength to rise from the floor and not have to look up at him while being judged and looked down upon from his moral high ground.

Get the fuck up, Desi. Fuck that.

With every bit of strength she could muster, like climbing a mountain, she did stand tall and step forward to lean her belly against the island. The distance between them was far longer than its length.

"Loren, you were the first man I slept with in five years. I own a dress boutique and showroom. I attend college," she said. "There is nothing else about me that you do not know as of the day we reconnected in class."

He frowned so deeply his brows seemed to connect. "Save the bullshit for your court case and give me the truth, Desdemona," he demanded. "Or should I say, Madam X?"

Desdemona eyed him and hated the tear that raced down her cheek. It spoke to a vulnerability she disdained. Loving him gave Loren a power she had never given to anyone since the day she watched Majig die of an overdose.

The bitter laugh she released only hinted at the bevy of bad people and even worse situations she had experienced. "You have no idea what the fuck I been through. What I fought, what I overcame. You have no clue," she spat out before releasing another bitter laugh that turned into a cry. "Shit you couldn't imagine. Shit you couldn't dare live through."

The countless faces of the men she'd serviced seemed to flash in her mind in rapid succession.

Fucking me.

Fighting me.

Raping me.

Going numb had saved her soul.

Desdemona was herself sinking under the waves of her emotions as she pressed her eyes closed and hugged herself. She let her head fall back as her tears weakened her knees. "Father God!" she cried as she felt her face wrinkle with despair.

"Desi."

She felt Loren's hands on her arms, but she jerked away from his touch. Never had she felt so raw and exposed.

"Tell me," Loren said.

"I can't," she said, guarding her life—her story—even amid her misery.

It had become second nature.

"Why?"

"I told you there were parts of my past I could never talk about with you. That fact has not changed, Lo," she said, moving over to the wine cabinet to remove a bottle of her favorite.

"Were you a prostitute, Desi, and then a madam?" he asked. "Is what MQ and the news saying true? Fuck that. Answer me."

She was trembling and set the bottle atop the island as she gripped the neck. "If it were, would it change us? Would you leave? Would you judge? Would you hate me?" she asked, her voice hollow as she stared at the label on the wine to avoid locking her eyes with his and seeing something in the dark depths that would shatter her even more.

At his silence, she found the courage to look up at him. His face was tense and stormy.

"Would you count the men I've slept with? Huh? Try to detect the miles on my pussy? Would you be bothered by what I could've done in bed with other men? Women, too, at times? Huh? Would you hate me for every trick I booked for someone else and made a fee? Could you forgive and forget? Could I trust you?"

Loren's eyes filled with disbelief. "Do you trust me?" he asked.

I trust no one.

"Would you be able to fuck me and not care who came before you?" she asked, releasing the bottle and undoing the belt of her wrap dress to fling back and expose the sheer undergarments she wore as she walked over to stand before him. "Would you still want a woman if she sold herself?"

"Did you?" he retorted before reaching to pull the dress closed.

It fell back open at her sides as she turned away from him and walked over to the counter to pick up the electric wine opener. "I will never answer that, Lo," she said.

"That's as good as an answer."

Desdemona looked over at him. "Not in court," she said, and then hated her flippancy.

He was hurt and angry. Understandably so.

"In court? You think I would sit my ass up in court and reveal things discussed between us?" he asked, his voice incredulous. "That's what you think of me? You really don't trust me!"

Desdemona gripped the bottle of wine to fling it to the floor to shatter. "I have never been in a position to trust *anyone.*" She spat her truth with fury at always having to be on her guard since the death of her father—maybe even her mother.

It was a long and tiresome road to travel on. Especially alone.

And now, her only safe space—with her Lo—was quickly disappearing.

Desdemona covered her face with her hands. Again. Felt lost, hopeless, desperate, angry, and sad. Again.

So many things she had buried deeply were resurfacing and she felt herself emotionally drowning.

"Lo, I have to fight for my freedom. Please don't make me have to fight you as well," she pled, her voice cracking. "Please."

"What should I do, Desi, pretend you haven't been in jail? Fake like your face isn't all over the news? Take pride that you fucked MQ and he bragged about it in a damn book with his motherfucking clown ass?" Loren asked. "Just stick my head up my ass and keep pretending like we *been* doing?"

Yes.

But she knew better.

Maybe it's for the best.

"I need you right now," she admitted, surprising herself.

"I need the truth from you right now," he countered.

They looked at each other.

Even in the midst of anger, judgment, and bitter disappointment, that energy they created pulsed between them. Around them. So powerful.

Desdemona's heart pounded and raced as her heart pained and was shredding. "I need you right now, Lo," she admitted again as she stared at him, vulnerable and exposed. "Please."

For a moment she saw all the love he had for her fill the brown depths of his eyes and hope began to pick up the pieces of her heart.

He shook his head and broke their gaze. "I need to get out of here, Desi," he said, turning to walk down the hall toward the foyer.

She followed him, but her steps faltered at the sight of the packed bags by the door in the foyer. "Lo, please, I need you right now," she repeated, going to him as she felt her world completely spin off its axis. She wrapped her arms around his waist and pressed her face against his chest with a desperation she knew she would one day regret. "Please. Not now. Please, Lo."

Loren reach around himself to remove her arms and set them at her side. "I can't, Desi," he said.

Hope faded and her heart broke as she stood before him with her hair loose, her makeup undoubtedly ruined by tears and her dress opened with a level of vulnerability like nothing she had ever known. Or ever wanted to know again.

She nodded and stepped back, fighting to bury her feelings once more and reclaim the façade that had shielded her over the years. "I guess you found the strength. Huh?" she asked, reminding him of his quandary that very morning.

"Because I can't find the strength to leave you."

Desdemona stepped in front of the mirror on the wall of the foyer and retied her dress, raked her fingers through her hair, and used her fingertips to clean up her makeup. which was just as clownish-looking as she'd assumed.

Fuck him, then.

Loren opened the door.

The little girl afraid to be left alone broke through the tough shell. "I need you. I love you," she admitted. "If you leave me now, I will never forgive you, Loren."

With one last long look, he did indeed pick up his belongings and walk out.

Desi moved to the closed door and grabbed the door-knob, ready to yank it open and plead with him. *No,* she told herself, resting her head against the cool wood instead as she gave in to her heartbreak and let hot tears race down her face.

Come what may . . .

Hours later, Desdemona awakened on the sofa, cloaked by a darkness only broken by the streetlights filtering in from the window. She welcomed the calm as she sat in the corner of the couch, with her eyes still pained and swollen from crying. She didn't bother with the television or checking her phone. For tonight, she welcomed the peace. Tomorrow was another day, though.

And with the rise of the sun, she was setting off on a warpath.

Amid her detainment and the search of the showroom, she had focused on one indisputable truth.

One of her consorts or courtesans had reported her to the police.

Tomorrow would be soon enough to find and destroy *that* motherfucker.

Chapter Six

Tuesday, April 6

*I don't have the time or energy for this particular piece
of bullshit.*

Desdemona closed her journal before she settled back
against the chair behind the large desk that also served as the
payment counter of the showroom. She eyed Patrice, sitting
across from her. It was clear the woman was nervous about
this confrontation.

"I hope you understand my point of view," Patrice said.
"I just don't see the boutique still being viable with the
scandal and you facing criminal charges."

"I offered you a partnership in this business because of
your hard work, your dedication, and your style," she said.
"Even though you hadn't bought into the business yet, I
considered you a partner and paid you a fifty percent share.
That's loyalty. I guess I expect the same in return."

Patrice nodded. "And I am grateful, Ms. Smi—uh, Dean.
Ms. Dean."

"Desdemona," she offered.

"Okay, Desdemona, why the alias? All these years you were Ms. Smith *to me*, and that was fake?" the woman asked.

"For my privacy" was all Desdemona offered.

Although she'd had the locks changed and had the entire space swept for bugs left behind by the police before reopening, she still was careful with her words.

"I'm just worried that if the business fails, I won't be able to help provide for my family," Patrice continued. "And my husband doesn't like me working here anymore, to be honest."

Of course he doesn't.

Desdemona shifted her gaze beyond the woman to the mannequins positioned at the front of the showroom. The sunlight blazed through the glass windows and caused the sequins on some of the expensive frocks to twinkle. It made her smile a little, and most days that was rare. To be cherished. "Listen, I completely understand. As a matter of fact, if I were able, I would walk away from the boutique altogether, but I can't right now. So, you do have a choice, Patrice, because I recognize the position you feel you are in. Leave now and chart a new path for yourself or continue working, because I will be cleared of these allegations."

Jynn had advised her to continue the operation of the boutique to maintain the appearance of propriety. The attorney had also assigned Desdemona a bodyguard, who now stood outside the door of the showroom, casting a rather large, imposing shadow against the floor and wall. Yusef was six foot five and broad.

"I think it's best I leave," Patrice said, her eyes dropping, as if she was unable to meet Desdemona's steady gaze.

I miss my courtesans. They were brave and loyal.

"Then I wish you well, Patrice, and in thanks for everything you have done to keep this business going when I was too busy to do it, I will offer severance pay of one year's salary," Desdemona said, feeling no ill will and enjoying the way surprise rounded Patrice's eyes. "Hell, open your own boutique and give me some real competition."

The woman's eyes welled with tears that she blinked away. "Seriously?" she asked with softness.

"Absolutely," Desdemona stressed. "I will have a check sent to you this week. Make a good life, Patrice."

"Thank you," she said as she rose and retrieved her purse, with several glances over at Desdemona before she walked to the door. She opened it and turned. "I'm not judging you for whatever you did or did not do. I know how good you have been to me these last five years, and I couldn't imagine you being anything but that to anyone else. I hope everything turns out good, Desdemona."

That touched her. The good she did for so many people that she never bragged about went unnoticed. It was nice to be seen for once for her goodness. She truly tried to be a blessing. "It will," she said with promise.

All she could hope was that she spoke the truth.

After Patrice left, Desdemona rose to walk over to the mannequins, weaving her way between them all as she enjoyed the feel of the sun against her face. When she reached the window, she looked down at the busy Manhattan street and the creeping traffic. The press was gone, but the paparazzi lingered.

The week had done nothing to weaken the curiosity about Madam X at all. Her face, name, and business were everywhere. The protective wall she had so carefully built around herself was gone and she was now completely alone in the bubble.

She hadn't heard from Lo since he left. It was truly over. Her longing for him seemed insurmountable. The desire to go to him was constant. But she fought it.

Her truth was out, whether she admitted it to him or not, and she could not make him love who she was—or had been. A streetwalker for a brutal pimp who went on to run his client list upon his death and then shed lowbrow johns for the wealthy and famous when the opportunity arose.

I am Madam X.

No formal arrest had been made, but the police—and possibly the feds—were investigating her. She skipped the last week of class. Her condo board let her know that with a conviction, she would be in violation of its bylaws. The comments section on the *Glitz* website had to be disabled because of trolls hurling vile and cruel insults. She lived in preparation of the police arriving at her home to arrest her, making it hard to fully sleep. She was bombarded with requests for comments and interviews.

It was hectic and bothersome.

She raised one arm and slid into a ray of sun, enjoying the glimmer of the diamond bracelets and the way the butterfly trinkets seemed to dance.

Change had truly come. What was next?

Desdemona turned and crossed the showroom just as the door opened. She looked to see Yusef, the bodyguard, entering with a huge bouquet of colorful flowers and a stack of mail in hand.

"Deliveries, Ms. Dean," he said, setting the flowers and mail atop the desk.

She frowned. As a storefront used mainly for deliveries, inventory, and occasionally private appointments, not much mail was generated. "Thanks, Yusef," she said, reaching for the message card with the flowers. " 'Forever grateful. My life is so different because of you,' " she read aloud as Yusef took his leave.

It was signed "The Other P."

Desdemona chuckled and tapped the card against her chin as she eyed the two dozen roses that could only be from Portia, a young woman who shared the same first name as her mother.

And at that moment, she truly felt Black girl joy and needed it so *very* badly.

On the back of the card were descriptions and instructions for the proper care of each flower.

"Snapdragons, blue stars, columbines, and gladiolus." She read about each before turning to bend and inhale the scent of the florae. Again, she chuckled. Each symbolized power. An obviously deliberate choice by the young woman she had saved.

One night, Desdemona had wandered back to the dark and deserted block where she had once sold herself. While sitting in her car and reflecting on the worst days, which were far behind her, screams filled with inflicted pain echoed. The sight of a woman being brutally beaten by her pimp reminded Desdemona of being the victim of brutality, and she rushed to use her trusted baton against him to intervene. The woman was no more than a teenager, and once Desdemona hustled the girl into her car and sped away from the pimp and his gun, she had made it her business to offer the help to a frightened teenager no one had offered her....

Desdemona settled back against the cracked leather of the restaurant booth. "What's your story, Portia?" she asked.

The teenager shrugged one shoulder before removing her puffer coat. "Stuff I wish I could forget," she said.

"Like?" she pressed.

"Why?" Portia countered, her voice soft.

She sounded and acted younger than her years.

"Because I can't help you on your journey unless I know where you've been," Desdemona said. "What have I gotten myself into?"

"You? Me too!"

"*Right,*" *Desdemona agreed.*

They fell silent as the waitress set their drinks and straws on the table and retreated.

Portia removed the paper from her straw and dropped it in her drink. "Junkie mom. Deadbeat dad. Molestation. Rape. Physical abuse. Rebel. Runaway. Kidnapped. Pimped," she said, her voice a monotone, as if she separated her emotions from the memories.

"*Beaten,*" *Desdemona added.*

Portia nodded and looked at her drink as she stirred her straw in circles. She looked distant. Her thoughts were elsewhere.

It was because of stories such as Portia's, and her own, that Desdemona never forced one of her paramours to do anything they didn't choose to. She thought of her own pimp. Majig. Violence had been his best friend as well. She flinched at the memory of one of his backhanded slaps.

"*So, he is all you have?*" *Desdemona asked, hating just how much she understood.*

"*Had,*" *Portia stressed. "And yes. I lived with him because I'm not old enough to get my own place."*

"*How old are you?*"

"*Sixteen.*"

Still a kid.

"*I'm not going back to foster care. Before I do that, I will go back to Papo and just recover from that ass whipping.*"

Desdemona had placed the teenager in her own small apartment with a stipend, paid for a lawyer to help the teenager file a petition for emancipation, and encouraged her to get a job. Her one requirement? No more prostitution. Even as a madam, a life of prostitution was the last thing she wanted for the teenager with the same name as her mother. And in time, once she was fully on track, Desdemona had simply faded from her life without revealing her true identity or profession to Portia.

The headlines had made short work of that anonymity.

Sometimes she wondered about Portia, who had to be nearing eighteen or nineteen now. The flowers meant she was doing well. "Thank God," Desdemona said, moving the colorful arrangement to the edge of the desk and tucking the card away inside her bag.

Wanting to live in the goodness for a little bit longer, she turned on music to play via the wireless speakers. Beyoncé's "Daddy Lessons" filled the space. The bass-driven song had an upbeat country feel that always put her in a good mood. Always.

Even with her heartbreak.

Missing Lo.

Afraid of jail.

And unsure of the future.

She danced.

Fuck it.

All of it meant nothing in those four minutes and forty-eight seconds, as she got lost in the music and allowed herself to *be* happy.

"'Tough girl is what I had to be,'" she sang off-key along with the diva as she worked her hips down to the floor and back up again.

The horns fed her. Blessed her. Burst inside her.

Fuck. It.

She spun and noticed Yusef standing outside the show-room, looking at her with a bemused expression. She just shrugged at him and kept moving, using any available space to glide, slide, and two-step until the song ended.

Desdemona made her way back to her desk and turned down the music before picking up the mail to flip through. There were mostly advertisements and coupons, but it was clear Portia wasn't the only one anxious to reach out to her.

The phone had rung so incessantly in the showroom that she'd had it temporarily disconnected.

Claiming the seat, she set three envelopes of varying sizes side by side atop the desk.

Now what?

Desdemona pinched the bridge of her nose and leaned back in the chair to eye the envelopes. "And they went old school too," she said, nudging the corner of one of the envelopes with her index finger to send it in a semi-turn.

Feast or famine?

She selected the one with an Atlanta postmark and used a gold letter opener to find a handwritten card. "A friend," she read, recognizing the slashing handwriting as that of Denzin.

When it took a month for him to reveal to her that his mother had passed—and only because she asked about her—she had learned that this man she trusted as much as she was able did not consider her a friend.

"You only know my mother was sick at all because you asked me why I wanted to get into the business," Denzin had said. *"Hell, I don't even know your real name."*

No offense given or taken. Just truth.

On the card was a number, and she would bet a million dollars it was to a prepaid phone.

Friendship. More goodness.

Still, she wasn't ready for even her friends.

Desdemona reached into her bag and removed her phone. There were a dozen missed calls and texts from Melissa.

What can I say? What will she say?

If there was anything she'd discovered during the entire ordeal, it was that she felt no shame for her past—just for the lies and half-truths she'd told to protect herself from arrest. To people she cared about.

Like Melissa.

And Lo.

Desdemona set the phone face down on the desk and looked at the remaining two envelopes. She eyed the postmarks. One from New York. The other, a large, padded manila envelope, had none. "Weird," she said.

Ding.

Desdemona eyed the iPad connected to the boutique's ordering software. She was surprised to find a new order for a Marchesa embroidered tulle gown with an A-line skirt. She busied herself removing the dress from the mannequin and preparing it for shipment, thankful for the distraction. It wasn't until she printed the shipping label that she noticed the recipient.

Number 9.

The first john to ever make her climax, and also the last man she serviced before her celibacy.

Antoine Pierre.

The tall, handsome Haitian businessman with an arousing French accent had wanted her in his bed—and that was only when he wasn't in a relationship. During those times, Antoine would remain faithful, but as soon as it was over she would get a call to do business again.

Her heart raced a bit as she remembered the very last time she'd seen him. It was aboard his private jet, where she had personally brought three dresses for him to choose to purchase for whatever woman he was dating as a very eligible bachelor. They sipped champagne and flirted as he begged her to name her price—any price—to sex her again.

The memory of his demand echoed and caused her to lick her lips at the memory.

"Nommez votre prix."

She had still been celibate back then and so very tempted, but she left with her celibacy intact, nearly nine thousand dollars for all three dresses, a little cum on her cheek from her allowing him to masturbate in front of her, and an order for him to never contact her again as she blocked his number.

Knock-knock.

Desdemona looked over at the glass wall. "Oh no," she said with a shake of her head at the sight of Antoine standing beside Yusef.

The sexy Haitian was the wealthy owner of a multimillion-dollar tech business in Paris and he was smiling like a cat about to lick a bowl of warm milk. She rose and smoothed her hands over the Whitney Mero camo pencil skirt she wore with a sheer, black T-shirt tied in the back to expose a bit of her belly and emphasize her hourglass shape.

His eyes missed none of it, and it was then she knew the man was still doggedly in pursuit of bedding her. When she stopped servicing consorts, it made him want her even more—perhaps to brag to the others on the list that *he* had brought Mademoiselle out of retirement.

Or is he here to set me up?

She paused at the door with her hand on the clear handle.

No. Not Antoine. Or was it he who betrayed her? Angry that she would not relent—not for any price she could have named?

To make the order with the Madam X scandal swirling like a shark to chum was odd.

But then, so was Antoine.

Was this a sting, with Milligan and Wilson hoping she would discuss the good old days with Antoine—maybe even agree to fuck him—only to be arrested for being caught in the act of prostitution while he wore a wire?

No, not Antoine. There were a few consorts I kicked off the client list that I suspected, but not Antoine. His obsession was with fucking me, not sending me to jail.

Right?

Trust no one.

"Sir, this is by appointment only—" Yusef was saying.

Desdemona opened the door but leaned in the doorway. "Hello, sir. He is correct, this is a private showroom by appointment only," she explained.

Antoine slid his hands into the pockets of the slacks of his pinstripe suit and looked down at her. "I just placed an order and hoped I could pick it up since I need it for this evening," he explained smoothly with a hint of a French accent.

She looked at him. "Pat him down, Yusef, please?" she asked.

Antoine chuckled and raised his hands. "Whatever is necessary," he said.

Desdemona looked on as the bodyguard did a quick, light pat down before she stepped back and allowed Antoine to enter. And, of course, he smelled divine. "I'll get your dress for you, Mr. Pierre," she said, moving past him.

"The name Desdemona suits you," he said.

She gave him a brief look over her shoulder. "Really? I've learned that it means misery," she said.

"Well, this isn't Shakespeare, so I declare it means beautiful," Antoine said.

She gave him a chastising look that he returned with a devilish smile. "What are you doing? Especially now?"

He shrugged one broad shoulder. "I am purchasing a beautiful gown for an even more beautiful boutique owner," he said, rocking on the heels of his handmade loafers.

She arched a brow. "For or from?" she asked.

"The dress is for you to wear to dinner with me in Paris," he said.

"Antoine, you cannot be serious," she said. "A date?"

"*Tout à fait*. I think more than ever you deserve to be pampered, Desdemona."

Grown-man shit.

Desdemona turned to open the box in which she arranged the dress. "Thank you, but I can't, Antoine," she said, even as she traced the delicate edge of the décolletage. "I am in love."

"Lucky man," he said.

Is he?

To cling to loyalty to Loren when he was no longer in her life seemed foolish.

"I would never date a boutique customer, Antoine, and you know that," she said, refolding the tissue paper back atop the dress before replacing the lid of the box.

"Let me take care of you," Antoine said as he walked over to bend a bit at the waist to press a kiss to each of her cheeks before he whispered in her ear, *"Nommez votre prix."*

Name your price.

Foolishly, he thought she was still for sale. As a concubine.

A whore in residence. Same difference.

Kept woman. Streetwalker. Under the guise of a masseuse. High-class call girl. Woman dating a man simply for his wealth. All the same.

Desdemona gave him a chastising look before easing past him. "Should I have the dress delivered somewhere else?" she asked.

Antoine chuckled. "Keep it," he said, walking past her and letting his finger lightly draw a path across her back. "One day I plan to take it off you and make love to you for hours. *Au revoir*...for now."

Antoine was not the only consort who had sought to have her in bed again. Just the most persistent.

I really shouldn't have fucked him so well. My clever tongue has him obsessed.

She revised the address and reprinted the label to have the frock shipped to his villa in Paris. It would be awaiting him upon his return and, hopefully, help to make herself clearer to him.

Desdemona busied herself again, selecting one of the dresses in inventory on the racks behind the desk for the mannequin. The newer, most expensive stock was prominently displayed on the glossy mannequins, but there were a hundred pieces of inventory. Each was more beautiful than the last.

But Desdemona found no happiness in working with the clothes. For her, the boutique's purpose came and went with the end of Mademoiselle. Patrice was better suited for the passion for this work. She was already missed.

"Fuck this shit," she muttered, even as she arranged the skirt around the base of the mannequin.

I'd rather be back in class. Taking steps forward, not backward.

She made her way back across the showroom to gather her bag, phone, and the two remaining envelopes. She had no more energy, time, or effort to give the showroom that day. Although the condo seemed barren without Loren's presence, she was eager to go home.

Fuck it.

Desdemona left the showroom. Yusef stepped aside to make room for her to turn and lock the door. "I'm just heading home and then the rest of the day is yours, Yusef," she said as they began walking down the long length of the hall to the elevator.

When the metal doors slid open and several people occupied the space, she slid on oversized black shades and stepped on among them, with Yusef taking position to tower behind her.

"That's her," a voice whispered to someone else.

"She should be kicked out of the building—"

Desdemona tensed.

"Don't do that," Yusef warned them, with his big voice seeming to reach and press against the walls of the elevators.

Worth every cent.

The short ride was uncomfortably silent.

"Who are you?"

Dr. Ophelia's question came to her as they strode across the sun-blessed lobby.

Resilient.

There were a few flashes of cameras and a small crowd that had to be held back as they made the trek down the street and around the corner to the nearby parking garage. She was thankful it was staffed and had valet service because she wasn't sure she could have arrived without people surrounding her vehicle.

"Can I say something?" Yusef asked as they awaited the car.

She looked up at him through the dark tint of her shades. "Depends," she said.

"I love you, Madam X," a male voice shouted from a passing car with a long lay on his horn.

"You are fierce. No disrespect. I love my wife. I'm not on some low-key begging bullshit. It's just you're a warrior. You know. It's in your eyes. Your walk. Your demeanor. It says don't *fuck* with her. It's a vibe, Ms. Dean. Definitely a vibe. Warrior shit," he said as the valet pulled up in her Maserati.

I'm a warrior? Is that who I am?

As she slid into the passenger seat and Yusef closed the door to come around the front of the vehicle, Desdemona thought on that. "Warrior shit?" she asked when he slid into the driver's seat.

He chuckled. It rumbled. "Definitely," he assured her.

She fell silent as they rode and reached in her bag for her journal to add "warrior" to her list.

"Does your wife mind you working for me?" she asked as she tucked her pen back inside the pages and closed the diary.

"No," he said without hesitation. "Like we're good, you

know? It's *her* for me. And my kids. Hell, it's *us* for me. You feel me?"

Desdemona smiled. That was something Loren would have said.

"We're locked in," he continued as he checked the mirrors as he drove. "So she's good. She trusts me because she should. You feel me? Same way I trust her. Without question."

"That's what you think of me? You really don't trust me!"

"I have never been in a position to trust anyone."

She closed her eyes behind her shades at the heated memory with Loren. It was quickly followed by another.

"I need you. I love you. If you leave me now, I will never forgive you, Loren."

And he left.

That still stung.

Ding.

Desdemona pulled her phone from the side pocket of her vintage, monogrammed tote and used her thumb to swipe until she reached the newest Google alert. She frowned at the photo of her leaving the building just minutes before. *What the*, she mouthed as she scrolled.

It was a social media account dedicated to her daily fashion called Madam Fashion. Today's post already had two thousand likes.

People are crazy.

She slid the phone back into her bag.

Being so exposed, without any power to stop it, was doing something to her—and not in a good way. She didn't miss the irony of longing to step out of the shadows that once protected her to now wishing to disappear.

When they reached the underground parking of her building and Yusef left in his massive pickup truck, which he'd left parked there this morning, Desdemona climbed onto the elevator. A man stepped on beside her. She gave him a perfunctory glance and moved over to put distance between them, but she felt his eyes on her profile. Watching her.

Long-honed instincts kicked in.

She slid her hand inside her tote and wrapped her fingers around her new retractable baton. But then she released that and grabbed the Taser instead.

"I bet you're worth every cent. Aren't you?" he asked. "I'd drink your piss."

See? Dumb. Weird. Goofy. Idiotic. Bullshit.

In a quick one-two move, Desdemona jacked her tote onto the crook of the elbow of her right arm and extended her left to press the Taser to his throat with her thumb, ready to release high-powered voltage into him. "Say another word to me," she dared. "Say one more motherfucking word to me. Fuck with it."

His eyes were wide. And wild. Like his fear turned him on. But he said not one more word.

Oh, definitely a warrior.

And she had been the same about her courtesans. While they were on duty, she had stayed on alert to go to the side of any of them who felt fear. And there had been a few times a consort lost every bit of his mind and had to be brought back to reality with a good jolt or hit.

Disgusted with him—and men in general, who were led by their dicks—Desdemona thrust him away into the opposite corner. They stayed that way until the elevator stopped on her floor and she stepped off.

"Bitch!" he called out to her just before the door shut.

Desdemona kept walking.

Now Yusef would have to escort her to her front door, effectively making her a prisoner in her own home.

As she entered her condo, she made a note to add being

a protector to her growing list. Once the door was closed, she bent over to gladly unzip and step out of her polished black leather heels before heading to the kitchen. She set her keys and bag atop the island to pour herself a full glass of her favorite Rieussec wine. She carried the goblet into the bedroom and entered the walk-in closet. Like her last condo, it was equipped with a safe. This one was inside what appeared to be a slender shoe closet. She unlocked it swiftly as she sipped from her drink. Inside was a million in cash, her beloved journals from the days before prostitution claimed her life, several prepaid telephones, and a black billfold. She reached for the last. It held yet another set of fake credentials that would make it possible for Desdemona Dean to disappear and for Janet Anders to appear.

A backup plan for the backup plan of the backup plan...

Her madam protection program.

Without Loren in her life to worry about, it was becoming more and more of an option. She thought of him. Longed for him. Tried to understand him. Loved him. And hated him.

The line was always thin.

Desdemona set the billfold back in its place and locked the safe. Back in the kitchen, she removed the two envelopes and checked her phone. It was on "do not disturb," but there were a few voice mails and messages. She hated the quickening of her heart's pace, thinking one of them might be from Loren. She placed the phone on Speaker atop the island before walking over to the fridge.

"This is Desi. Why are you still leaving voice mails? Go ahead. I guess."

She removed leftover prawn fried rice and smiled a little at her outgoing message.

Beep.

"This is Trevor. With all due respect, lose my number."

Desdemona smirked. "It's *not* in my contacts, boo," she said, emptying the food onto a plate before sliding it into the microwave.

Beep.

"Desi. Melissa here. I wanted to see you. I'm giving you space, but you're still shutting me out after weeks. We need to talk. I do have questions, but I also have a huge glass of wine, a hug, and a place for you to hide for a while if you need to. What hurts most is you ignoring me. I miss your crazy, funny, smart, shit-talking ass. Let's at least talk about it. *Call* me."

I miss you too.

Desdemona reached to pause the voice mails. She stared at the phone as she stroked the lip gloss from her bottom lip with the side of her thumb. It was the questions and the curiosity over just how she became a madam she had to avoid. It would mean admitting something she would not.

I am Madam X.

She deleted the message and went on to the next.

Beep.

"Desdemona. Call me. Let's get together this week and strategize."

Jynn. No Loren. Okay. Cool.

But it wasn't.

Desdemona removed the plate and grabbed a fork to dig in and feed her hunger. In between bites, she opened the envelope with the postmark.

"'Ask God to forgive your sins and you will be saved. God bless,'" she read before turning the typed page to find the back blank. No signature.

Okay. Thanks.

"Father God, please forgive my sins and see into my heart in a way that only You can," she prayed with her head bowed.

Can't hurt. I could use some of God's grace.

She tossed the letter and its envelope in the trash and washed her hands. She paused before reaching for the last envelope.

As she opened the flap with her pinkie finger, she felt a nervousness shimmy over her. Inside was a cheap prepaid phone and a letter. With each movement of opening the folded paper and every passing moment, her trepidation was confirmed.

PAY ME $100,000 OR THE NEXT TIME I SEND THE POLICE FOR YOU, YOU WON'T WALK FREE, MADAM X. YOU CAN'T HIDE NOW. I'LL BE IN TOUCH.

"Shit," Desdemona swore as she let the paper fall onto her plate of food to slowly be soaked with grease.

Chapter Seven

Friday, April 9

Africa sounds like a plan right about now. Motherland, anyone?

Desdemona stepped inside the lecture hall of her history class. It was her first day back on campus and, thankfully, security did not allow paparazzi to go any further than the front gates. She had blissfully ridden past them in her rideshare, knowing her flashy car was now well-known. Murmurs raced across the students already assembled in their seats. Many turned to gaze at her excitedly. A few held up their phones in her direction until she gave them a hard stare and a jaunty point of her finger, like *Don't get fucked up.*

It was clear that news of her being Madam X had pervaded her life even further. She stopped watching television and checking social media, so she had no idea just what was being revealed about her life. Being a college student was one of the tidbits offered.

Desdemona claimed a seat at the front and gave them all her back.

Obtaining her college degree was important to her—just

as much as her hard-earned GED had been. She would not let conjecture keep her from doing just that.

The professor entered the hall. Gail Orli was a tall, thin woman with pale red hair, oversized glasses, and a dull tan suit. Beneath the dowdiness, Desdemona spotted a beauty. With a session with a colorist to deepen the red hues of her hair, better glasses, and vibrant colors, she could be a stunner.

Truly, any woman could with the right accessories.

As she began to teach about the role of women in Colonial America, Desdemona focused on taking notes and made sure to answer every question she knew, even as the whispers and snickers continued.

It reminded her of being fifteen, homeless, and barely clean but fighting sleep and the judgment of Majig to go to school every day. Until the teasing had become unbearable when word of her prostituting spread through the school. Seeing "Desdemona's price list. Blow job $10," on the chalkboard and the cruel laughter had been more than she could take anymore.

She never returned to school again.

That was sixteen years ago, and she was a grown woman now, with plenty of fortitude, more than to be bothered by classmates younger and more immature than she.

I won't be chased from school again.

When the class drew to an end, Desdemona was proud of herself. The shame she had never healed from about the teasing had her nerves on edge, but she reminded herself of everything she had overcome in her thirty-five years. More than many would be able to handle or rise above.

"Ms. Dean, may I speak to you, please?" the professor asked as she peered at her over the rim of her spectacles.

Desdemona paused for a moment before hitting Record on the laptop she used to take notes. She then made her way toward the podium. "Yes?"

The woman cleared her throat. "I think you could tell

that your presence in class caused a lot of disruption today," she began.

Desdemona frowned.

Another brief clearing of the throat. "Under the current circumstances, perhaps a little time off from your coursework would be beneficial to all," she said.

Desdemona ran her stiletto nails across her baby hair. "Or perhaps you could set guidelines in your classroom that would not allow disruption while you're teaching?" she offered. "I did not disrupt your class, so perhaps this conversation should've been saved for those who did."

The woman looked taken aback. "Ms. Dean—"

"Professor, I paid in full for this course and all my other ones—without loans or grants. Are you offering to personally refund this semester's cost back to me as you stand here and discourage a woman—like those you were just teaching about—from bettering herself?" Desdemona asked as she eyed her. "Because it's very much giving off a that-woman-deserved-to-be-raped-for-going-to-a-man's-hotel-room vibe."

"There's no need for aggression, Ms. Dean," she said with a lick of her lips.

Desdemona chuckled. "Telling choice of word, Professor. Careful. Because what was aggressive was you daring to ask me not to attend a class I paid for. Oh, that was *real* aggressive. *I* feel attacked. Triggered. Belittled. Harassed. Should I continue?"

"Most definitely not!" the woman snapped, her neck and back stiff.

"I enjoy your lectures—on *history*. I'm learning a lot. I look forward to next Wednesday's class. Hopefully, you will ensure a more respectful learning environment. Have a good weekend, Professor," Desdemona said before turning to close her laptop and slide it inside her bag.

Even though she knew she'd won that tiny battle, Desdemona's heart was still beating furiously. She had another class in two hours. Would there be more of the same?

Do I belong?

As she walked the hall and stepped out of the building, Desdemona looked around at the campus. Normally, she used her free time between classes to find Loren if he wasn't teaching a class or hit the campus café in the student center to eat while catching up on studying. Without her car and trying to escape lurkers waiting outside the gates of the campus, Desdemona felt trapped.

She slid on shades and headed in the direction of the library. As she was jogging up the steps of the modern glass building she stopped when the door opened and Loren stepped outside. He did the same at the sight of her.

What now? she thought, surprised at her nervousness.

What did ex-lovers do when their world was blown up by scandal? Speak and keep it moving? Ignore each other? Spontaneously run to each for a heated kiss and clutch of bodies?

Desdemona had never been in a relationship before, so she let him lead the way as she smoothed her lips against each other. And he looked so handsome in a crisp, striped shirt under a blazer with denims, with his hair pulled back into a low ponytail and his spectacles in place.

He hitched his book bag up higher on his broad shoulder and kept walking toward her. "Desdemona," he said as he passed her by.

She hated her desire to look back over her shoulder at his hasty retreat. But she didn't do it.

"I could never hate you. There is nothing you could do to make me hate you, Desdemona. Nothing."

A lie.

A bald-headed, raggedy-toothed, funky-breathed, no-good lie at that.

And then she did glance back.

In the distance, she could see that Loren did stop and turn to watch her, then turned and kept moving when she spotted him.

Fuck him.

Better said than done.

"Ms. Dean."

She looked forward to find Dr. Ophelia walking out of the library as another teacher held the door for her. And like that, Desdemona smiled and felt a comfort she couldn't explain but needed. The woman was soothing for her soul. The fuchsia blazer she wore over a lime-green T-shirt and wide-legged turquoise pants with bold gold accessories were *everything*.

"Hello, Dr. Ophelia," she said. "How are you?"

"Still in the number," the woman said, coming to stand before her as she looked at her. "How is your walk? Any more direction?"

Hopefully not straight to jail.

"Challenging," she admitted, curious if she too had heard that she was the notorious Madam X.

Dr. Ophelia smiled. "That builds character if you're open to learning the lesson," she said.

What lesson? Not to sell my ass or help people sell theirs?

"Are you free? I just came from a silly faculty advisory board meeting and I'm starving," the woman said, easing her arm through Desdemona's to steer her in the same direction. "I brought some oxtails over rice from home and there's plenty for two."

"You cook, Dr. Ophelia?" Desdemona asked as they walked together.

"The amazing thing about *any* woman is that there is nothing she cannot do. It's all in what you allow and disallow," she said.

Is this what having a mother feels like?

As they walked together and talked about nothing and

everything, Desdemona felt shielded inside an emotional bubble the woman created without even knowing she did so.

Does she know? *She couldn't. Thank God.*

Being in the woman's presence felt like a haven from the judgment all around her.

This is a catch-22 like a bitch.

Desdemona eyed her attorney as she sat in her posh office in Midtown Manhattan. Although Jynn carefully awaited a response from her, Desdemona wasn't sure whether to tell the woman about the blackmail. She was still waiting for the bastard to reach out with his demand.

Jynn set down her rose-gold stylus atop her iPad. "Listen, whatever we discuss is covered under attorney-client privilege. I could lose my license for betraying that privilege. To defend you, I need the truth, Desdemona. So, again, are you Madam X?" she asked.

Desdemona cleared her throat. The action reminded her of her professor doing the same thing during their conversation earlier that day.

"I think you could tell that your presence in class caused a lot of disruption today."

"You have to trust me," Jynn said.

Trust no one.

"I am Madam X," Desdemona said aloud for the first time, claiming her truth. "But I stepped away from the business over a year ago—nearing two."

"I thought so. No worries, though; nobody's gonna know," Jynn said with a nod, reminding her of the TikTok audio.

"I've never admitted that to anyone," she confessed, feeling light-headed and a little shaken.

"That's smart. Keep it that way."

The blackmailer could be a game changer, though. Unless I pay him or her and use whatever info they provided for payment to catch them. I just need to know who it is because no one is safe from the secrets I keep. No one.

"So the boutique is now completely legit?" Jynn asked in disbelief.

Desdemona nodded. "It is," she said with emphasis.

"Explain to me how it worked," Jynn said, leaning back in her chair as she crossed her arms over her chest.

And Desdemona did. But there was plenty she didn't reveal. So much. Names. The brothels she operated over the years. Locations for trysts. Her worldwide reach. The powerful allies. That info would die with her.

Jynn eyed her. "With just a GED, huh?" she asked.

Desdemona raised one shoulder and nodded.

"Your story *would* be interesting to read, Desdemona," Jynn said.

She shook her head adamantly. "It will never be told. It was bad enough living it, believe me," she said.

Do I tell her about the blackmailer? No, I won't. It's not like we can involve the police. Admit my crimes to catch someone else in theirs? No haps.

"There haven't been official charges. It's still just an investigation. Of course, if that changes, sit tight and I will jump right on getting you bail and then out of jail," Jynn said as she used the stylus to write notes on an app that converted her scribblings to typed words.

I need that to journal with, Desdemona thought, having always loved the feel of writing her thoughts and not typing them.

"Your downfall could be this person who told the police that the business was a front. Any clue which client or woman who worked for you—"

"All genders," Desdemona corrected her.

"Madam motherfuckin' X," Jynn said with a chuckle and

a shake of her head in wonder. "Any clue who that person could be?"

Tell her.

Her gut told her not to. "Not yet. No," Desdemona lied.

"The police did question Marquis Sanders, and he made it clear he never knew the true identity of the madam," Jynn said.

He kicked this shit off, so triple fuck him and every ball in his life. Still.

"One last issue to deal with," Jynn said, looking down at her tablet as she swiped through screens. "Do you know a Zena Dean?"

Desdemona gave herself a five-count and a low, sarcastic chuckle as she smoothed her chin with her fingertip. "She's my stepmother, who I haven't seen since I was fifteen and ran away from her house of hell. Why?" she asked, hating how she felt caught off guard.

Jynn's eyes filled with compassion. "She contacted the office and made it clear that she believes you stole money meant for her and wants it repaid," she said. "What's that about, Desdemona?"

Unable to sit still for that bullshit, Desdemona rose and began pacing as she slid her fists deep into the pockets of the dark gray, belted shirtdress she wore with her hair in a sleek topknot MiMi styled to be nearly six inches tall. She was trying to walk off her rising anger and failing horribly. "Evil has a face and it's *that* bitch," she spat.

Jynn stayed quiet.

Desdemona was thankful for the time to process and cycle through all the emotions that were present, with hate lingering behind. "To make a long story short," she said, finding her hands were trembling with rage. She tightened her fists to stop it. "My father died and left everything to me, but I was ten, and that bitch was appointed my legal guardian. I think he knew it was the only way to ensure I was taken care of, with my mother dying when I was five."

Desdemona grunted and pressed her lips together at the pain that radiated at the memory of her mother's death.

Damn. Still? Still.

"She did the bare minimum financially and barely spoke to me after my father died. At fifteen I ran away and was homeless. She never reported me missing because I went to school for weeks after that, until I dropped out. At twenty-one, when my inheritance was my own, I went to the estate's executor and claimed the remainder of what was mine. The crazy bitch is a liar. A thief. And an opportunist. I owe her nothing."

But a good beating with my baton and a few hits of that Taser for good measure.

"Goofy bitch," Desdemona muttered.

"I think she has brought more trouble on her hands than she wants if she continued to use your inheritance, knowing you were not living with her—"

"Did she leave a number?" Desdemona asked.

"I can handle this for you," Jynn said, her eyes showing her trepidation at her client contacting the woman herself. "You're in a sensitive situation right now—"

"She feels I owe her something. We agree about that," Desdemona said.

A Cardi B lyric came to her: "Bitches be pressed!"

Jynn sighed. "I just forwarded her contact info to your phone," she said, before swiping and then tapping her stylus on the screen. "Listen, do I think you were dealt a rough hand from the deck called life? Absolutely. Could you have made other choices? Possibly. Would I ever be a lady pimp? No. But for a high school dropout without any backup in this world since you were *fifteen* to build what you did in the

organized manner in which you did it is not to be over-
looked. It's methodical and smart. Don't be stupid *now*. Please."

"Thank you. I think?" Desdemona said with the hint of a
smile. She looked down at her phone to see the text message
sitting there, waiting for her to open it. "But I do want to
make it clear that I was never cruel, mean, manipulative, or
hurtful to anyone—not the way people were to me. No one
was ever forced or coerced. This was grown-folks' business."

Jynn nodded in understanding. "I'm still glad you're out
of the business," she said.

Desdemona locked eyes with her. "For my own reasons,
me too, Jynn. Me too," she said, before turning and leaving
the office.

*Ten-year-old Desdemona stood in the doorway of Mrs.
Zena's bedroom, hating the nervousness she felt about
talking to this woman who had become a stranger to her
again. Her eyes darted to her father's side of the bed and she
missed him like crazy. It had been just a month since he
died, but everything was different.*

She is different.

*Desdemona eyed her stepmother, sitting on the foot of
the bed, rubbing lotion on her arms in her nightgown. She
stopped suddenly, and her face became tight with annoyance. Desdemona stiffened.*

*"What?" Zena snapped, looking straight ahead, as if
avoiding even laying eyes on her.*

*At that moment, Desdemona wished she didn't have to
bother her at all. But she did. She had no one else to rely
on. "Could you do my hair?" she asked, her voice soft and
hesitant.*

*She didn't bother to add that her fuzzy and unkempt
braids were drawing too much attention from classmates.*

Zena released an agitated breath before rising from the bed to retrieve the comb, brush, and hair grease from the adjoining bathroom. "Come on," *she said with barely concealed irritation.*

That was how it always was. The new normal. She would do what was required: cook, clean, wash clothes, and send her to school, but every second of it was laced with her annoyance. Her coldness. It was clear she did what she did out of obligation and not love.

She hates me.

Desdemona walked into the bedroom, her feet bare and her steps padded by the plush carpeting. She sat down on the edge of the bed, already knowing to hold her neck stiff because Mrs. Zena's rough movements would cause her head to jerk back and forth. It was why she waited to remind her about her hair every two weeks.

"If your little behind wasn't so grown, you would tie your hair up like I said and make it last longer," Zena said.

"I will," she said softly, hating that pang of hurt she felt.

Mrs. Zena never hit her, but there were no hugs either. Not anymore, not since her father died.

Why do you hate me? *Desdemona mouthed, wanting to give voice to the words. To her feelings.*

But she didn't.

She knew the answer. Kinda.

The day of her father's funeral, she had overheard Zena telling someone how she was stuck raising the child her husband had with another woman when she wasn't able to ever have one of her own.

"Maybe, in a weird way, she is your chance to be a mother, Zena," the woman she spoke to had said.

"Or she's a daily reminder shoved down my throat," Zena had replied. *"His will leaves everything to her and for*

me there's a stipend every week, but I have to agree to be her trustee. I don't have any choice but to raise her. Daniel fucked me over once again."

Desdemona wished the scene didn't replay in her head, but it did. Her hurt caused by the woman stung. Still. Memories of neglect. Humiliation. Disdain.

No child deserved to be made to feel like a burden. Not even the child of your husband's mistress.

"Don't be stupid now."

Desdemona squinted as she eyed the small house in northern New Jersey. It was a long way in miles and values from the house where Zena Dean had once lived with her husband and stepchild. She continuously flicked the acrylic nail of her middle finger with her thumb as she sat behind the wheel of her crossover and eyed the house. And then the street. The 'burbs it was not.

She had wondered just what Zena could hope to gain with her lies, but looking at the drop in financial status made it clearer with each passing moment. The info Jynn sent was a phone number and address. Desdemona took that to mean her stepmother *wanted* to be contacted by her.

She climbed from the vehicle and came around the rear of it to cross the cracked pavement of the sidewalk. The blare of a television echoed from inside the house. Without a second for regrets, she knocked on the metal security gate of the front door.

Here I is.

"Well, well, well," a voice said via the Ring doorbell.

Desdemona eyed the device. "You didn't leave your address with my attorney to talk via a doorbell," she snapped.

After several locks were undone and the front door opened, there stood Zena Dean with just the security gate between them. Desdemona was taken aback by the silver-haired, aged woman standing before her. In her mind, Zena had been frozen in time from when she'd last seen her over fifteen years before.

"You got my money you stole?" Zena asked as she slid her hands into the pockets of the purple sweatsuit she wore with socks and slippers.

"You got mine that you stole all those years after I ran away. By the time I was old enough to claim my inheritance, it was clear you were still eating off of it," Desdemona countered. "You lucky I don't sue you and Hervey's short dick ass for my cash."

Zena looked her up and down with the same contempt as years ago. "Your father owed me that and more," she said with a coldness that only hinted at the depth of her hatred and anger.

And misery.

She wore it like a second skin. It radiated like a stink.

"There's plenty I owe you for the hell you made my life those five years," Desdemona countered.

Her laugh was bitter. "Your life? What about mine? My pain? My embarrassment? Cheating on me wasn't enough? He knew I couldn't have children and he knew why," Zena said with fiery eyes and venom in her tone.

Desdemona knew at that moment that the story of why Zena couldn't have children was deep and painful, scarring the woman. Physically and mentally. "What was he supposed to do with me when my mother died, Zena?" she asked, unsure why she tried to reason with her.

"Not bring you home to *me*," she said, with her eyes wide and brimming with tears that soon raced down her cheeks as she poked her chest with a finger. "Every damn day you were a reminder of him breaking my heart and then ripping through my soul because he knew how badly I wanted children. That motherfucker *knew* and did not give a shit that it was *too much* for me."

Zena turned her back to Desdemona and wiped away her tears, as if she wouldn't allow her stepdaughter to see her pain.

Desdemona was taken aback and lowered her head for a moment before looking back up to find the woman was facing her again.

"Your daddy wasn't shit. Let's call a thing a thing, little girl," Zena said in a harsh whisper through thinned lips. "Your hoe ass mama—"

"Don't," Desdemona warned with plenty of venom of her own.

Zena laughed. Her eyes were mocking, her face contorted. "Truth hurts. Huh? Tough titty, little girl, because your hoe ass mama wasn't the only bitch he screwed, and the disease he gave me killed my womb."

Desdemona grimaced.

Zena slammed her hand against the gate, causing it to noisily clang. "The last thing his whoring ass should have done was bring another woman's baby home for me to raise," she spat, with a bit of spittle hanging from her quivering bottom lip.

True.

"You need help," Desdemona said, honestly believing that.

Zena's anger was as visceral as if it all happened yesterday and not twenty-five years ago. It would continue to destroy her. And for that Desdemona felt pity for the woman who had been her tormenter. Her stepmother was incapable of rational thinking and behavior. Her pain and hurt would not allow it.

"You whoring ass bitch, what I need is my money," Zena said, slamming her hand against the security gate again. "You fuckin' athletes and shit, so I know you got it."

Desdemona's anger tried to push through the pity, but she refused to sink into the madness along with this broken woman. "What my father did to you was wrong, Zena. It was wrong," Desdemona admitted. "But what you did to me was no better. I was a child. I was innocent in all of it. I didn't ask to be born. I didn't ask to have every breath I took in your house cause you pain."

Zena's lip curled with cruelty.

"You hated me and made sure I knew it every day after my father died," she said, hating the residual pain still lingering. "So I ain't got nothing for you but a prayer that you will get the psychological help you need."

"Oh, you gone pay me," Zena said. The tears were gone and her gaze upon Desdemona was hateful. "I lost everything when you got the rest of that money. Everything. My house. My dignity. My sanity."

"That was gone before the house," Desdemona inserted.

Zena made a face of shock before another round of bitter laughter. "That was my husband and my money," she said, poking herself in the chest again.

"That was my father and, according to his wishes, it was *my* money," Desdemona countered with a calm that revealed she was done with the matter and with Zena Dean.

The woman looked like she wanted to open the gate and attack Desdemona like a savage. "You a slut just like your hoe ass mama," she said in a low voice, in a singsong fashion that hinted at her madness. "I was glad when the bitch died. Even more glad when your daddy died. Fuck 'em both. And fuck you too. I pray I'm alive to piss on your grave."

Desdemona realized the hatred Zena projected reflected just how deeply the woman hated herself. Her father had played a role in the woman's demise—loving the wrong person could do that—but the issues he worsened were already there. She had already lost the fight before the battle even truly began. "I forgive you, Zena. I forgive you because you don't know any better," she said, meaning it.

And feeling a bit of that burden she carried for all those years lift.

"Just stay away from me or I will have you pursued for spending that money while I lived on the streets," she said, to set a boundary she could only hope the woman didn't cross.

Desdemona turned.

The security gate rattled again before Zena released a shout. "Fuck your forgiveness, little girl, where's my money?" she roared, her voice echoing in the air.

Desdemona ignored her and walked to her vehicle, using the key to unlock it and slide inside.

"I'm gonna get my money, bitch. One way or the other, *hoe!*"

That was the last thing she heard before she closed the door and started the Maserati before driving away to leave her stepmother to stew in her hatred.

Desdemona freed her hair from the topknot and ran her fingers through her hair and across her scalp as she released a yawn. She pushed her textbook away where she sat at the dining room table and picked up her phone to scroll through the folder of photos she had of her and Loren.

Their interaction—or lack of one—did not sit well with her. When she allowed memories of him to stick, she swung between disappointment and anger. Still...

I miss him.

She couldn't fool herself into believing she didn't. She looked around the condo and could envision him there in a dozen different places. Like a ghost.

Cooking dinner in the kitchen.

Reading a book by the fireplace.

On the sofa, writing on his laptop.

Making love to her against the wall by the door.

And then on the bed, sketching her as she reveled in the afterglow of sex, still nude and sweaty.

His essence was still there, even if his presence was not.

She zoomed in on a picture of Loren shirtless and asleep, with an open book across his chest. Adorable.

Lo is done-done.

As she swiped through more photos of them, she wondered if telling him the truth about her past would have changed anything. Somehow, she found it hard to believe his judgment would have lessened.

Admitting the truth to Jynn had felt freeing. Afterward, anyway.

Could she do the same with Loren? Would it even matter? His bags had already been packed before she got home from the police station.

"So she's good. She trusts me because she should. You feel me? Same way I trust her. Without question."

Yusef's words just didn't sit well with her. The majority of her life had been about protecting herself. Vulnerability meant weakness.

"You think I would sit my ass up in court and reveal things discussed between us? That's what you think of me? You really don't trust me!"

And she should. She knew it. She believed Loren was deserving of a level of trust she had never fully given anyone. She just couldn't bring herself to do that.

It's over with Lo. Move on, Desi. Move the fuck on.

Biting her bottom lip, Desdemona deleted the folder of pictures. She deleted the fake accounts she'd used to follow him on social media.

It was time. The man barely spared me a glance today.

She thought of Antoine and how easy it would be to be spoiled by him—especially since he was well aware of just who and what she was or had been. It would be the best distraction for getting over Loren. And she knew whatever she asked for would be hers, including good sex. Not Loren level but satisfying.

Nommez votre prix.

"Take me away from all this bullshit," she muttered.

Brrrnnnggg.

Her eyes shot to the prepaid as her heart pounded. Setting down her iPhone, she reached for it and answered. "Yeah," she said, instantly putting her guard up and hoping her instincts were on high alert.

Who are you?

"I thought the throwaway phone was a nice throwback to one of your old tricks, Mademoiselle," the voice said.

It was distorted. Hard to tell if it was a man or a woman. Or a cop.

The anger of Detective Milligan replayed in her head.

"We are coming for you, Madam X."

Would they fake a blackmail attempt just to set her up to prove she had crimes to hide?

Stepping away from being a madam and enjoying vacationing, the world had dulled those instincts she once relied on. That slight feeling of unease. Stomach flutters. An inner voice.

She took a moment to relax. In the panic of all the recent events, she was reacting and not acting. A fatal flaw.

What would Mademoiselle do?

"You there?" the voice asked.

Desdemona stood up and walked over to the windows lining the front of the condo. "I think it's bullshit for the police to try every nasty trick in the book to try to make me look guilty of something I didn't do," she lied as her eyes watched the fast pace of the traffic on the street below. "I'm not falling for that bullshit, Detective. If it continues, I will sue the NYPD for harassment!"

She ended the call with a smirk.

It was time to shake some shit up. The same way she got shook up. Control was key, and it was time to reclaim as much of it as she could. She wasn't sure if the blackmailer was real or not, but it was one hell of a good excuse to rattle whoever it was.

Let the games begin.

Chapter Eight

Saturday, April 10

Lo. Dr. Loren Marc Palmer. My greatest love. It's so hard to say goodbye, but it's time . . .

Desdemona paused in writing in her journal, still trying to gather her thoughts on willfully releasing her love for him. Not just accepting that he was done with the relationship but choosing that she wouldn't want it back even if he changed his mind.

"'I don't deserve to be ignored or shunned. Like a pariah,'" she added to the page in her neat script. "'Not by Lo.'"

She released a breath and looked about the room as the morning sun radiated against the walls. Her gaze fell on the prepaid phone atop her bedside table. She set her pen in the groove of the journal to reach for it.

"Hmm," Desdemona grunted.

Nearly a hundred missed calls overnight.

It was very much giving off desperation.

She had slept like a baby during it all, with the phone on vibrate. With sleep and time came clarity. She was confident it was not the police. All her consorts were wealthy men. One hundred thousand dollars was nothing to them. Did that make the blackmailer a courtesan instead? The police? Or a person facing financial ruin?

The answer to those questions would help thin the herd of suspects.

And give her more control. Her arrest would cut off their hope for an influx of cash.

Bzzzzzz. Bzzzzzz. Bzzzzzz.

With a shake of her head, Desdemona looked down at the phone vibrating in her hand. She checked the time. It was just seven in the morning.

Back at it bright and early.

Was this about revenge or money?

She raised the crisp cotton sheet to cover her bare breasts, as if they could be seen while she was on the phone. The prepaid flip phone was definitely not video call–ready. "FaceTime? More like OldTime," she quipped before she answered the call and placed it on Speaker.

"Don't fuck with me, bitch!" the voice roared. "I will destroy you and fucking enjoy it. Now the price has doubled. Pay me or I will send—"

"I don't have it," she lied.

"You have one week to get me two hundred thousand dollars, Mademoiselle."

"That is a lot, Detective," she said.

"Cut the police bullshit!"

"You know my accounts have been seized," she lied. "Why are you doing this?"

The line went quiet.

Silence could be just as telling as spoken words.

Money is the main goal.

"Then sell that pretty ass of yours because I want my money."

Just as irrational as Zena.

Desdemona followed her gut and ended the call.

Bzzzzzz. Bzzzzzz. Bzzzzzz.

It was a gamble and she was taking it. It was time to flush out the rat. And the next time they talked, she would do the calling.

She put the phone on Silent and tossed it on the bed before slinging back the covers to leave her comfortable bed. She crossed the room to complete her morning rituals before selecting one of her dozens of silk or lace robes to pull on as she headed out of the suite. When she reached the guest bedroom, she paused in the doorway. Loren had set it up as his home office. Determined to move on from him, she closed the door.

That's not enough.

She reopened the door and strode in to remove one of the empty plastic containers in the closet. Starting with the office, she went through the entire condo, removing anything of his he'd left behind. Any reminder. A purge. Freedom from parts of him that lingered and haunted.

She held a pencil of his in her hand. Whenever he was nervous or lost deep in thought, he would drum the eraser against a hard surface. At times it drove her close to insanity. Who knew one day she would long to hear it echoing through the condo.

No more.

She dropped the pencil atop his other items and secured the lid on the container.

Only sparing time for a glass of juice and half a muffin for breakfast, Desdemona made her way back to her suite to get dressed. She chose a simple red T-shirt dress that clung to her curves with a cropped denim jacket and white leather low Chuck Taylors.

Just as she was filling a black tote with items, the doorbell rang. She knew it was Yusef. On time as always. Even on a Saturday. She could set a clock by his punctuality.

"Good morning, Yusef," she said, letting him take the container from her arm as she locked her front door.

"Morning," he said, ever professional in his black long-sleeved T-shirt and slacks.

Desdemona slid on her shades and followed him down the length of the hall to the elevator. "I need to go to Brooklyn," she said as the door opened and they stepped on.

He nodded in understanding.

Thankfully, the elevator was empty and they rode in silence, with Desdemona hating that a neighbor could feel comfortable demeaning her.

"I bet you're worth every cent. Aren't you?"

She shivered in revulsion, wishing she *had* tased him.

In the parking garage, Yusef held the passenger door for her until she was seated. Out the window, she eyed his pickup truck in the spot where Loren had kept his beloved raggedy Tahoe.

I wonder if it's fixed? Wait. Why would I care?

She gave Yusef the address of Loren's parents' house for him to input in the GPS. During the entire ride, she looked out the window and wondered just what would happen when she arrived. She would leave the container on the porch if she had to.

Yesterday Loren had made a bold move to show her it was over.

Today it was her turn.

Childish? Petty? Unnecessary? Perhaps.

But it was going down.

Right now, she thought as he pulled to a stop and parked in front of the house.

"You need me?" Yusef asked.

"No, but thanks," she said, exiting her car with the container under one arm.

Loren's truck wasn't in the driveway, but she forged ahead, not knowing if he'd had it fixed or not. As she climbed the stairs, the front door opened before she could reach it. Both his parents stepped out onto the porch.

Loren was practically his mother's twin, but he had inherited his father's build. He was born and bred from love.

What do they think of me?

In her haste, she hadn't considered that. And so she paused on the steps.

"It's good to see you, Desdemona," his mother, Bell, said with hesitancy in her voice.

"Sure is," Garee agreed, tucking the pen he carried behind his ear.

Her slight laugh was nervous. "You sure?" she asked, easing her shades off her face to look at them.

Bell's hazel eyes studied her face. "Now? With time. Yes," she admitted. "Just like when we had to get used to you being older than Loren."

"Bell," Garee said, soft but sure in his reprimand.

Bell turned her head, with her short, black curls, and gave her husband a quick look. "I'm human, Garee," she said.

"And thus capable of mistakes, just like Desdemona," he advised.

She missed their bond. They had made her feel like family. "I, uh, had things of Lo's I wanted to give to him," she said with a lick of her gloss-covered lips.

The couple shared a look.

"Loren moved back into his apartment, Desdemona," Garee said.

Moved *back*.

His apartment.

"W–what? Wait. Huh?" Desdemona asked in confusion.

They shared another look between them.

"The *studio*?" she asked in exasperation at the one-room apartment he had lived in before they moved in together. Eight months ago.

Desdemona turned and ate up the distance down the stairs and across the sidewalk to the car. "New plan," she said to Yusef once she was in the car again. She tossed the container over her shoulder onto the back seat without a care as she gave him the address.

Loren's address.

Every possible scenario for why he had kept that apartment played out in her head, and each one ended very badly. There was no explanation. It was a deception. Something she hadn't believed Loren capable of.

"You okay?" Yusef asked.

"No," she admitted.

He fell silent.

This is Loren. Loren wouldn't. He couldn't. Then why keep it from me?

And she asked herself that a hundred times over until the moment Yusef pulled the Maserati to a stop in front of the Brooklyn apartment building. She was out of the car almost before he brought it to a stop. Her feet ate up the stairs and she ignored the noises coming from the apartments she passed on her ascent. By the time she reached his front door, her heart was pounding from exertion and lingering shock.

The door opened before she could knock. Loren stood in the doorway, looking down at her with a solemn expression. His hair was loose and he wore nothing but basketball shorts as she studied his face with eyes she knew had to show her disbelief and disappointment.

"It seems I'm not the only one keeping a secret, Lo," she finally was able to say.

"Desi, it's not what you think," he began.

She nodded several times and twisted her mouth in derision. "You owe me an explanation, just like you owed me a better goodbye than what you offered me," she said, her emotion straining her voice. "It's over. We're done. You want me to ignore you like you damn near ignored me. Fine. Cool. But this *shit* right here needs to be explained."

"Come in," he said, stepping back to make room for her to do so.

"You sure you don't have company?" she asked with sarcasm as she entered the studio apartment and looked around.

Polished hardwood floors anchored the small but organized studio apartment. The brick accent wall and tall, brightly lit windows made it seem bigger than its limited square footage. A khaki leather sofa bed. Plenty of books. The drawing table. His small but stylish kitchenette with chrome appliances.

It was exactly the same as it had ever been.

Desdemona turned to face him as he leaned against the closed door with his arms crossed over his chest. For a moment—just a moment—she understood all too well sinking into the abyss of crazy like Zena, but she refused to sink. "You said your stuff was in storage," she said shaking her head in disbelief.

"I knew you wouldn't agree with me keeping the apartment, Desi," he said. "But it's a sorry rabbit that only has one hole."

Desdemona's eyes widened and she took a deep inhale of breath in shock. "Hoe?"

"I said hole. Not hoe. H–O–L–E," he said.

"What holes? Whose hole?" she asked.

Loren dared to smile, but he erased it when she arched a brow at him. "Not pussy holes," he said, walking over to lay his hands on her upper arms.

She shrank away from his touch.

"'It's a sorry rabbit that only got one hole' means a person should always have another place to go," he explained.

"To fuck bitches?" she asked. "To lay up in side pussy?"

Loren threw up his hands in exasperation. "Now you believe I would cheat on you. First snitch. Now cheat. Wow," he said. "You don't know me at all."

Desdemona shook her head. "No. I don't," she acquiesced. "I never thought you would deceive me, and for damn sure I didn't know that after everything we've been through that we couldn't still be friends even after it was over. That you would see me and treat me like a stranger. So no, I don't fucking know you at all."

"We didn't know each other," he countered in a low tone.

They locked eyes.

She felt overwhelmed by sadness. "How would we work if you had a backup plan the whole time, Lo?" she asked.

"How would we work when you kept such a huge part of your life from me—still do?" he countered.

She bit her bottom lip and looked down at the tip of her sneakers. "I thought love was enough."

"Loving you is not my issue," he said. "I love you so much that seeing you again makes me weak. Makes me want to forget what I know about you and come home."

"*This* is your home," she said, waving her hand around at the small space. "It's where you pay rent."

"It's where I can *afford* to pay rent, Desi," he drawled.

The condo is costly.

They were able to share a smile.

"I got some of your stuff you left. I'll go get it," she said, easing past him to open the front door.

She felt him reach behind himself to touch her free hand.

The small contact was as electrifying as ever. She shivered and felt a tiny jolt, as if some switch had been clicked on.

Antoine could give her Paris, but he could never give her *that*.

She broke the connection and continued out of the apartment and back down the stairs to retrieve the container.

Yusef was scrolling on his phone as he leaned back against the front of the vehicle. "I'm good, Yusef," she said before he could ask.

He chuckled.

Desdemona closed the door and made her way back inside the building. She was thankful for having worn sneakers as she jogged up the stairs again. Loren was standing by the window. He glanced back at her.

"That's your new dude?" he asked.

Desdemona set the container on the counter of the kitchenette. "Would you care?" she asked.

"Care? I'm willing to go down and *try* to whup his ass," Loren quipped.

Desdemona moved over to stand beside him by the window. "That's my bodyguard and he is happily married with three kids," she explained.

Loren tensed beside her. "Bodyguard?" he asked.

She nodded as she looked up at him. "Shit is mad wild right now," she said.

"I've been avoiding it," he admitted, reaching to stroke her chin as his eyes studied hers.

"Me too," she said.

"Will there be charges?" he asked as his eyes dropped to her mouth.

He used to love kissing her.

"I don't know," she admitted.

"Are you worried?" he asked as his thumb caressed her bottom lip.

"Sometimes," she confessed. "Do you want me to be?"

Loren frowned and shook his head. "Hell no, Desi," he said. "Please think better of me."

"I could ask you to do the same," she countered.

His eyes locked with hers.

"What *do* you want, Lo?" she asked, seeing his desire for her heating his dark brown eyes.

"In a perfect world? You," he said, before pulling her body against his in a tight embrace as he lightly rested his chin atop her head.

She fought the desire to wrap her arms around his familiar body. She was afraid she wouldn't want to let him go. But neither she nor the world were perfect, so that wasn't a possibility. He was already gone.

Desdemona opened her eyes in surprise.

But his erection is not.

The feel of his hardness pressed between their bodies was undeniable. And that awakened her bud, as it swelled to life, seeking release and causing a deep ache that radiated throughout her body.

She tilted her head back, bringing her hands up around him to splay against his strong back. The thought of his long strokes and intimate kisses aroused her. Even if only for one last time.

Fuck it.

She gripped the back of his head and raised on her toes to lick at his mouth. He grunted in pleasure and gave her his tongue to suck deeply. She felt him tremble as she lightly dragged her nails down his bare back to ease her fingers inside the rim of his basketball shorts. He didn't have on boxers, and she gripped his hard buttocks before jerking the shorts down below them. With both hands, she held his inches and stroked him from root to tip, one after the other.

Loren released a short cry of pleasure as he closed his eyes and tilted his head back.

Desdemona looked down at *it,* loving that the skin was darker than the rest of his medium brown complexion. The thickness. The curve. The smooth tip. The throbbing veins.

A beautifully perfect dick.

She hungered to lick it.

With a wicked little bite of her bottom lip as she glanced up at him, Desdemona lowered her body into a squat and tilted her head to the side to lick him from his balls to the tip before taking it into her mouth to circle it with her tongue.

"Desi," he cried out as he weaved his fingers through her hair to lightly grip it.

She hummed and purred as she alternated licking and sucking his hardness until she felt his thighs quiver in reaction to her skill. "You like that?" she asked in a hot whisper against the tip before sucking just it into her mouth.

"Wait," Lo said before he pressed a hand to her forehead. She looked up at him. "What's wrong?" she asked.

He shook his head, as if to clear it, and then squeezed his eyes with his fingers. "I can't. I don't want to," he said.

Desdemona was taken aback as his dick lost its hardness before her very eyes.

Loren stepped back from her and jerked his shorts back up around his waist—in fact accidentally so high that it would have been comical if Desdemona felt like laughing.

She didn't.

She wiped the dampness from around her mouth as she stood up.

Loren paced the brief distance from the sofa to the stove. "I can't. I love you, but I can't get past it," he said, running a hand through his hair and then gripping it like he wanted to pull it out from the roots.

"Past what?" she asked, her voice a monotone.

He stopped and looked over at her. "You sleeping or doing that with other men for money," he admitted. "I can't get the image out of my head."

Reality hit that she didn't feel safe with Lo right then. There wasn't a fear of physical harm. But judgment. Scorn. Rejection.

Like so many other times in her life that remained unforgotten and unhealed.

She forced a smile she knew didn't overcome the hurt that had to be reflected there in her eyes. "If you see me on campus, let's speak to each other. Let's respect what we once had. Can we do that?" she asked, even as her heart broke.

He looked regretful and torn.

That was some solace.

She walked over to the door, glad he could only see her back as she pursed her lips to release a long stream of air that she prayed helped keep her from falling completely apart. With the door open, she paused. "I did what I had to do to survive," she admitted, finding herself unable not to.

She didn't look at him. She kept her gaze on the door.

"Goodbye, Loren," she said with finality before stepping out into the hall and closing the door behind her to grapple with her hurt and to leave him with his.

"The police called me, Desdemona."

She eyed Antoine, sitting across from her in the show-room. After another pat down, she had allowed Yusef to admit him when he popped up expectedly. She massaged her palm as she eyed him. "And?" she asked, back under the shell of her cool demeanor. "Do share."

"They wanted to know if your business was indeed legitimate and if called upon to do so, could I provide to them each dress I purchased," Antoine said, handsome as ever in all black, with that French accent she found wickedly delightful. "I told them unless they wanted me to reach out to some angry exes to reclaim gifts, that would be impossible."

She nodded. *The police are still on my trail.*

"Others have been called as well," he said.

She cut her eyes over to him. "Anybody worried?" she asked.

"No. Not yet. The majority of the wives have confirmed receipt of the dresses," he said. "Quite a few of the clients are upset at MQ. He'll be feeling the chill for a quite a bit and probably experience some financial losses. He pissed off the wrong people."

"Good," she said without remorse. "He deserves it."

Desdemona's client list of prominent wealthy and famous men had been built on referral only, and many of her clients were friendly with one another. She didn't doubt that there had been plenty of communication between her former consorts regarding anything to do with their Mademoiselle.

Antoine crossed one leg over the other and eyed her. "You're very talkative today," he said.

She smiled. "Am I?" she asked, enjoying the distraction of their cat-and-mouse game.

"Why?"

"I need information from you," she said.

He nodded his head in understanding. "Good thing I am still in the country," he said.

"Why *are* you still here, Antoine?" she asked.

"Waiting for you to change your mind," he said, pressing his hands together in a plea.

Desdemona chuckled. "It cannot be that serious," she said.

"It is. I promise you, it is," he said, easing his body forward to the edge of the seat to lean in over the desk a bit. "Ever since you took away the *chatte*, I have not been able to find anyone to fuck me the way you did."

"*Chatte?*" she asked.

Antoine locked his eyes with hers. "Pussy," he said with a slight lift of his square chin.

"Oh. Okay," she said with a chuckle.

"And I know it was good for you too. I felt you climax," he said.

"I did," she admitted.

"Oooooooh!" he moaned as he twisted in his seat and made a face like it was sweet torture. He swore in French and made a tight fist that he bit down on. "I *knew* it!"

Ding.

She laughed as she checked the tablet. Another incoming order.

"Tell me, Desdemona, was I the only one to make you climax?" he asked.

Desdemona rose to come around the desk. She paused by his desk and stroked the side of his face. "You were the first," she admitted with a wink. "You taught me that my pleasure was just as important as theirs."

Ever the playful charmer, Antoine straightened his legs and crossed his arms over his chest like a corpse.

That made her belly laugh as she walked over to remove the gold-sequined strapless gown from one of the mannequins. Antoine could be such a perv about bedding her, but he was also charming and likable. And perhaps he had info that could be useful.

"Listen," she said as she draped the dress over her arm and came back across the showroom to hang it on the rack to be bagged. "Anyone on the list hurting for money? Any requests for loans or favors?"

"I don't know everyone on the list, but those I know are doing exceptionally well," he said, back in serious mode. "In fact, I've done business with a few while I'm in the country."

Desdemona feigned a hurt expression. "Oh. And I thought it was just for my *chatte*?" she teased.

"One stone. Two birds," he said with a shrug.

She set about properly packing the dress for shipment.

"*Fuck* that dress. *Fuck* this showroom," he said, almost in disgust.

"Trust me. I feel the same way," she drawled.

"Let's go have dinner. I'm starving," he said. "And I could use some beautiful company."

She left the dress box open on the table used for shipping and reclaimed her seat. "You know my rule on that, Antoine," she said.

"It died with the business. You are Desdemona, a beautiful boutique owner. Mademoiselle? Not anymore."

"True, but no, Antoine. I can't. I have to get home to check on something important," she said, thinking of the prepaid phone she'd left behind and avoided thinking about all day. "But any info you can give me about anyone with money troubles would help me."

"Then I'll see what I can find," he assured her. "Anyone in particular?"

She was trusting her gut again and just hoped she finally had it recalibrated to help her.

"I have a few ideas, but I'd rather not say and have you mistakenly alert them that I'm asking about them," she explained.

"Listen, let's be serious for a moment," he said. "Do you know how much of a coup it was to make it onto your list?"

She did, but she remained silent.

"Everything about it was top tier and exclusive," he said. "I'd find it hard to believe any of us betrayed you for any reason—if that's what you're trying to root out."

"What about someone kicked *off* the list?" she asked.

"Possibly," he said.

If memory served her, over her five years as Madam X, only six men had been removed from her list.

"*Tu es spectaculaire,*" he said with his eyes locked on her face.

Desdemona smiled and shook her head. "Translation?" she asked.

"You are spectacular," he said, almost in awe.

She shifted her gaze away for a second before looking back at him. She warmed under his gaze. She was a woman who fought her way out of the gutter to run a multimillion-dollar enterprise and did it on her own terms. The last thing she should need or want was validation from anyone, but after the stunning blow of Loren's rejection, Antoine's attention struck a chord with her.

He knew of her past and was still able to desire her—probably because his heart wasn't involved. Still...it felt redeeming to be wanted. Pursued. Adulated.

Desdemona rose with her eyes on him as she gave him a tempting smile. "Still hungry?" she asked, turning with a flirtatious look over her shoulder before she slowly walked to the small room in the back where they kept supplies. "I'm going to feed you."

"*Dieu merci!*" he exclaimed.

His steps were fast and echoed.

She opened the door and leaned back against it as she beckoned the Haitian further with the bend of her finger. He entered and turned to grab her wrist. With a slight tug, she was inside the small space with him. She kicked the door closed.

Antoine pulled her body close and bent to press kisses to her neck.

Desdemona closed her eyes, wishing his body didn't feel wrong. There was no perfect fit. No blazing chemistry.

No Loren.

She winced and eased back from him to pull her dress over her head.

Antoine swore at the sight of her curves in delicate, barely there, sheer lingerie as she pressed her back to the door and struck a pose meant to drive him wild. And it did. Next, she eased out of her panties with a snakelike move. She understood—and taught—the assignment.

Desdemona had schooled each of the courtesans in the art of seduction. That sex was also about passion and anticipation. Touch. Tease. Restraint. Focus. Thrill. Climax.

Antoine released a string of French expletives as his dick strained against his pants.

Desdemona reached to press her hand atop his head and pushed down until he squatted before her. Slowly, she eased her back down the door a little and spread her knees before thrusting her hips forward. He pressed his face to her plump, waxed mound to inhale the scent of her.

"Eat me," she demanded in a moan.

He placed one thigh on each of his shoulders and then lifted her as he stood to his full height. She reached up to press her hands to the cool ceiling as Antoine licked her lips before opening them with his tongue.

"Jack your dick," she told him.

Soon sounds of him freeing his inches echoed. The belt undone. The zipper lowered. The boxers pulled down under his balls. Never once did he relent at tasting her.

She rolled her hips and arched her back as he slowly brought her to one climax and then another before he roared with his own.

"Merci. Merci," he moaned in between kisses to her quivering inner thighs. "Merci, Desdemona."

She was thankful for the sexual release but very aware that it had failed in making her forget Loren Palmer.

Desdemona leaned against the wall and looked out at the city night as she held the prepaid phone in her hand. She took a sip of wine from the glass she held in one hand and dialed with the other. It rang several times. She was just about to end the call when it was answered with noises of fumbling and jostling.

She smiled at catching them off guard. There had been so many missed calls, she was surprised the phone had not gone dead.

Looking for me? Here I go.

"Why are you fucking playing with me?" the voice said with anger.

"Why are *you* fucking playing with *me*?" she countered, her tone calm. "Prove you're not the police."

"You're not running shit," the voice snapped.

"Ain't I? Money makes the world go 'round, mother-fucka, and right now your broke ass ain't moving nan-nathan," she said, pulling from her reserves of being Angel the streetwalker.

Hood shit.

"Broke?" the voice chewed out.

"Busted. Disgusted. All of *that*," she said, moving her head as she claimed her cocky. "You want this money, then you meet me to get it. Face-to-face. Bring your proof. If not? I'll take my chances. Do a bid. Get out to live lovely as fuck without worrying about this type of goofy, lowlife, struggling bullshit ever again. Understand? Good. *I'll* be in touch."

She ended the call.

This time there was no instant callback.

She took another deep sip of wine and tossed the phone across the room onto the sofa. As time ticked by, her eyes kept going to it. Nervousness crept in. Had she played the wrong hand?

Only time would tell.

Chapter Nine

Wednesday, April 14

What have I done?

All contact with the blackmailer ceased.

There were no more calls and Desdemona's attempts to reach out were met with silence. She was apprehensive, some of her bravado fading as she wondered just what would happen next. Her doubts about her bold move to take control of the situation plagued her.

She could barely focus in class. Twice she nearly sent dresses to incorrect addresses. Her appetite was waning. Her hair was shedding.

I should have just paid the motherfucker.

All of that, plus the open police investigation, missing Loren, being bombarded by crowds wherever she went, the press attempting to get an exclusive interview or statement, feeling trapped in her home or the showroom, still unable to pick a major, haunted by Zena's show of madness, feeling like she was being watched constantly...

Desdemona released a shrill little cry of frustration.

"Shit," she swore as she rubbed her face before massaging her temples.

She yearned for a glass of wine but fought the urge, feeling it was becoming a vice.

Gone were her normal luxuries. No friends. No exercising. No traveling. No dinners at her favorite eateries. She hadn't had her hair done since the scandal broke. No spa treatments. Her nails were ragged. She needed a bikini wax—badly.

Another yelp escaped.

She pressed her lips together and drew her knees to her chest in the middle of the bed, knocking the science book she had been studying onto the floor, where it landed with a loud *wham* that startled her.

I gambled. Did I lose?

"Fuuuuck," she said, straightening her legs and rolling over to Loren's side of the bed to bury her face deep into the pillows, wishing his scent lingered. It didn't. He was gone, the pillowcases laundered many times over since he left.

And like always recently, any thought of him brought on an ache that radiated. Like the police investigation of her, she wondered when it would end.

It needs to.

A seductress by trade couldn't keep a man hard.

"Ego breaker," she muttered into the downy softness.

With another deep breath, she rolled out of bed and happened to catch her reflection in the mirror. "His loss," she said, feeling her apple bottom and firm breasts. Loving herself. Until her eyes fell on the untrimmed bush that covered her intimacy.

"Troll hair," she said with a shake of her head before she turned to pick up her iPhone.

It was still on "do not disturb."

The voice mailbox was full. She didn't bother to check any of them, knowing they were from strangers who had somehow gotten her number and were anxious for access to Madam X.

I hate that name. I'm not fucking Madonna. I'm Mademoiselle, bitches.

She opened the text messages from known senders.

ANTOINE: No news yet. On it, though. Call me.

Damn. I need that tip-off more than ever.

JYNN/ATTY: God bless you cuz your stepmother is bananas. Like completely fucked in the head.

And is.

MELISSA: I miss my friend. (Sad face emoji)

I miss you too.

ANTOINE: Tonight. My hotel suite. I need to taste you again. Feed me.

Not. Well . . . maybe.

SECURITY: I made The Shade Room because of you! #SexySecurity Thankful the wife finds it funny.

The Shade Room? I can only imagine the comments. Not fucking with it.

Yusef included a link to the post with the headline: **MADAM X'S SEXY SECURITY GUARD FOUND. Y'ALL ASKED. WE DELIVERED! #Boom #SecureMe.** There were a dozen slides of her being guarded by him.

She frowned at the comment from rapper Big Craze, which she saw without scrolling: *Fuck him. Tell her to drop the pin. I'm tryna see something. (Tongue emoji)*

She shook her head. With the continuing coverage on social media almost making her a legend in the streets, she knew the police would not let up anytime soon. Detective Milligan was just being stroked to take her down. She was clueless as to why he was dogged about it. Personal history with prostitutes? Scorned by a woman? Small dick?

You know what? Fuck it and fuck him.

JYNN/ATTY: Call me. More offers are pouring in—

Desdemona winced and dropped the phone.

Reality TV gigs.

Brand endorsement offers.

Offers to design a capsule fashion collection.

More book deals.

Interview requests.

Managers wanting to promote her.

Agents wanting to represent her.

Reps for celebrities reaching out with offers for glamorous dates.

After five years of having a direct line to celebrities and politicians, none of it moved or impressed her. At all. Instead, she was annoyed by the evidence of America's obsession with notoriety.

She looked down at the phone to finish reading the message. "'And the police want you to come in for more questioning,'" she read aloud.

What have I done?

"Now what?" she asked, even as her heart beat a little faster.

She dialed Jynn's private line. It rang three times before the attorney answered.

"You are a savage for that DND," she said by way of greeting.

Desdemona laughed. "And I sleep like a baby," she said.

"What if there is an emergency?"

"'Me, myself and I. That's all I got in the end,'" she sang the Beyoncé lyric, hating the hint of sadness that panged her.

"How are you doing with everything?" Jynn asked after a brief pause.

"I'm good," she said.

Fake it until you make it.

"Let me know if it becomes otherwise."

"Got it," Desdemona said as she entered her closet and began to select her wardrobe for the day.

"The detectives want to see us ASAP. I say let's head

down now and get it over with. I don't have court, so I'll accompany you. I'd prefer that," Jynn said.

What do you wear to be arrested?

"Do you think I will be charged?" Desdemona asked as she selected a simple and classic, khaki long-sleeved dress topped with a large, structured corset belt to add interest.

"Honestly, I think if they wanted to arrest you, they wouldn't wait for you to stroll in to them. But I could be wrong," Jynn said. "Let's go in together. My car can be there in thirty minutes."

Desdemona laid the dress atop the island, along with leather heels that matched the belt. "Let me call you back first?" she asked as she moved over to her concealed safe. She opened it and reached in for the false credentials.

"Okay. But let me know soon."

The call ended.

Run, Desdemona. Run.

Another fork in the road.

It would be so easy to flee and leave it all behind.

Why not? What reason did she have to stay? Who was worth risking jail time when she could choose to be free and live a good life abroad? And the thought of that made her feel more at ease, like it was the clear solution.

She had long since collected the cash she used to keep in safety deposit boxes in several banks. That money had been secured in an offshore account during her world travels, just waiting for her if she needed it.

I could walk in that police station and not be able to leave out in the same way.

Desdemona did not want to go to jail. Even though the limits put on her life since the scandal hit were torture at times. What would she do in a six-by-eight-foot jail cell?

Lose my mind.

She leaned against the wall and stared at the money stacked there. Time ticked by as she wrestled with what to do. When she checked her phone, there were a couple of missed calls from Jynn. She didn't return them and instead used her phone to check for private flights to Bali, Indonesia.

It was a perfect choice.

Beautiful lands. Rich culture. Delicious foods. Inexpensive cost of living. No extradition treaty with the United States. And a contact there that would help her remain in the country on a permanent visa.

Everything was set and put in place a long time ago. All it would take would be one phone call to an ex-consort. Number 47. Heir to his family's vast, billion-dollar tobacco empire.

She had nothing to lose and absolutely everything to gain.

Fuck it.

Moving quickly, she grabbed her laptop and tried to charter a private jet, not wanting to ask Antoine for use of his. When that failed, she checked commercial airlines. There was a 1:15 p.m. flight leaving out of John F. Kennedy International Airport. She checked the time.

11:03.

If I rush, I can make it.

She booked the flight with the credit card assigned to her new identity and then rushed to pack. When she eyed the massive amount of cash, she knew she couldn't take it on a commercial flight and risk getting flagged by the TSA. That could lead to questioning by law enforcement about why she was carrying so much cash and where she got it from.

It has to stay.

She grabbed ten thousand dollars and the journals to shove into her carry-on before locking it. It would be a huge financial loss. Not including the million Jynn had access to in case of an arrest and bail needed to be paid.

"Shit," she swore, feeling rushed and knowing she wasn't fully prepared to flee.

Just like the condo she would never be able to sell. And the bulk of her belongings she would be unable to take. The pricey cost of freedom.

I can't enjoy those things in jail either.

She forged ahead and continued rushing around the condo, choosing what to leave and what to take.

Ding-dong. Ding-dong. Ding-dong.

Desdemona paused in placing her diamond jewelry inside cases before packing them. She left her bedroom and made her way to the front door. A brief look out the peephole revealed it was Jynn. She walked away, planning to ignore her until she went away.

Knock-knock. Knock-knock. Ding-dong. Knock-knock-knock-knock—

Exasperated, Desdemona turned and went back to the door to jack it open. "Is all of that necessary?" she asked as the woman brushed past her to enter.

"Don't do it. Running is a mistake," Jynn said, facing her with her hands on her hips in the all-black pantsuit she wore.

Desdemona closed the door and leaned back against it.

"And don't lie and say you weren't. I've been at this too long not to know the signs," the other woman said. "Right now, the investigations are not working. So far, you are ahead of the game. Not appearing for questioning and then fleeing makes you look guilty, Desdemona. *Think*, please. You're smarter than that."

Desdemona crossed her arms over her chest and walked over to look out the window.

"Do you really want to be on the run for the rest of your life?" Jynn asked. "Hell, even being charged doesn't mean you will be found guilty. And being found guilty is not a lifelong sentence the way being on the run would be. We're talking prostitution, not murder. Relax."

Easy for you to say.

"I need a minute," Desdemona said before turning and leaving the living room.

When she reached her bedroom, she looked at the open suitcases on the bed as she paced. The feeling of anxiety was overwhelming. "Wait, wait, wait," she said in a soft rush, splaying her hands and forcing herself to breathe deeply.

For years Desdemona had survived by being smart and methodical. Rarely had she moved in haste. That shouldn't change.

I panicked.

Admitting that removed the tension from her shoulders, neck, and back.

"Desdemona," Jynn said suddenly from behind her.

She glanced back over her shoulder to find the woman standing in the open doorway. "I was out of here," she admitted. "There's a blackmailer who threatened to turn over evidence to the police and I would only pay out on my terms. Hadn't heard for them in a few days—"

"And now the police want you to come in, so you figured the blackmailer turned over the evidence," Jynn finished, strolling into the room to look down at the suitcases. Her eyes widened at the sight of the jewelry. "Good *Lord.*"

Desdemona gave her the hint of a smile as she shook her head. "If I do get charged today, how much time am I looking at?" she asked.

It was a question she had deliberately avoided up until that point.

"Depends on the charges and how many counts are brought against you. Whether the feds become involved," Jynn said. "I will say that I think if the blackmailer had turned you in, the police would have already issued a warrant for your arrest and you would be in jail."

I hope.

"Running is not the answer," Jynn added.

I hope.

"So, you ready to go answer some questions?"

"No," Desdemona said, even as she picked up a solid black designer tote.

Jynn gave one of the expensive baubles one last stroke. "Selling pussy sure pays," she joked before they left the bedroom together to go to face Desdemona's fate.

She gave a stealthy look down the length of the hall before knocking on the door to the suite of the luxury hotel in Midtown. She adjusted the large shades she wore with a baseball cap as she waited for the door to be opened. She slipped inside as soon as it was.

"That's quite a getup," Antoine said as he closed the entry door to the expansive suite finely decorated in shades of slate blue with hints of gold.

Desdemona removed the cap and shades. "I'm here," she said, raking her fingers through the ends of her hair.

"And dressed to burgle," he teased, taking in the black leggings and matching long-sleeved T-shirt she wore. "I've never seen you in pants."

"I wear them to exercise, Antoine," she said.

"As good as those look on you, I have something else for you to wear," he said, walking over to close both sets of covered balcony doors, shutting out the afternoon sun and the noise of the city. "It's in the bedroom."

"Three things first," Desdemona said as she walked over to stand before him to pat him down.

Antoine spread his arms and legs as he tilted his head back and laughed. "You still don't trust me?" he asked, sounding amused.

Trust no one.

"The second?" he asked when she rose and took a step back.

"No talk of the Madam X mess," she insisted.

He gave her a nod of acceptance. "And the third?"

"No sex," she stated.

Antoine frowned. "There's much more to me than my mouth, Desdemona," he said.

She turned and scooped up her hat and shades to slip on before she headed to the door.

"Fine," he said, sounding bored. "What made you accept my offer for a late lunch?"

"I need to relax," she admitted. "My avenues for that are limited lately."

Antoine walked over to a room service cart to pour two glasses of champagne. "Glad to be of service," he quipped as he came over to hand her a half-filled flute. "I canceled a very important meeting when you called."

She didn't doubt it.

"Do I *need* to change?" she asked before taking a deep sip.

"Trust me, you'll love it," he said, moving over to claim a seat on the sofa.

Why not?

Desdemona carried the flute with her into the bedroom, closing the door behind her. "No, he didn't," she said aloud as she eyed the same dress he'd ordered and she'd shipped to him in Paris. Sitting beside it was a box of matching heels.

Antoine was always determined to have his way.

When she first laid eyes on the evening gown, she had wavered between purchasing it for herself or adding it to the inventory for the boutique. The design was exquisite and perfect for highlighting a woman's curves.

It seemed Antoine was determined to see her in it...and then out of it.

He was wonderful for a woman's morale.

She looked around the room and then headed toward the en suite. It was as luxurious as the rest of the suite. She began a bath in the soaking tub and soon had removed her clothes and slipped beneath the water with a sigh.

She was determined to enjoy herself. If only for one day. Opportunities to have fun had been few and far between lately.

Desdemona draped her hair over the side to prevent it from getting wet as she sank to rest the back of her head against the smooth rim. She lost track of time and did not care.

"*D'une beauté exquise,*" Antoine's voice said, erasing the quiet.

That one she knew. He told her she was exquisitely beautiful often.

Desdemona opened her eyes to find him leaning in the doorway, watching her. She raised one leg high in the air. "Even more than the supermodel?" she asked of the Swedish model he'd dated for five years.

Antoine walked over to kneel by the tub, raising the sleeve of his lightweight silk sweater to lower his hand under the water. "That was love" was his delayed answer to her question.

"And this?" she asked as he slid one finger and then another deep inside her.

"Is obsession," he whispered as he watched her closely for her reaction to the strokes of his fingers.

Desdemona gasped and arched her back, raising the dark and taut tips of her breasts to peek above the water.

"Love lasts. Obsession fades," he said, lowering his head to capture one tight nipple in his mouth.

She brought her hands up to press to the back of his head as he deeply sucked first one breast and then the other with hunger. She closed her eyes and enjoyed the fantasy that it was Loren who was seducing her. That intensified her passion and she ached for release. For him to make her cum.

She needed the bliss.

But Antoine withdrew his hands and rose to his full height.

Her anticipation had her panting as she looked up at him, his erection straining against his slacks.

He looked amused. "It's my turn to make you wait," he said before he sucked the fingers that had nearly brought her to climax, and he turned and left the bathroom.

Desdemona bit her bottom lip and released a shaky breath as she fought the urge to finger herself to completion. She didn't. Leaving her dangling that close to explosion and then withdrawing his pleasure left her excited.

She finished her bath and smoothed her body with lotion before entering the bedroom to pull on the dress, not bothering with undergarments. She tucked her hair behind her ears; the simple makeup she wore would have to suffice. In the mirror, she studied her reflection.

Desdemona felt beautiful and wished it was Loren who was waiting for her on the other side of the door.

"Love lasts. Obsession fades."

Was that true?

Then what was it that Loren felt for me? Mine was love.

Pushing aside a hurt that clung, she left the bedroom to find Antoine standing beside the large window that gave a view of Central Park. He turned to watch her cross the room.

Their playful exchanges were fun but lacked substance. A distraction, but like drugs, the avoidance didn't last, just prolonged things until later.

"Dance with me," he said. "Any preference on music?"

"Chopin—"

He looked surprised. "Chopin?" he asked.

"Yes," she stressed before chuckling. "Opus 55 No. 1."

Soon music filled the suite.

Antoine held out his hand for her.

She took it, and he settled the other on her lower back and pulled her close. "There's a lot you don't know about me," she said.

He pressed kisses to her neck and shoulders. "I know everything I want to know," he said.

"Like?"

"I love making love to you," he said as he slowly danced her around the living room.

She leaned back and looked up at him. "That's *it*?" she asked.

Loren would have asked her why she wanted Chopin. He would have listened intently and even asked more questions if he didn't fully understand the story she was telling. He had always been so engaged and caring.

She had mentioned her love of the composition to him once and he had remembered that tiny nugget and played it for her the first night she spent with him in his tiny studio apartment.

So thoughtful and loving. So Loren.

"I don't care about anything else," Antoine said with the utmost seriousness as he looked down into her eyes.

Desdemona smiled. "And if I told you that you're just a distraction for me as I get over having my heart broken?" she asked.

"You have, in so many words," he said with a shrug.

True.

She lowered her head to his chest and listened to the piano arrangement that had resonated so deeply with her since first hearing it. During her days as Angel, one of her johns, a wealthy white lawyer of seventy, just wanted to listen to music as they lay in bed naked with their limbs entwined. He sought comfort, and in time, she realized she received the same because one night a week she felt safe.

But it was Loren she thought of, and how they made love as the music swelled in the air as he blazed a blunt. They had gotten so lost in each other with their sex and their vices.

Antoine brought his hand up to notch her chin. He pressed his mouth to hers, and for the first time, she allowed him to kiss her. She closed her eyes with one hand cupping the back of his head as he sucked her tongue.

"Let me put you in a house. Anywhere you want in the world," he whispered against her lips. "I want you all to myself."

She slid a finger in between their mouths. "And if the model—"

"Astrid," he provided.

"And if Astrid wants to take you back?" Desdemona asked.

He raised his head "I would go back," he said.

"And where would that leave me?"

"Cheating is for little boys. I don't cheat," he announced.

"I know, Antoine. So what would happen to me if Astrid wanted you back?" she asked again, just wanting him to see his folly.

"I would make sure you were taken care of, but I would never see you again," he admitted.

Desdemona stroked his bottom lip with her thumb. "I believe that," she whispered up to him. "I really do."

He looked hopeful. "So you'll do it?" he asked.

"No, of course not," she told him.

"Of course not," he agreed.

They danced and kissed. When Desdemona took his hand and led him to the bedroom, she let him undress her and plant kisses along all of her erogenous zones as she lay on her back and then her belly. She was thankful for getting lost in the enjoyment he offered and surprised them both by offering him the same. Protected by a condom, she pressed him down onto the bed and rode him until they reached a slow climax, clinging to each other as they used each other to replace the ones they missed.

After a brief nap, Desdemona cleansed herself and moved quickly about the hotel suite to dress in the clothing in which she'd arrived, her shades, and her baseball cap. "Goodbye forever, Antoine," she whispered to him before bending to press a kiss to his forehead.

"Au revoir, Desdemona," he said, opening his eyes.

She smiled. "Is the chase over?" she asked, hoping she had finally freed him from his obsession with bedding her.

"Perhaps," he teased.

"And perhaps you will have your Astrid and I will get over my Loren," she said.

"Perhaps," he teased again, before closing his eyes and soon reclaiming slumber.

With one last look back, Desdemona left Antoine for the last time.

Hours later, Desdemona stepped inside the hair salon. It was empty save for MiMi, sweeping the floor. The woman looked up and placed her hand on her hip to give her a chastising eye. "Hey, MiMi," she said.

"Lock the door. You paid for a private appointment," she said.

And she had.

Earlier that day, she had discovered the detectives asked her to come in to offer her a deal to avoid charges in exchange for turning over her client list. After claiming no client list existed because she was innocent, she had been weak with relief when she was allowed to leave. Desdemona had been so elated that she decided to treat herself to an after-hours private appointment at the salon.

Desdemona did secure the door before setting her tote in one of the empty chairs. She ran her fingers through her hair, then shook it out. "It needs some attention," she said, trying to gauge the other woman's feelings about her client being revealed as Madam X.

MiMi gave her an eye. "I never said you wasn't welcome here no more. You been my client for a long time," she said. "Even when your money changed, you kept coming."

Desdemona paused in her walk over to the shampoo station, where MiMi now waited for her. "Are we good, MiMi?" she asked.

Yet another reckoning.

The woman shrugged a shoulder. "Yeah, I guess," she said with a comical curl of her top lip. "I mean, you coulda put me on. Long as I been doing your hair. I wanna make some of that money too. MQ coulda get it—front and backward."

Desdemona arched a brow. "Are you upset that you *weren't* asked to sell ass?" she asked in exasperation.

MiMi dropped down and twerked. "Yup! Lizzo not the only one out here reppin' for the big girls. Shit," she said as she continued her butt movements.

Desdemona pinched the bridge of her nose. "MiMi, I am not a madam," she said.

Anymore.

MiMi gave her a wicked side-eye before her face filled with understanding. "Oh. O-o-oh-oh. Okay. Right. *Riiiiiight.* I get it," she said with an exaggerated wink.

Desdemona stayed quiet and just sat on the shampoo chair as the hairdresser covered her with a cape. She hadn't come to talk. She just needed to be pampered, and the feel of the stream of water from the spray hose was everything she needed. That and the sweet scent of the shampoo put her at ease, and she didn't stop a little grunt of pleasure at MiMi's skilled fingers working her scalp.

"Answer me this?" MiMi said, breaking the silence. "Is MQ's thang as long as it looks? He gives off big dick energy."

Desdemona frowned. "I wouldn't know, MiMi. Sorry," she lied, wanting the silence again.

"He's tall and strong like he could just take a big bitch, you know, and flip her on the dick," MiMi said.

It was a vision Desdemona didn't need to have planted in her brain, and now she felt plagued by a hundred kaleidoscope-type images of MiMi twerking on MQ while sticking out her tongue like Cardi B.

Lord help me.

"In MQ's book it said you—I mean *Madam X*—retired," MiMi continued. "But *if* she got back in the biz and was looking for juicy girls, I sure would be down. Hint-hint."

Damn. Do I have to find a new hairdresser?

"Your skill is doing hair. Stick to that," Desdemona said.

"Yeah, you're right," MiMi agreed. "*But* being paid to fly all over the world and fuck a celebrity that I'm crushin' on anyway does not seem like the same hard work as standing on my feet twelve hours a day. That's *all* I'm sayin'."

"I really can't help you with any of that," Desdemona said as MiMi raised the chair and wrapped a towel around her hair. "And I'll be glad when this big misunderstanding is cleared up and my life can get back to normal."

"That would be wild *if* someone was lying on you," MiMi said.

Desdemona didn't miss the huge emphasis on *if*. She would almost laugh if she hadn't been seriously considering going on the run with a permanent move to Bali earlier that day.

"The girls all sure do miss you," MiMi said as she began to comb Desdemona's hair.

Desdemona stayed quiet.

"Especially after that day you were in here when we was talking about Madam X," she added.

Desdemona released a heavy breath of pure annoyance as

she opened one eye while pressing her index finger atop the lid of the closed one. "MiMi, is five hundred dollars enough for you to do my hair, not mention Madam X or MQ or *any* of that shit, and then also not mention to *the girls* that you even saw me? Will that do it?"

In the mirror on the opposite wall, she could see the woman's face fill with shock.

The price was worth it for some peace.

"Ab-so-fucking-lutely," MiMi assured her.

"Done deal," Desdemona said.

Chapter Ten

Desdemona stepped off the elevator on her floor but paused to see Loren leaning against the wall beside her front door. Instantly, she felt guilty about Antoine but pushed that thought aside.

He left.

You're single.

He doesn't want you anymore.

He doesn't love you.

Maybe never did.

"Love doesn't fade."

Loren looked up from scrolling on his phone at her approach. His eyes took her in—quickly but thoroughly—before shifting away.

Her mind had registered that it was over. Her body needed to catch up because her reaction to him—his presence, his nearness—was just as profound as ever. All the bells and whistles of awareness went off.

"Hello, Lo," she said as she reached him.

"Can we talk?" Loren asked, his gaze everywhere but on her.

"Can you not stand to lay eyes on me?" she asked as she used her key to unlock the door and enter, leaving him to do the same.

He did.

She set her bag and keys on the table in the foyer and turned to look up at him as he closed the door. "What can I help you with?" she asked.

He shifted to move past her, but Desdemona stepped in his path. "Damn, can I get past the entry?" he asked.

She shook her head. "Your freedom to move about *this* space ended when you left and moved back into *your* place," she explained, crossing her arms over her chest and tilting her head as she looked up at him.

He then did match her stare.

It tugged her heart.

"How could you do it?" he asked, with a passion that was a mix of his clear anger and disappointment. "How could you sleep with people for money?"

To survive.

She covered her mouth with one of her hands. It was a fight not to tell him her story and how she had to work to forgive herself for the things she was forced to do and then chose to do when it was all she knew how to do.

"Are you still doing that shit?" he asked, with emotions that shaped his face as he splayed his hands. "Were you safe? Were you out here raw dogging strangers? Were you walking the streets? Do I need to get tested for some shit? Are motherfuckers still hitting you up? Like what *the fuck* is going on, Desi?"

She winced at his anger. "Or?" she asked, her voice soft.

Loren did a double take. "What?" he asked, seemingly confused.

"What happened to weighing if a situation is as bad as

you think *or* is it something else going on. Remember?" she said, trying to remind him of the days when he found the good in everything and everybody. "If it seems a woman is mad at me, I should ask myself: '*Or* is she not mad at me but having a bad day? *Or* is she sick and grouchy in general? *Or* is she going through something and could use a friend? *Or*—'"

He nodded at his own words being given back to him.

"I am so sorry that the thoughtful, sweet kid with such a big, beautiful smile and spirit is gone. I did that to you. That is truthfully my *biggest* regret. What stands before me is someone who has lost that outlook on life that helped change me. Helped me to grow. To dream. To go after what I wanted. To conquer my fears. To make friends for the first time. To believe in God's plan for me and the greater good. To skydive. To travel. To live. And to love," she finished softly.

Loren was pacing but stopped to look down at her.

"If you being so tormented by me has changed you so much, I'd rather you forget me and move on and get back to being the dreamer and the optimist," she said with soft eyes as she reached to squeeze his forearm.

He clenched his jaw and then released a breath. "I want to forgive you. I want to forget," he said, his eyes filling with his torment. "I love you, Desi."

Her smile was sad. "No, you don't," she said with a tightness radiating across her chest. "And now you don't even desire me. It's...over, Lo. It's hard to swallow, but it's *so* over."

Her vision blurred with her tears, and with a blink they raced down her cheek.

He reached for her face, but she shook her head and stepped back. "I have always been regularly tested. I have never had sex with anyone without protection except you. I did not sleep with anyone in the five years before I met you. I never cheated on you. I have never loved any man but you.

All of that is the truth, but of course, feel free to get tested and feel free to move on," she finished with a finality she forced into her tone.

Here was yet another man she hoped to set free.

"Good thing you kept your place, huh?" she asked.

He looked around at the condo. It was hard to deny its luxury. "This never felt like home. I always felt like I was sleeping over or visiting," he admitted with a shake of his head.

"I never meant to make you feel that way, Lo," she said.

"You didn't. You never did. It's just how I felt. It was my shit to deal with," he admitted with another look around the space and then up at the lofty ceilings.

"We had a love stuff working against us," she said, disheartened by that.

He eyed her and then smiled. "A lot of," he said.

"Huh?" she asked.

"You said that we had a love stuff working against us and you meant a lot of stuff working against us," he said, with a smile that also touched his deep-set eyes.

He was such a handsome man and his dimpled smile made him radiant.

Her heart couldn't take it. "I, um, got some studying to do," she said, fighting the desire to lightly poke one tip of her nail into one of his dimples.

Loren nodded and turned to open the door.

"Maybe we shouldn't see each other anymore," she said, needing to free her heart of him and the ache of not having him.

He paused. "Is that what you want?" he asked.

"What I want is for the last few weeks to disappear," she admitted.

Loren stepped out into the hall and turned. "If you could change the past, would you?" he asked.

Desdemona made sure to look him directly in the eye.

"No. Not one thing, because this path got me here. It got me to you even though it didn't last. It was hell, but I wouldn't change a thing," she said.

And meant it.

Regrets? Plenty.

Shame? Not as much. Not anymore.

"I am able to live a good life and I have helped a lot of people, Loren. That more than made up for what I went through," she said. "See, you taught me to be grateful for it *all*."

His eyes filled with concern. "What did you go through? Can you at least share that with me? I was ready to be with you for the rest of my life and I don't know shit about you. Where you grew up? How you grew up? Why you dropped out of school? What were you like as a kid?" he asked, his voice rising.

She reached for his wrist and pulled him back inside before sticking her head out to make sure none of her neighbors were in the hall. "I'm already walking on thin ice in this building, Lo," she said as she closed the door.

His look said: *I'm waiting.*

"Why does it matter now when it's over?" she asked. "You agreed that—"

"Yes. I agreed to not knowing your past, but you shouldn't have asked that of me and I shouldn't have agreed," he said.

"Oh, you switching it up now?" she asked. "Where they do that at?"

"Right here." Loren motioned a finger back and forth in the space between them. "Right now."

Tell him.

"Mother dead at five. Father dead at ten. Raised by a wicked stepmother. Cheated out of my inheritance. Ran away at fifteen to survive. Homeless. Hungry. Tricked. Used. Abused," she said.

"Damn, Desi," Loren said, reaching for her.

Again, she stepped away from his touch. "'Y'all gotta bear with me, I been through some things,'" she quoted the Cardi B lyric from "Best Life" before giving him a weak smile that she knew didn't reach her eyes.

His brows touched as his face was marked with concern.

"I went from sleeping in laundromats and starving—tempted to eat out the trash—to all of this," she said as she waved her hand around the condo. "I came from the gutter and crawled my way up and it's *stuck*."

Loren opened his mouth to speak. Desdemona raised a hand to stop him.

"You lived. I *survived*," she said with fiery eyes. "We do not have the same background and thus we do not make the same decisions about life. We are not the same. You had parents. You had a home. You had love. You had security. Hell, you had the basics with a fucking bed and food to eat. *Stop* judging my life based on your life."

Loren looked uncomfortable.

Good.

"So you don't want to be here, then don't be here. You don't want to be with me, don't be with me. You don't want to fuck me, then don't fuck me," she railed. "It's all *good*."

Loren studied her as he ran his long fingers through his wild curls. "I am different. I changed. That's all true, Desi," he admitted. "I just wanted it all to be different. I love you. I do. I think of you. I miss you. I sketch you. You are in my dreams. In goals. Marriage. Babies. Our family. I want you there. I just—"

"Want it perfect and I'm not, Lo," she said, always alluding to the truth but never fully claiming it. "You would have to take me as I am. Flaws and all. And you can't. And that's okay."

Their eyes locked.

"When you ended things first, I already knew I loved you. And then you disappeared for a year. I thought of you every day. I missed you. I wanted you. I *ached* for you," he admitted, his deep voice swelling with passion. "And when you popped up in that English class that day, I was so damn happy to see you again after all that time, I would have accepted anything for you not to leave again."

Desdemona's closed her eyes and released a shaky breath.

"Don't tell me I don't love you," he stressed.

She looked at him again and she gasped at the raw emotion in his eyes. "Lo," she sighed.

"I didn't fuck nothing since that last night you were at my apartment," he admitted.

That surprised her. "You never told me that," she said.

Loren pressed his finger to her chest. "Don't tell me I don't love you," he repeated.

He brought the hand up to cup her neck and draw her close, pressing a kiss to her brow as he liked to do. "I just wanted everything to be different," he whispered once he lowered his head and settled his mouth near her ear. "But I do love the hell out of you."

With one last kiss on her cheek, Loren turned and left the condo.

Desdemona turned and eyed her wine cabinet but fought the urge, knowing she would easily finish a bottle in one sitting. She stepped over to the table to remove her cell phone from her tote. As she opened the side pocket, she noticed the note from Portia and the card from Denzin. She hadn't worn that particular bag since the day she first received them.

It was the card that she picked up with the tips of her stiletto nails.

As if it were a gift, she had happened upon the card and the offer of friendship at just the right time. Denzin understood why she had sold herself and then become a madam—offering others the opportunity and protection to do the same. And she needed that.

I need Denzin.

She rubbed her thumb across the words he wrote before she quickly turned up the rest of the lights and moved through the condo to retrieve one of the prepaids from the safe. With her heart beating with loud thumps, she dialed Denzin's number on the activated flip phone.

It rang just once.

"Hello, stranger," Denzin said, warmth coating his deep voice.

"Hello to you, sir," she teased, smiling like a fool.

"I didn't think you were going to call me," he said.

"At first I wasn't," she admitted as she sat down on the bench she used to put on her boots. "That was our deal, remember?"

"How *are* you?" he asked.

"In need of a getaway. How's Atlanta looking for the weekend?" she asked, glancing at the open suitcases stacked atop each other, which she had yet to unpack.

Thursday, April 22

Welcome to the A

Desdemona barely caught the last flight out of New York into Atlanta's Hartsfield-Jackson International Airport. When she arrived with just one of her rolling carry-ons, Denzin was awaiting her at curbside in a metallic-red Audi R8 sports car. He climbed from the driver's seat, tall and muscular, with a deep brown complexion and broad, handsome features.

He stopped short of pulling her into a hug to extend his hand. "Nice to meet you, Desdemona," he teased.

She swiped his hand away and hugged him. Tightly. "You looking like new money," she said, leaning to the side to eye his whip.

Denzin took her carry-on and opened the trunk to slide it inside. "I told you those years at the mansion I was saving money," he said, holding the passenger door for her. "And my catering business is doing well."

She had not discovered her stud had graduated from culinary school until their final days together. "Is that the *only* business?" she asked when he slid into the driver's seat.

Denzin smiled. "I kept a few of my select clients," he admitted.

They fell quiet.

"What you been up to besides trying to stay out of jail?" he asked as he maneuvered his sports car into the heavy flow of downtown Atlanta traffic—it gave New York a run for its money.

"I traveled the world for a year before starting college," she said, giving him a glance. "Fell in love. Now I'm falling out of love because of the bullshit. Running the boutique legitimately. Just out here trying to stay free."

"I just got back from a week in Dubai with Number 25," Denzin said with a wink.

Monica Harcourt. World-renowned comedian, actress, and talk show host who sold out coliseums around the world and was recently listed on *Time*'s list of top influential people.

"Good money. Good sex. Good times," Denzin added.

"Ain't nothing wrong with that," she said, having approved of her courtesans remaining in contact with consorts when she ended her business.

"She wanted to make sure I wasn't still connected to you," he added with a brief look over at her.

"I don't blame her," Desdemona conceded. "Right now, I'm sure there's quite a few from the old list feeling a little nervous. Maybe some courtesans too."

Denzin nodded in agreement as he drove.

"Do you think any of them would turn on me?" she asked, letting her eyes study his rugged profile. "Would *you*?"

"Whoa," Denzin said giving her a wide-eyed look. "I thought you came to chill, not interrogate me."

Desdemona eyed the brightly lit scenario as he sped the car up the interstate. "I did. But the questions are still hanging."

Denzin gave her another look like: *Bet.*

He took the next exit with a swift dip move and pulled over on the side of the road.

Not this again, she thought, remembering Loren doing the same on the way to the resort.

She climbed from the car to join him as he sat on the hood with the engine softly purring. The night winds felt good and she closed her eyes as she took a deep inhale.

"I'd do a bid before I turn on you," he swore.

She looked over at him. "Right now. I don't know who or what to trust," she admitted.

"You can trust me, Mademoiselle," he said.

She looked out at the towering buildings in the distance. "Trust is not in my DNA anymore," she said, thinking of Loren.

"You used to trust me," he said.

"To a point," she confessed with a little laugh.

Denzin leaned over to rest his head on her shoulder.

"It's just after fifteen years I stepped away from it all on *my* terms," Desdemona said, giving voice to her frustration. "I could've kept going, but I stepped away. And now, after two years of being legitimate, I'm dealing with being betrayed by someone I know I have protected at some point. It feels so unfair sometimes and other times as if I brought it on myself by all the people who were hurt by their spouse or their lovers cheating on them."

"Don't beat yourself up," Denzin said, rising and turning to stand before her. "You are not responsible for the actions of grown people that came to you hunting up pussy."

Desdemona shrugged one shoulder. "I don't know," she said, looking up at him. "I honestly thought it was all I knew. All I could do. I was so caught up in it."

"Listen, everybody grows up, learns better, and does better," he said.

She thought of Loren's judgment. "You ever feel less than for being a sex worker?" she asked.

"*Hell* no," Denzin said with emphasis. "I promise you, there are way more dudes out there fucking more than me and still borrowing somebody's car to drive while *she* at work."

Desdemona laughed.

"Is that about the falling-out-of-love part?" Denzin asked.

"Look at you, being all observant," she said.

Denzin raised his arms and flexed them. "I have two heads, you know," he said, before unfurling his tongue and giving her a body roll. "Then again, you would never give me a shot to prove it to you."

She arched a brow. "Trust me, I saw *plenty* of your dick. Okay," she said with a dismissive hand wave.

"Seeing and feeling are two different things," he said, taking a bold step forward.

Desdemona pressed a hand to his chest to stop him. "I have had dick today. Thanks, though," she said.

A car sped past them so fast, she felt like this car shifted a bit. "Can we get off the side of the road?" she asked, rising to open the door. "Before we get hit and go flying."

Denzin laughed and came around the front to slide into the driver's seat. "So, you are never going to have sex with me?" he asked, so blunt and direct.

She missed that about him.

"I'd rather have the friend than the dick," she said.

He eyed her.

She wondered what he was thinking as the moments ticked by.

"I think you scared you would love it," he said, choosing to tease her as he put the car in Drive.

She released a sarcastic yelp. "I would have you walking to New York barefoot with your dick in one hand and a flashlight in the other *looking* for me," she told him. "Calling out my name. 'Desi! Desdemona, where are you? Please give me some more. *Pleeeeease.*'"

"I can believe it," he agreed with a deep chuckle as he drove off.

"Don't play with me. Like it or love it, it was my occupation and I'm good at what I do," she said with confidence.

Bzzzzzz. Bzzzzzz. Bzzzzzz.

Her eyes dropped to her tote. The light of a phone illuminated the interior of the bag. Her heart raced.

The blackmailer.

She rushed to pick it up. "Don't say nothing," she said to Denzin before answering.

He nodded in agreement.

"Let's meet up," the distorted voice said.

Got 'em.

"I'm not in town," she said. "I'll be back Sunday night, though."

"Damn," the voice swore in a whisper.

"Who are you?" she asked.

"You'll see when we meet. I'll call you Sunday with the time and place."

"No, I'll pick the time and place. You bring whatever evidence you got and you'll get your two hundred thousand."

Denzin reached over to cover the hand on her thigh with his own. *Two hundred thousand dollars?* he mouthed.

Desdemona placed a finger to her lips to ensure he stayed silent.

"Don't fuck me over," the voice warned with malice. "Or I'll make sure they bury your ass *under* the jail."

The call ended.

She dropped the phone back inside her tote. "I got this. Just leave it be, Denzin," she said before he could start.

"Evidence? Two hundred bands?" he said in disbelief. "Are you being blackmailed? Who else knows about this?"

"No one," she confessed before letting her head back on the seat with her eyes closed.

"Not even your lawyer or the person you're *falling* out of love with?" he asked in disbelief.

"Loren," she supplied. "And no, I haven't told him much of anything. Hell, nothing at all."

The silence that followed caused her to open her eyes and look at him. "What?" she asked.

"Did he know already?" Denzin asked.

"No."

"Damn!" he said emphatically. "Ma–da–moi–selle! Come *on*."

"Desdemona," she corrected him.

"I kinda like Madam X."

"I'll settle for Desi," she said.

"Cool," he said. "Now, back to you trying to hide the biggest part of your life from the man you love. Not fair. Not cool."

She said nothing as she looked out the window as Denzin drove through the streets of Midtown Atlanta.

"It should have been his choice to forgive and forget," Denzin added, his voice tempered, as if he thought he was treading on sensitive ground. "We have every right to use our adult bodies as we see fit, but it can be difficult for some to handle. You needed to know that going in before your heart got involved."

I know.

"You love him?" he asked.

"Like crazy, but it's over," she said. "Plus, we had other differences we couldn't overcome."

"I'm sorry to hear that," he said as he made a right turn at a red light, after checking for oncoming traffic.

"Yeah right," she drawled with a playful pinch of his arm.

"I want to fuck you, not hurt you or see you hurt," he said. "I said one time before that we weren't friends, but we were—in our way. I missed you. We were a team. At least you made me feel that way."

"Same, Denzin," she said, with softness reaching over to cover the top of his hand with hers.

They fell quiet again.

An SUV with a booming, bass-filled beat passed by.

"You ever feel like we're dirty? Wrong? Like, shitty people? Fucking criminals or some shit?' she asked, knowing it was that question that made her seek him out. A kindred spirit. Another lost soul.

"Legally, we are criminals," he said. "Dirty? Far from it. Especially with all the drug and STD testing you made us all take. We're grown, Desdemona. And your body autonomy allows you to do with it as you please and/or be as sexual as you please."

But she thought of herself at fifteen, forced to use her body to repay a debt for things she assumed Majig had gifted her. That had not been sexual freedom. No freedom at all.

Until I let him die.

And when she claimed his client list and took control, it was then she *chose* to continue her work.

"Now there's no reason not to stay in touch," he said, pulling to a stop in front of a building with glowing red lights around the trim.

"What if I go to jail?" she asked.

"Then I will put money on your books and come visit as much as I can," he promised, raising their hands to kiss the back of hers. "You made it possible for me to make good money to take care of my mother when she was sick and still have time to spend with her. I lived in a beautiful mansion, fully stocked with food and drink for free for years, and I saved so much money because of that. I saw you pay off school loans and bills for people. Helped with major medical costs. For nothing in return but gratitude. There is *nothing* I won't do for you, Desdemona Dean."

"I could use a big brotha," she said.

"See? As badly as I want to know if you're as good in bed as you look, I will even do that for you," he said with a smile before releasing her hand and shutting off the car. "Come on. Let's have some fun."

Desdemona peered through the windshield to look out at the building. A sign flashed "Burlesque" in the window. "What the hell?" she said aloud as she looked around at the crowded parking lot.

Denzin waved her out of the car.

She exited. "Denzin, I would love to get to my hotel to take a shower and change before we conquer these ATL streets," she said as she stood by the car with the passenger door still open.

"Hotel? You're staying with me at my condo. Second, if we don't go now, we'll miss the last set," Denzin said, coming over to grab her wrist to tug her as he closed the door with a push with his free hand.

Desdemona resisted, looking down at the black matte

jersey dress she wore with black ankle socks with fur balls and black designer slides, just to travel in. Thankfully, with much effort to remain incognito, large shades, and her long hair tucked away under a black baseball cap, no one had recognized her.

"It's damn near one in the morning," Denzin said, reclaiming her wrist to tug her behind him. "No one will care."

"I care," Desdemona said. "Open the trunk."

He shook his head as he used his key fob to open it as requested.

Desdemona opened her carry-on and removed a pair of gold heels she brought to wear with a flirty metallic dress. She changed in the car, quickly checked her armpits for freshness, brushed out her hair, and reapplied lip gloss before looking at her reflection in the tinted glass of the car. "Not my best but better," she said, turning this way and that in the formfitting dress.

He eyed her from head to toe with a woeful head shake. "Right, *Sis*," he said with dry sarcasm before opening the door and holding it for her.

Desdemona entered the dark interior with spots of lighting offered by red wall sconces on the black brocade–covered walls. They stopped at an ornate, bronzed theatrical booth manned by a beautiful woman in a gold-metallic corset and matching miniature top hat with dramatic make-up. The music was slow, jazzy, and swelling in the air, which was scented with something sweet but not cloying.

She wrapped one arm around Denzin's muscular one as he paid their cover charge and they moved through gold-trimmed, black velvet curtains. She looked around at the dimly lit, double-level club, which somehow still seemed to be intimate. And the décor was over the top. Red chandeliers. Small gold lamps on each table. Brocade walls and tablecloth. Gold-trimmed leather chairs. And in the center of it all was a large, round stage that currently rotated.

Denzin guided her to an empty table near the middle of the lower level just as the lights went out. The first refrain of a bluesy song began to play just as the sound of a sultry saxophone overlaid the beat. The stage opened and light streamed upward to the ceiling. First, sequined gloves began to emerge in snakelike motions to the music. Inch by inch came the reveal. Crystal headwrap. Beautiful made-up face. Skin as dark and glistening as freshly made chocolate. A body to die for draped in nothing but an iridescent thong, white feather-tail fans, and incredibly high, crystal-adorned heels with pert breasts exposed. She looked about the crowd as she danced with the fluidity of ocean waves. Boldly, she made eye contact. Mesmerizing all with her talent, her beauty, and maybe even a spell. Slow splits. Seductive removal of her gloves. A peekaboo dance with the feather fans before the music built to a crescendo and she dropped to her knees, fell backward, and then arched her back as she flung her arms wide and exposed her breasts before slowly covering them again as the music lowered.

Desdemona was unable to take her eyes off the smooth movements of the dancer as she took control of the stage and everyone in attendance for her performance. She could tell why the woman was the headliner.

A chair was set on the stage and with liquid moves, she claimed the seat. "There is nothing grander than the beauty of a woman—*every* woman's body," she said, even the flow of her words in sync with the music as she worked her shoulders back and forth with her knees pressed together.

"Whether purely existing, making love, or giving birth, worship the vessel you were given," she continued, turning sideways and leaning back to extend one leg high into the air with pure flexibility.

Desdemona was surprised at feeling her sexuality stir, not from desiring the performer but in awareness of her own sensuality. Her being. Her power—or at least one of them.

"Own your sexuality in whatever way you see fit," the performer said as she sat up, pressed her hands to her thighs, and slowly eased her knees open wide. "Own your body freely, of your own choice. It is a part of being human. Alive. Passionate."

As the woman continued her sensual dance, her talk of sex positivity blew Desdemona's mind.

"Who are you, Desdemona?"

It had been a while since Dr. Ophelia's question had come to her mind and at the moment, she had an answer readily available.

Sexual.

"*Be* safe. *Be* in control. *Be* free," the performer said as the stage opened again and she was lowered down into the floor to thunderous applause.

Desdemona rose to her feet to join in. "That was amazing," she said, looking down at Denzin, still eyeing the stage though nothing more of the woman could be seen.

His look was so intense.

Desdemona sat back down and leaned in close to him. "You okay? You look like you ready to take her home," she said.

He looked at her. "Oh, I'm already fucking the hell out of her," he said. "For *free.*"

Of course.

Desdemona imagined them going at it and just knew it was electric.

"Good thing I don't swing that way because I would take her from you," she joked.

"Or we could share," he said, locking eyes with her. "A threesome is a very freeing expression of sexuality."

Desdemona just ignored that as they rose to leave. "If you have plans, I can find something else to get into," she said.

"Nah, she has lovers. I'm just one. I'll have my turn Sunday night because this weekend I'm chilling with you. Ready?" he said, wrapping an arm around her shoulders in a way that was brotherly.

Thank God.

Chapter Eleven

Monday, April 26

*No call. No show. What now? I hate being in the
dark. When it comes to this part of the drama and
every player in it: What are the coordinates?*

"What happened to the butterflies?" Desdemona whispered aloud.

Just as swiftly as they came to her, they had disappeared.
Was her transformation over or stalled?

She sighed and picked up her phone to eye her lock
screen. On it was a colorful meme she'd saved off Instagram.
"'Adversity is meant to launch you forward,'" she read
aloud.

Toward what, though?

She eyed the notifications on her screen. She took note
that calls and texts from Melissa had stopped. Truly, she
couldn't blame her for not reaching out anymore.

Desdemona's plate was full. Maintaining a friendship at
that time was not a priority, even if she missed her like crazy.

I just can't juggle all the balls again.

Still.

She quickly typed: Melissa. Thank you for not turning your back on me. Miss you, friend. Hopefully, when the mess is over, we can reconnect.

She hit Send.

Whoosh.

Next was a voice mail from Jynn.

Before she could open it, she saw that her friend already had responded to her text.

MELISSA: Not sure what to say or feel. Maybe I will know by the time you finally reach out to me. We'll see then. Good luck, Desdemona. Praying for you.

More than fair.

Desdemona opened the voice mail.

Beep.

"A little birdie told me the police wanted a warrant to search your condo. It was denied for insufficient evidence by Judge Harrison Young. The witch hunt is falling apart, kiddo. Call me," Jynn said on the recording.

Desdemona stiffened and sat up straighter as she frowned.

Search my condo?

She thought of the cash and false credentials in her safe. Very incriminating.

And very stupid to have there while being investigated by the NYPD.

"I am losing it," she muttered.

With a shake of her head, Desdemona leaned back in the chair behind her desk in the showroom as she looked across the divide out the window. The sun was beginning to set above the city, casting the skies in deeper shades of blue. She was lucky for a break in the heights of the building across the street from her to be able to enjoy a partial view of night falling.

Up until then, it had been an uneventful day. She had

attended classes earlier and then shipped a few orders when she arrived at the showroom. But pulsing with a life all its own behind the surface was the fact she had not heard from her extortionist last night upon her return to New York.

Now what?

There were connections she'd made over the years, favors to be returned, and secrets she could hold over the heads of very powerful men, but she had vowed never to betray the trust put in her. Not even to avoid prosecution and jail.

Besides, without her prepaid phone system, contacting them would require using direct means that solidified a relationship between them. Right now, she was avoiding all courtesans and consorts. And they all were doing the same. Well, most.

Save for Antoine, Denzin, and Red.

It was the latter who surprised her with an order today.

She opened the tablet linked to the boutique's website and pulled up the completed order for an emerald-green asymmetrical sequined gown that would look dynamic on the svelte, redheaded beauty. There was a gift message that Desdemona had just printed off and included in the packaging without reading it in her haste to get out several orders.

"'I owed you, and it's time to repay the favor. Signed, Red,'" she read aloud.

Desdemona scrunched her face in confusion. Red was a moniker she'd assigned the woman when she joined her roster. Her real name was Erin.

Her eyes darted down to the delivery address. It was indeed the town house where Red lived. A gift message to herself?

Or to me?

An attempt to be covert?

Or one to sabotage?

Desdemona felt the flutter in her belly. Her instinct said there was more to it than just a former consort purchasing a dress. Still cautious after the police used Patrice to lure her to the boutique, she fought the urge to reach out to her former consort in case of another setup.

"Damn," Desdemona swore, setting the tablet back on its stand, wishing she could be sure she wasn't looking too deeply into things.

There was no doubt Red owed her and buying a three-thousand-dollar dress would not equate—*if* she had been looking for a return on the favor. Plus, Red was linked to one of the consorts Desdemona believed was angry with her.

Red had left working for Mademoiselle to become the concubine of one of her consorts, Hunter Garrett, a Republican political pundit who was "happily" married and a zealous Conservative. Desdemona had used sources to find the secret town house where he kept Red and then confronted him there about paying her fifty thousand dollars for the lost revenue from her lineup.

There had been no lost revenue. No debt to be paid. She did not own anyone.

Her true intent? Desdemona kept just 10 percent of the money and secretly gave the rest to Red for her to have a backup when—and not if—Garrett left her behind one day to fend for herself.

Hunter had been angry, but enough for revenge and blackmail?

Desdemona rose from the chair and came around the desk as she pulled her hair up in a ponytail. She began to pace and nibble at her bottom lip. Not knowing how deeply she was being monitored by the police, she was hesitant to even search for current info on the pundit via her Wi-Fi. Them just knowing she had typed his name in the search bar could kick off an investigation into possible connections between them. Especially after learning they had tried to get a warrant to search her home.

"Shit," she swore.

I need help.

"Everything okay?"

She looked over at Yusef, leaning inside the now-open glass door.

"Just thinking. Don't mind me," she said with a smile.

He gave her a nod and closed the door to reclaim his position blocking the entrance.

She hated feeling as if her hands were tied.

Couldn't reach out to Red.

Scared to hire someone to research Hunter.

Too worried to even jump on the internet now.

They could be on my ass.

Her life felt like that old Rockwell song: "Somebody's Watching Me."

Paranoia is not fun. Neither is incarceration.

Desdemona retrieved her phone and pulled up her contacts before making a call.

The phone rang for what seemed endless moments before going to voice mail. "Hey, Antoine. Dinner tonight? Let me know?" she said before ending the call.

She hadn't spoken to him or heard from him at all since the afternoon they spent together the week before. And were it not for her needing him to get some intel on Hunter Garrett, that would be fine by her. She had no idea if he was still in the country now that he had finally succeeded in getting her in his bed.

The glass door opened again. Yusef held his lit phone in his hand.

"You might want to turn on that Maria Vargas show," Yusef said, his eyes apologetic.

"Fuck Maria Vargas," she said.

He chuckled.

I am sick of that particular bitch.

He closed the door as Desdemona reached for the remote and turned on the television on the wall. She flipped through the channels until she saw the face of the woman she had come to disdain. Her resilience in stirring the Madam X mess was fanatical.

"Welcome back to Celebrity Spotlight. *Ever since the explosive autobiography of NBA superstar Marquis "MQ" Sanders revealing his past relationship with an upscale prostitution ring, the world has been riveted by the revelation of the identity of Madam X."*

Desdemona leaned against the edge of the desk and winced a bit at the sight of the photo of her now on the screen.

"There isn't much to be found about Desdemona Dean. No criminal arrest records. No social media accounts. Not much of a digital imprint at all. And yet the police—based on a tip not yet found to be credible—believe this woman, Desdemona Dean, to be Madam X.,"

"Here on Celebrity Spotlight, *we've put out calls for anyone willing to come forward with details about Dean but were unsuccessful . . . until* now. *Please welcome Zena Dean, stepmother of Desdemona Dean—"*

Desdemona stood up. "That. Crazy. Bitch," she snapped, eyeing the sight of Zena in a pink church suit, complete with a matching hat tilted to the side as she sat on a white pleather couch with a framed photo of Black Jesus on the wall above her head.

She slid her hands inside the pockets of the flared skirt of the crimson strapless cotton dress she wore under a matching car coat with raised lapels. The backs of her fingers slid across the satin lining as she balled her hands into fists. Tight ones.

"Welcome to Celebrity Spotlight, *Ms. Dean."*

"Thank you. I am happy to be on with you." Zena's voice echoed from the television.

"I just bet you are, you motherfucking lunatic," Desdemona muttered.

"First, tell me about your relationship with Desdemona."

"Well, it did not start easily. My husband had an affair with this woman—this intruder in my marriage—and when she died from her sins my husband asked me to let the child—she was five at the time—live in our home with us and to raise her and love her, which we did."

Zena's eyes were wide and she licked at her thin lips as she lightly rocked back and forth as she spoke.

Never had Desdemona been filled with a rage that made her feel cold with chills. It was weird. She hoped it wasn't the sign of a stroke, but she definitely felt a coldness deep inside that left her body rigid.

"And my husband died five years later. That left me to step up again to raise my stepdaughter."

"So how was Desdemona as a child? Tell us, Ms. Dean."

"Um, a little willful. A little disobedient—"

Desdemona didn't know why she was shocked by the woman's lies, but she was.

"But I'm a God-fearing woman and a lover of children and there was no one else to love her through losing her parents, and so I did what I had to do."

Maria solemnly nodded.

"She lived with me until she was fifteen. Had become fast and promiscuous, like her mother, of course, and when I set rules and tried to help her stay on track she ran away. She ran away. I never heard from her again despite efforts to locate her. And to now learn that she became a prostitute and madam is, I have to admit, not shocking. Not at all."

"Oh *hell* no," Desdemona snapped.

"And so you believe these allegations about your stepdaughter?"

"Absolutely! I can't name all the boys I caught her sneaking into my home. Yes, yes, I believe it. Yes!"

Desdemona's eyes darted down to the crawler at the bottom of the screen with the phone number for the show's tip line. 1-555-TALK2ME. "Fuck the dumb shit," she said, reaching in her tote for the prepaid phone she used to call Denzin.

With her heart beating a little faster and before she could change her mind, Desdemona dialed the number.

"When was the last time you talked to Desdemona?"

"She came to my house about two weeks ago. Here's a snapshot of her on my doorbell camera."

"*Celebrity Spotlight* tip line. What do you have for us?" a young man said, answering the call.

"This is Desdemona Dean," she said. "I want to ask my stepmother a question live on the air."

"Say what now?" the voice said.

"Let Maria Vargas know you have Desdemona Dean on the line," she said, making her voice firm, like she was talking to an employee.

"H–h–hold on."

Elevator music suddenly was playing over the phone line.

Fuck her. Fuck it. Fuck that.

Desdemona paced. *"She was trying to convince me not to come forward—"*

"One moment, Ms. Dean. Ladies and gentleman. We are live on the air and my producer has informed me that we have the Desdemona Dean on the line. Now, let me be clear, we have not confirmed the identity of the person on the phone—"

Knock-knock-knock.

Desdemona turned. Yusef was holding up his phone. *This you?* he mouthed, with wide eyes.

She nodded and turned back to the television.

"Hello, Desdemona. Welcome to Celebrity Spotlight."

Desdemona focused her gaze on Zena's face on the television and enjoyed the discomfort slowly lining her face. "Hello. Let me just say due to the current police investigation, I will not address any questions or make any comments about that," she began, hating the nervous tremor in her voice even as she forged ahead. "But since you have chosen to give this lying, deceiving, and hateful woman a platform to speak about me, I have called in to ask Zena to please explain how there was never a call made to any authorities about me being missing after I ran away. An easily proven fact—something I wish your investigation show would have investigated before giving this woman an opportunity to spread lies about me."

Zena's eyed widened and her lips curled with rage.

"Liar! You lying bi—"

BEEEEEEP.

Zena's mouth was moving, but she was muted.

"I ran away after years of neglect by Ms. Dean, who was angry that my father left the entirety of his modest estate to me. The only way she would receive a stipend from it, she would *have to* serve as my trustee. Something she did with clear disdain of me every day of the time I was in her home. I was never disrespectful. Never a bad child. *Never*," Desdemona stressed as Zena's feed disappeared and a paparazzi photo of Desdemona climbing into a vehicle was displayed instead. "I ran away when I overheard her asking the executor of my father's estate about ways to get control of the money without having to deal with me or have me in her home any longer. And let me add, they were having sex at the time. She asked what would happen if I went to jail and then asked what would happen in the event of my death. Of course I ran...*for my life.*"

Maria Vargas splayed her hands and took a visible swallow over a lump in her throat.

"And a lot that should have been confirmed before she was booked for an interview," Desdemona said with condemnation, feeling bolstered that the tremor was gone. "This woman continued to collect money even in my absence, until I claimed the rest of my inheritance six years later. Even though you have made it your business, Maria Vargas, to help destroy my life and my privacy, I want to thank you—*at the very least*—for getting this horrible woman to admit on television that she knew I ran away at fifteen and thus had no legal standing to pilfer from my inheritance in my absence."

She saw a brief moment of compassion in Maria's eyes before it was quickly covered with the cool façade.

"*Ms. Dean, how are you holding up during what is clearly a difficult time for you, as you may be criminally charged as a madam in the state of New York? What are you hoping to be the outcome?*"

Desdemona arched a brow and placed the phone on Speaker before setting it on the desk. "I am *hoping* that more focus is put on journalistic integrity on this show than time being squandered on salacious gossip, Ms. Vargas, but I doubt it because it's very clear that nothing matters to you but ratings. Now you have a blessed day," she said before ending the call with a hard punch of her finger.

"*Ms. Dean? Ms. Dean?*"

The woman's voice echoed into the quiet of the showroom as Desdemona watched her holding her hand to her ear.

"*It seems Desdemona said what she had to say and has ended the call. Let's head into a commercial break and then we'll be back to see if Zena Dean would like to address the accusations lodged against her. Then I will take a moment to address the judgment also placed on me and this show. Right after the break.*"

Desdemona pouted her lips and released a long breath from puffed cheeks as she sought calm.

What have I done?

That would become social media fodder and only add more life to the frenzy over Madam X.

Her phone was still on "do not disturb," but she saw the notification for a missed call hit the screen. And then again. And again. Next was a voice mail. Then a text.

She checked them.

Jynn.

"Shit," she swore, looking out the door to find Yusef giving her a thumbs-up.

She smiled, but it felt weak. Like her knees. She squatted down and let her head hang between her thighs. "Shit, shit, shit, shit," she repeated.

Desdemona heard the door open behind her, but she held up a hand to alert him to leave her be. The door closed, and she knew she was alone again. She had lost control. Gone was the cool-headed, methodical Mademoiselle, to be replaced by an emotional wreck who let anger, hate, and resentment spurn her to destroy her wicked stepmother on live television.

She felt she was drowning under the waves of her regrets.

The rise of tears surprised her.

Under attack from strangers and an enemy.

"*Welcome back to a very shocking episode of Celebrity Spotlight. During the break, it seems Ms. Zena Dean chose not to speak on the matter any further. She is no longer available for a follow-up comment. Again, we cannot confirm the identity of the woman on the line claiming to be Desdemona Dean. It's a live show and we felt we could not let the opportunity pass to hear from one of the most talked-about people in the world right now.*"

Desdemona settled an elbow atop a knee, then placed her chin in her palm as she looked at the television screen.

"Lastly, before we move on to our next segment, let me state that here at Celebrity Spotlight, *we have in the past and will continue to bring you nothing but the very best in entertainment news. We work very hard and long hours to break entertainment news stories to keep our fans engaged. That is our mission here. And now, on to our next story."*

Not journalism, in other words. Bullshit.

The glass door opened again.

Desdemona stood to her full height in her heels. "Yes, Yusef?" she said, sounding as emotionally drained as she felt.

"It's Ms. Nkosi," he said, handing her his phone.

Desdemona took it. "Not now, Jynn," she said, her voice a monotone. "I am literally going numb from the neck up as we speak."

"What the hell were you thinking?" Jynn exclaimed.

"I was just sick of not being a part of the narrative about me," she said, going to her desk to gather her things and shut down the showroom for the day. "And you can lecture me tomorrow because I can't, Jynn. I swear, I just fucking can't."

Desdemona heard the emotional strain in her own voice, and that struck an even deeper, more painful chord inside. The weight of it all was buckling her.

"Okay," the attorney said quickly and softly. "Okay. Give Yusef the phone."

Desdemona felt she barely had the strength to do that. Thankfully, he reached for it.

"Yeah," he said, walking away.

Truly, Desdemona felt like dropping everything, including her body, to the floor and just giving in.

To despair.

To depression.

To stress.

To a mental breakdown.

She didn't know whether to scream or cry—she didn't have the strength for either. The blows seemed to be coming from all around and weakening her like a video game character with each one.

Marquis's autobiography.

The police investigation.

Facing jail time.

Loren leaving.

Antoine's attention.

The blackmailer.

Classes.

Working at the showroom.

The press.

The lies.

The broken expectations.

The past she couldn't escape.

And even more than that.

Everyone has a line where it all is just *too* much.

With one last gasp, Desdemona's eyes closed and she fell into the abyss of unconsciousness as she finally met that line.

Desdemona opened her eyes.

The room was pitch-dark, but she knew the feel of her bed and her sheets.

I'm home.

She reached out to turn on the lamp before sitting up in bed, thankful she was fully dressed sans her heels. "How did I get here?" she asked.

The last thing she remembered was the moment before she passed out at the showroom.

She shifted on the bed to sit on the side and let her feet

dangle before she rose and removed the car coat and loosened her hair from the now disheveled ponytail. "Anyone here?" she called.

Moments later, Loren came to stand in the doorway to the bedroom.

His hair was loosened and shaped into an afro by his wild curls. He wore his spectacles and was still in work clothes, a striped shirt and khakis. "Hey. Good, you're up," he said, removing the thick tortoise frames that she once thought he wore just for style.

"Yeah, yeah, I'm up," she said, looking down at her feet and then back up at him. "And you're here."

"I am," he said with a boyish smile.

"Because?" she asked, drawing out the question.

Loren chuckled. "It was all over the news that you had to be carried out of the office building by your bodyguard," he explained. "Melissa saw it. Told Benjie. He called me."

"Melissa?" she asked in surprise. "I thought she hated me."

"None of us who *really* know Desdemona Dean could ever hate you," he said, leaning back against the door frame to look at her with those deep-set eyes.

There her pulse went. Off to the races.

She looked away from him, seeking a reprieve.

"Anyway. I came here to wait—yes, I did use the key I still have," he admitted. "A doctor came to your showroom to check you. He said you had a panic attack. You came to, but he gave you a sedative. They brought you here. He'll be back in the morning to check on you again. Your bodyguard and the attorney left too."

"A doctor making house calls?" she said in surprise.

"A favor for your attorney," he supplied.

Desdemona nodded. "What time is it?" she asked.

"Eleven," he supplied.

"Damn!" she spouted in shock.

Loren chuckled. "Hungry?" he asked. "I made you some soup."

"Were you still up or did I wake you?" she asked before moving from the spot where she had seemed rooted to lead him into the kitchen.

There was a convertible sofa bed in the office.

"I'm finishing my book tonight," he said as he moved to the stove to keep an eye under a huge stockpot. "I want to finally get it to that agent tomorrow."

"Loren, that is amazing," she said, feeling joy for him as she crossed the kitchen to grip his arm and look up at him. "I'm so proud and so happy."

He looked down at her and studied her. "You really mean that. Don't you?" he said.

"Of course!" she stressed. "I want you to get a huge deal and then all the writing awards. To have all your dreams."

His eyes lost some of their shine. "Not all," he said, looking down at her eyes and then her mouth before turning away.

Forgive my past and let's start again.

But she bit her bottom lip to keep from saying that, knowing the matter of them having children was still there, pressing between them as well.

Desdemona gave his arm one last squeeze before moving away from him to look for her bag. It was sitting on the living room sofa. She sat down beside it with one foot tucked beneath her bottom as she unzipped it.

"Tell me about your book again, Lo," she said as she checked her iPhone.

No calls from Antoine.

Damn.

"It's a story about Bongani, the first African captured and sold into slavery in the mid-1500s, who was a king back in his native land," he said as he came into the living room with a tray holding a bowl of homemade chicken noodle soup with plenty of broth. "It spans the entirety of his sixty-three years in America. Love. Loss. Rebellion. Freedom."

Desdemona watched the play of emotions on Loren's face as he described the major plot points of the book to her. And what she saw—and felt—was conviction, excitement, passion, and profound love for his work and his art. The blend of two of his loves: history and creative writing.

The man was deep. The way his mind worked. And his dedication to his craft and his belief. His handsomeness was surface. The true beauty of this man was his soul and the very essence of his being.

He shrugged. "Sorry. I get so caught up in it. I love the story. I *love* it," he said.

And I love you.

"No, it's amazing. I can't wait to read it," she said, so truthfully.

He had been insistent that she never do so until the book was in print. She respected his wish.

"I think my favorite part is the love he has for Sena, and how he fights for that love," he said, locking eyes with her. "Even when she's sold away. And loses their children. And even at one point her mind. Still, he loves her. He fights for her."

Desdemona wanted to look away and couldn't. She imagined Loren—her Loren—aged, with his hair silver and his face lined with wrinkles but still dignified and handsome. And she was beside him. Still loving him. Still fighting for him. Her Sena to his Bongani.

That resonated with her. It just felt right.

But it was never to be.

Desdemona rose from the sofa and walked over to her wine cabinet to retrieve a bottle of Rieussec.

"Sedatives," Loren reminded her.

"Right," she said, setting down the bottle and the wine opener she was about to put to work. She moved back to the couch and picked up her bowl, sitting on the low-slung, modern glass coffee table of hand-forged iron, with bronze end caps.

"The doctor wants you to take it easy," Loren said. "Maybe close the boutique until you're finished with classes this semester, or at least until this investigation is officially closed."

She dropped her phone back into her bag. "Yes, but when will that be?" she said, stirring the soup with her spoon.

Loren walked back into the kitchen and returned with a bowl of soup of his own. He sat in one of the club chairs by the unlit fireplace—across the room.

Desdemona took note but said nothing about it. "Should I assume you saw or heard about *Celebrity Spotlight* today?" she asked as she looked down at the hearty noodles, veggies, and shredded chicken as she continued to stir.

"Not live, but yes, I saw it later online," he said.

Desdemona took a sip of the broth. It was seasoned well. She had another.

"The upside of your health scare on the news was there has been a shift in the narrative," Loren said, covering his mouth as he chewed.

"A shift?" she asked.

"Someone checked. You were right. The police were never called about you being missing and you were never placed on the missing person's register," he continued. "That shit blew up in Maria Vargas's face big-time and didn't help the NYPD one bit about the possibility of you being lied on about the prostitution ring."

"You don't say," she said.

Loren gave her an indulgent smile.

Desdemona took a huge breath. "My life with my stepmother was really hard. And sad, Loren," she admitted in a whisper. "She was so cold. So spiteful and mean. She did not want me there and that was clear. Losing my mother and then my father before being left alone in the world with a woman with so much misery in her DNA was tough."

He rose to come over to the sofa.

She was thankful for his closeness. "When she mentioned me dying, I knew I had to get out of there before she poisoned me slowly or some shit," she said, remembering the night so clearly and the many nights before that one when she suffered in silence. With grief. With loneliness. With anxiety and fear.

Desdemona felt overcome with emotion and knew it was her unresolved issues. With her parents. With Zena. Maybe even with herself. "To see her lie on me like that. I just had to *say* something. I had to stand up for myself with her. She lied. That wasn't true, Loren. I wasn't fast. I didn't have boys in her house. I wasn't disrespectful," she admitted as her tears fell and her voice broke because of them.

He pulled her body back toward him with his arm so that she rested against his chest. She welcomed the comfort, hating how gripped she felt by the same emotions she wrestled with as a child.

"I wanted her to love me like when my dad was alive, but she changed after his death," she admitted in a whisper, feeling her heart break for the sad little girl she used to be— and maybe deep down still was. "I tried to be *so* good. I was neat. I would fix my own food. I would try to wash my own clothes and clean up behind myself. At night I stayed in my room so she didn't have to see me and hate me. I tried to never ask for anything. I tried to be . . . invisible. I just wanted her to love me. And she wouldn't. She *wouldn't*."

Desdemona freed a cry of misery, and her body shook with tears she'd needed to shed years ago.

"Aw, poor kid," Loren whispered, pulling her body into his lap as he nestled his chin atop her head and held her close.

It was everything Desdemona needed at that moment, and there in his safety, she let down her guard and freed her desolation.

Chapter Twelve

Desdemona awakened with a few slow blinks of her eyes. She hated the taste of her mouth, and her body felt cramped, still sitting in Loren's lap like a child. Careful not to awaken him, she rose, smiling down at his arms stretched out across the back of the sofa, head tilted back, and mouth wide open as he slept.

He looks uncomfortable.

"Lo. Lo. Lie down," she whispered to him as she tried to guide his body to do that.

He stirred awake instead and released a yawn as he stretched. "What time is it?" he asked, his voice deeper, having just woken up.

She reached in her bag for her phone. "It's just after two," she said.

"Damn," he swore, rubbing his eyes with his hands. "I need to work on my book."

Desdemona eyed the missed call from Antoine. "Use the office," she said. "I'm gonna get out of this dress and take a bath."

She turned to leave.

He rose and followed her down the hall.

Just as she passed the open door to the office, she felt his fingertips graze her wrist.

"Desi."

She turned.

"I'm sorry about what happened to you. Yesterday. Thirty-one years ago. Twenty-six years ago. Sixteen years ago," he said with solemn eyes. "It's a testament to your inner strength that you didn't let any of it destroy you."

Confronting Zena on live TV.

Her mother's death.

Her father's death.

Running away from home.

Huge imprints on her life.

That was Loren. So attentive. Thoughtful. And kind.

But also fierce when need be. With his loyalty. His protection of others. His lovemaking. And his love.

"Thank you," she said before turning and heading to her suite to bask it with overhead light.

She removed the strapless dress she'd had on since yesterday. She drew a bath and then sat atop the closed lid of the commode as she returned Antoine's call.

It's eight in Paris.

"How am I supposed to get over you?" he asked when he answered after the first ring.

"You were doing just fine," she said, casting a glance out the bathroom to ensure the doors to her suite were indeed closed. "Listen. I have a name. I need some intel. Can you do that for me without shaking too many trees?"

That gift message had to mean something, and she was following her gut instinct.

Nothing else but that makes sense to me.

"Anything you ask me is yours," he assured her.

"Hunter Garrett," she said, rising to turn off the faucets and drag her fingertips across the water to make ripples.

"I don't know him personally," Antoine said. "He's not in my crowd."

That's an understatement.

"Give me a few hours and I'll see what I can do," he said.

"Where are you?" she asked.

"Back in Paris. Before I continue to chase you to be a *femme entretenue*, I need to try one more time with Astrid," he said.

"*Femme entretenue?*" she asked.

"Kept woman," he explained.

She smiled and shook her head. "I truly wish you much luck with Astrid," she said, truthfully.

He chuckled. "*Têtue!*" he exclaimed good-naturedly.

Stubborn!

That one she knew. She had heard it plenty from him before.

"Let me go bigot hunting," Antoine said.

"*Merci,*" she said before ending the call.

Am I right to be on Hunter's trail? But it can't be him. He is wealthy and well-connected. Why would he bother with a blackmail attempt? A hundred or two hundred thousand dollars is a drop in the bucket to him and his wealthy wife, an oil heiress.

She slipped beneath the scented water and enjoyed its steamy caresses until the water began to cool before she bathed. By the time she was finished and dressed in a robe, she found Loren closed in the office with the *tap-tap-tap* of his fingers against the laptop's keyboard seeming to fly with speed.

Desdemona fixed herself a rare treat of a cup of Ghanaian coffee—fixed light and sweet—before moving back into the living room to stand beside one of the large windows. Even at such a late hour, the familiar sounds of New York City filled the air. She pulled her phone from the pocket of her robe and searched for her name.

The number of videos, articles, memes, retweets, and shares of her impromptu call to *Celebrity Spotlight* were too many to count. As she began to open some to watch or read the commentary, she felt emboldened by the number of people questioning the role Maria Vargas and the show played in pushing a stressed woman closer to the edge. Of course, a few TikToks were using a clip of her words for audio on their videos.

Desdemona even smiled at a few.

Others offered long, venom-filled think pieces on the delivery of karma after participating in the sex trade.

All was fair in being a public spectacle, and she'd made one of herself by calling that show.

But it also led to her revealing more of herself to Loren—and that brought on a breakthrough she felt she needed when it came to her issues with Zena Dean. Stepmother from the very bowels of hell.

Okay, maybe not all of that. Some children had fared even worse than being ignored and hated, but for her, it had been enough.

Her truth had brought on a victory.

Facing Zena and Maria on the show had brought on compassion.

"Who are you, Desdemona?"

Honest. Inherently so.

And going against that had brought on plenty of heartaches. Under the darkness of privacy and secrecy, she had begun to wither like a flower without sun. The truth could only be found in the light.

She looked at her phone.

A missed call ten minutes ago.

"Antoine," she said, unlocking the phone and returning the call.

It barely rang once.

"Any chance you'll tell me why you need this information?" Antoine asked.

"No," she stated firmly.

"It was worth a try," he said. "Okay. Moving on. Your client list was sizable. Once you gave up a name, I knew exactly where to get the info. A reliable source on the political circuit out of DC said Garrett's assets are frozen, making him desperate for money—and in a position to need cash by *any* means."

Broke son of a bitch. But was he the blackmailer?

Desdemona stood a bit taller, pressing her flat palm to her stomach. "What happened?" she asked as she began to pace.

"He was under federal investigation for insider trading, tax evasion, and fraud," Antoine informed her.

Damn!

"Quite the trifecta," she said dryly.

"He's in talks for a plea deal," Antoine added.

"And you didn't let on why you asked about him?" she asked.

"I lied and told him Garrett wanted to borrow money from someone close," Antoine said. "I got the feeling there is even more going on. Something big."

Desdemona's mind was in overdrive, formulating and then tossing aside every conceivable notion of Hunter Garrett being her blackmailer. Each time she always came back to Red.

Were they still together?

Was the message . . . a *message*?

The timing could not be denied. The night before she's supposed to meet with the blackmailer—who doesn't show—and the next day she gets a dress order from Red.

Was it a setup?

I have to know for sure.

"Thank you, Antoine," she said, moving back through the dimly lit house.

"Tell me what is going on, Desdemona," he said. "Let me help you."

"How about I help you instead?" she asked, as she passed the closed office door again.

Tap-tap-tap-tap-tap

"With?" he asked.

"Propose to Astrid. Five years is a long time to feel like an option," she told him.

The line went quiet.

"You there?" she asked, turning the light on in her walk-in closet and removing her robe.

"Marriage?" he asked.

"It never crossed your mind?" she asked, chuckling a little because she knew he was on the other end frowning. Deeply.

"Wow," she said at the continuing silence.

She pulled out black leggings and a long-sleeved T-shirt, not even wasting time with undergarments. "I gotta go. Good luck with Astrid," she said.

"But I—"

Desdemona ended the call before tossing the phone onto the leather bench to get dressed. Her heart was racing—with excitement and not fear. It was time to ask Red just what was going on with Hunter Garrett.

And that *she does owe me.*

She pulled her hair back into a ponytail, tugged on some flat ankle boots, and pulled one of her crossover bags over her head before easing both her Taser and retractable baton into it.

"What the hell is going on *here*?"

Desdemona turned to find Loren standing there holding two flutes of what appeared to be champagne. "What is going on *there*?" she countered with a chin lift toward the glasses.

"I finished my book," he said with a deadpan expression. She gave him a smile that was wide and genuine as she took a flute from him. "Congratulations, Loren," she said warmly, holding up the glass in a toast. "To the first of many more."

They touched glasses.

Ding.

"Your turn," he said, not taking a sip of the vintage champagne like she did.

Desdemona slowly tipped her head back as she emptied the glass. "Loren, I have to go out," she said, setting the flute atop the glass jewelry case in the island.

She eased past him to leave the closet.

"What's wrong? Where are you going?" he said, coming back around her to stand in her path.

Desdemona set her hands on her hips and tilted her head to the side as she looked up at him. "Loren," she began.

"No. No, fuck that. *Fuck* that," he stressed, his voice deep and his eyes fiery. "Tell me what is going on, Desdemona. You just passed out from a panic attack yesterday and now—whether I'm your man or not—I'm supposed to stand here like a straight pussy and just let you leave in the middle of the night with no questions asked. You really trying to handle me like that?"

"*Let* me leave?" she asked with a cock of her head.

"I'm younger," he stated. "But I'm stronger."

Desdemona felt a thrill that she hid well, remembering the night he stood while lowering and lifting her body as he delivered one wicked thrust after the other.

"You not getting past me and we both know it," he said with confidence.

The lips of her intimacy figuratively applauded him and her fleshy bud throbbed to life while she considered dipping low, sweep kicking his legs, and landing him on his ass just to prove she could.

"Don't," he said. "You're plotting how to get me out the way and I can see it in your eyes."

Sure am.

"Why not try the truth?" Loren asked before taking a sip of his champagne.

Desdemona released a heavy breath and leaned back against the door as she crossed her arms over her chest.

"Why not trust me?" he added before another sip.

She eyed him.

With him, she had shared a hurt she long ago pushed down deep inside and afterward he had held her. Made her feel safe. Took some of the burdens off her shoulders.

In a way she had never allowed anyone to be there for her before.

"No questions?" she asked of him.

Loren eyed her for a few moments before finally nodding. "No questions," he agreed.

"I am being blackmailed for two hundred thousand dollars and I got a tip on his or her identity," she said. "I'm headed there now to confront someone who might reveal if he is guilty or not."

"Two hundred *thousand* dollars!" Loren exclaimed.

Desdemona gave him a chiding look. "No questions. Remember?"

"Technically, that was not a question," he pointed out as he finished the rest of his drink in a huge gulp that raised and lowered his Adam's apple.

"I'll be back," she said, pushing off the door to move around him.

He sidestepped in front of her. "Call the police, Desdemona," he said.

"And tell them—while I'm being investigated as a madam—that someone is blackmailing me to not turn over evidence of my being a madam?" she asked.

"Um. Oh. There's evidence?"

"No questions," she reminded him again.

Loren scratched his scalp as he shook his head.

"I gotta go," she said.

"Then I'm going with you," he said.

She shook her head. "No, Lo."

"Nolo? What's that?" he asked with a quizzical expression. "Like YOLO?"

"No, *Loren*," she stressed. "I'll be back."

"I'm going with you," he repeated.

She leveled her eyes on his face. "I don't have time for this, Loren," she said wearily.

"The sooner you agree, the sooner we can leave," Loren said.

Desdemona gave him a soft look. "Loren, so far your name has not been in the middle of this mess. You're innocent. Keep it that way," she said.

"And you're *not* innocent," he said.

This was the moment. *To trust or not to trust?*

"No, Loren, I am not innocent," she admitted, keeping her gaze locked on his eyes as she fully stepped into her truth.

And in his eyes, she saw him cycle through his feelings about her admitting to her past. Some she recognized. Others she did not. The one that lasted the longest was his conflict.

To love or not to love: that was his *question.*

Desdemona reached to grasp his wrist. "Stay out of it, Loren," she urged him before moving past him to cross the room.

She stopped suddenly.

Loren walked into her back.

She dropped her head.

"I'm going with you," he said from behind her.

"With or without your glasses?" she said, admittedly childish.

Loren stepped in front of her and led the way to the front door to hold it open for her. "You didn't worry about my glasses, if I had them on, while I was laying *dick*," he said as she bent under his arm to step out into the hall.

"Touché," she said with a quick, impish look back over her shoulder at him as they made their way to the elevators.

During the drive, Desdemona lost any sign of playfulness. Thankfully, Loren was quiet with his own thoughts as she wrestled with hers. She could only hope that Red was useful. It was a power play she couldn't afford to lose.

She parked down the street from the town house where Red was "kept." A four-story town house with a street-level garage on the Upper East Side. The first time she'd been there it had taken using valuable allies to gain the address. Hunter Garrett did everything possible to keep his owner-ship of the two-million-dollar home covert. Because of the shell company that owned the shell company that owned the shell company that owned the town house, she wasn't sure if anyone knew about the home ... or that Red was living in it. She'd barely got the heads-up about it.

Was Hunter being watched and followed?

Am I?

She checked the rearview mirror, not even sure what she was looking for outside of any other moving car on the street. There were none.

"I left this all behind, Loren. I want to be done with it," she said in a voice barely above a whisper.

"Then why are we here?" Loren asked.

She felt his eyes on her profile, but she kept her gaze locked on the brick structure. "Because I need to know so I can fix it and be *done* with it," she said, her hands gripping the steering wheel. "And then get back to the life I was trying to build. I swear, I want to be done with my past. I *was* done with it. Until the book. And then the snitch."

Loren covered one of her hands with his. She turned it over to grip it tightly.

"When I ran away from home, I was sleeping anywhere at night that was still open. I was so scared and alone, but I could not go back to that house," she confessed. "I was in a laundromat when this dude tried to talk to me. He said all the right shit. Looked good. Smelled nice. Was driving a fly whip."

Loren stroked her inner wrist with his thumb.

"He knew I was young and dumb and homeless. He offered to give me a place to stay and clothes and food. I thought he liked—I thought he loved me. Until he brought a man to the house," she said, pressing her eyes closed. "And told me I owed him for everything he *offered*."

She flinched, remembering the first feel of her pimp's fists and feet on her body.

Loren leaned over and pressed a kiss to her temple.

"Having someone hold something over my head and threaten me to do what they want just puts me back to when I had no power. No control. Of my own body. Of what to say. What to do," she continued, shuddering and releasing a breath. "I need this to be over. I need this to be *over*. I can end this bullshit. I just need to know who is trying to blackmail me. I need to know and then I can fix it, Loren."

"Then let's go fix it if we can," he told her.

Desdemona shook her head as she removed a pair of leather gloves from her crossbody and tugged them on. "Not we. Me," she said, reaching for the handle of the driver's door. "I'll be back. I just need to ask her a few questions. I'll do better alone."

"You sure?" he asked. "I thought you said you're checking if the blackmailer is this man you think it might be."

"He's married. I doubt he's here this time of the night. That's why I came now," she said, opening the door to exit.

Loren looked skeptical.

"I'm good," she said, closing the door before it became another debate and doing a light jog to cross the dark street.

Desdemona fast walked up the block. A quick glance back revealed Loren had exited the crossover and was leaning against the door, watching her. She reached the town house and climbed the stairs to ring the doorbell.

Red has to help clue me in on Hunter.

After another long ring, the door was snatched open.

She gasped a bit at Hunter Garrett standing there, disheveled, wild-eyed, and clearly drunk or high. He was a short, pale, balding white man, thick at the waist and reddened from whatever he'd imbibed.

"Here to delight in my downfall, Mademoiselle?" he asked, his eyes glassy and his words slurring as he held a snifter of some brown liquor.

"Where's Red?" she asked when he turned and walked back inside the home with an odd, zigzag pattern.

He is fucked up.

She stepped in but left the door slightly ajar in case she needed to get away fast. The house was dimly lit and in total disarray. The furniture, of French country décor, wasn't neatly arranged; the pillows were here, there, and everywhere. As were empty alcohol bottles and half-empty takeout food containers. On the table was an open vial of cocaine, with a credit card obviously used to line up the product for snorting. Nothing but the residue of the drug remained.

Hunter released a laugh. "That bitch left me today. No money—no *motherfucking* honey," he spat out before turning and tossing his glass into the unlit fireplace.

"Is that why you tried to blackmail me?" Desdemona asked as he slumped down onto the sofa to cover his face with his hands.

He laughed. It was maniacal.

She winced at it.

Hunter lowered his hands and exposed the lines of his already weathered face. "What you going to do, bitch? Huh? Go to the police?" he asked before another round of laughter.

"No," she answered calmly, trying valiantly to control anger that would cause a foolish misstep. "We both know I can't do that."

"The great and powerful purveyor of prime pussy, ladies and gentleman," he slurred, grabbing the neck of a spilled bottle of tequila to guzzle. "Madam—who gives a fuck—moiselle."

"True," she said, stepping farther into the room with her hand already inside her crossbody purse. "I'll even tell you what I don't give a fuck about, Garrett. You. Your fucked-up life. Your jail time that's coming. Not even that motherfucking plea deal you working on."

He cut his eyes over at her with his wet mouth still around the opening of the bottle.

It was her turn to chuckle a little. "I know about it. Did you think I wouldn't?" she asked, her voice low and cold as she walked to stand over where he sat. "Did you really think you would threaten me and get away with it?"

Hunter looked up at her. "Did you think you would steal my fifty grand and get away with it?" he asked. "How's that investigation going? I hope they lock your ass up."

"You first," she said, still calm, but it was lit because inside she raged.

The urge to backhand him was consuming her.

And the look in his eyes showed he probably wanted to do the same to her.

"Please give me even more of a reason to *fuck* you up," she snarled.

He laughed. "How?"

"Physically," she began. "*Or* I can contact the feds and get your plea deal voided and some extra charges thrown in for drug trafficking."

Garrett's eyes widened in shock and fear.

"You want a name? John Wicks," she whispered to him, enjoying the fear breaking through his bravado and high.

His thin lips quivered.

"I am the keeper of secrets. Did you forget?" she asked. "You better forget me. As far as I'm concerned, your ass is already forgotten. Let's keep it that way. Am I clear, or do I have to finish destroying you?"

Hunter Garrett glared at her even as his upper body wobbled a bit. He breathed heavily—huffing and puffing with no house to blow down. As the seconds passed, his eyes changed to some other emotion than anger and his top lip curled. Suddenly, he slipped his hand beneath the sofa cushion and brandished a gun.

"Shit!"

Desdemona looked back to see Loren had been leaning in the doorway and was now racing across the room to pass her.

Hunter raised the gun to aim it at her.

She drew her Taser with her left hand to stick it to his neck, but before she could, Loren grabbed his wrist and pushed his arm up into the air before delivering three swift, solid punches to Hunter's jaw.

Bap!-Bap!-Bap!

The gun dropped to the floor and spun away as Loren thrust him down onto his side on the sofa like a rag doll.

Loren turned to look down at her. "You got your answer. Is it done?" he asked in a hard voice.

Desdemona nodded as she slid her Taser back into her bag.

Loren took her hand in his and led her toward the still-open front door.

How much had he overheard?

She looked up at his profile. His face seemed carved in stone and his brows were down over his eyes as he frowned. Deeply. She glanced back over her shoulder. Hunter was on the floor on his belly, making his way toward the gun.

She snatched her hand away and took long strides just as he slid the barrel into his mouth as his body jerked with ragged tears. She stepped on his hand.

"Ah!" he cried out.

She bent and pried the weapon from his fingers. "I won't let death save you," she said before rising and leaving him behind as she removed the clip from the gun with plans to toss it over the bridge into the river

Desdemona stepped out onto the porch ahead of Loren but leaned past him to securely close the door, cutting off the echoes of Hunter Garrett's sorrowful tears. She paused before she descended the stairs to take a deep breath. At the very least, the blackmail was over. For *that,* she was weak with relief.

"That's a side of you I haven't met before," Loren said as they descended the stairs together.

Desdemona glanced at his profile. "Thoughts?" she asked, unsure of what else to say.

"I'm not sure yet what I think," he admitted as they crossed the street.

"Okay," she said.

They reached the car.

"I'll drive," Loren said, using the key fob to unlock the passenger door to hold for her.

Like always.

Desdemona climbed in and he closed the door before coming around to claim the helm of the Maserati. She turned the satellite radio to a jazz station. Soon the sounds of the melodic voices of Ella Fitzgerald and Louis Armstrong filled the silence.

Jazz always reminded her of her parents during those rare

moments she'd seen them together. She would sit on the floor, playing with toys, and watch them dance to jazz records. Smiling, laughing, and sharing tender kisses as they moved together around the living room.

It wasn't until she was older that she pieced together their story. He was a pediatrician and she was a nurse. As best she could assume, they worked together and began a dalliance. Seeing each other every day had made them give in to a temptation that his marriage to another woman should have forbidden.

Desdemona could only guess because back then she had been too young to wonder about her parents. After her mother's death, her name had never been spoken in her father and stepmother's home. Soon she caught on to the tension it brought to the house and she stopped mentioning her as well.

But I never forgot her. And never will.

"'Dancing cheek to cheek,'" Loren sang in a low voice along with the radio.

Desdemona gave him a side-eye. "What do you know about Ella and Louis?" she asked.

"My parents," he said with a wink.

"Me too," she said.

They fell silent again, but it was a bit more relaxed as he drove them toward Midtown. When he pulled the vehicle into her parking spot, she smiled at the sight of his battered Tahoe sitting in the other one assigned to the condo. It felt so normal when *everything* was anything but that.

Loren left the car running and got out to open the passenger door. He extended his hand to her. "Dance with me," he said.

Billie Holiday's "All of Me" played.

Desdemona took his hand and he guided her behind the rear of the crossover as the music resonated out of the open car doors. He held her hips while she crossed her wrists behind his head, lightly playing with a loose strand of his curly hair. She looked up at him as they swayed in sync to the music.

"I'm no good without you," she mouthed along with Billie, singing to the man she loved, about taking all of her because he'd already taken her heart and broken it.

So true.

His eyes studied her face.

Long after the song ended, they continued to hold each other and sway, as if both were afraid to let go.

"You ready to talk?" Loren asked.

Desdemona nodded.

Perhaps it was their last dance.

Chapter Thirteen

"I am Madam X."

They sat on opposite ends of the living room sofa but faced each other. When they'd entered the condo just minutes ago, Loren had claimed his spot first and Desdemona followed, wanting to see his face and offering him the same. It was required for the level of truth she was finally ready to give him.

He nodded and looked down to the hand-knotted silk area rug, as if letting the weight of that fully rest upon him. "I figured as much, of course, but thank you for admitting that to me," he finally said, still not looking up.

Trust no one? I have to. There is no other way to live.

"Ask me anything," she said. "*But* I cannot reveal the names of clients. Just as I would not reveal intimate details about ex-boyfriends. I don't believe a woman has to reveal every page in the book of her life to be seen or respected by the man in her life. But other than names, ask away."

He did look over at her then. "Were you ever forced? Violated?" he corrected.

Desdemona kept his stare. "Yes," she said, unable to stop her flinch.

Loren's hand atop the sofa balled into a large fist and he clenched his jaw. "Wasn't the Majig motherfucker supposed to protect you?" he asked, his eyes rimmed red with his fury.

"He didn't feel that way about it," she said, feeling so uncomfortable but fighting through the urge to run from their conversation.

He grunted in what could only be frustration. His gaze went across to the unlit fireplace. "So, you know you were a victim of sex trafficking?" he asked.

"Yes," she answered.

Loren rotated his shoulders, as if shaking something off. "I would kill someone for putting their hands on you, so this is hard," he said, his voice strained.

"Yes. I know," she said, thinking of how he'd protected her earlier. She hadn't needed it, but she had to admit that after years of taking care of herself, it felt good to be safeguarded.

"You didn't deserve that," he said with a shake of his head. "No girl does. Hell, no boy. No kid."

"Agreed," she said.

"Damn," he swore, looking away from her again.

"I was always clean. Always safe. Tested. Condoms," she offered, to ease any worries. "Always."

He looked over at her. "I don't want to know the years you did it. I don't want a number," he said, almost pleading.

Desdemona nodded. *I wish I could forget*, she thought.

"How did you become a madam? What happened to Majig?" he asked.

I let him die.

"He overdosed on heroin and I took over," she said.

Loren looked confused at that.

She could imagine the questions speeding through his mind.

You were free. Why not leave?

Why didn't you run?

Did you want to have sex with men for money?

"No, Loren, what really happened is I had worked my way off the street—"

He flinched.

"And," she continued, "I became his in-house girl and was just happy to be off the street. He got hooked on heroin and I started to run the business more and more. One day I went into his room and he was on the floor, OD'ing. All I could think right then was *I'm free.* No more abuse. No more bullshit. I left the room and shut the door, but then I went right back in to help, but he was dead already."

Loren's eyed were wide.

Desdemona was too deeply entrenched in her own emotions to rally for him. She tilted her head back, pressed a hand to the racing pulse at the base of her throat, and released a breath through pursed lips. For a long time, she carried guilt about those three seconds she left the room before returning. She felt his death had created symbolic blood on her hands. "For a moment, I was *relieved* he was dying," she admitted in a harsh whisper.

"Fuck him," Loren said. "You live by the sword, you die by the sword."

She lowered her head to look at him. "I was so determined to do it differently," she said, looking down at her wrist. "Instead, I should've walked away. Gone back to high school and then college. Healed all the brokenness of my past. Focused on me. Been able to answer: *Who are you, Desdemona?*"

"You sound like Professor Ophelia," he said.

"Cool," she said, having imitated that last line in her voice. "That's what I was going for."

She held up her wrist to show him the tattoo, *No Regrets.* "This changed me, when you came into my life with your positivity. I was already so bored and so done with being a madam. Going crazy. I stopped servicing clients five years before that just the way I told you, but I was tired of juggling a hundred balls to keep everyone safe, protected, and out of jail—including myself. Trying to be the mama to everybody that no one was to me."

"That's deep," Loren said.

"Yeah, it was, wasn't it?" she said, surprised by the revelation.

"And that's why you feel you don't have it in you to mother a child?" he asked.

She rested her head in her hand. "And I wasn't sure I wanted to be responsible for someone else," she said. "What if I fuck them up? A parent's job is to raise a good human being."

Loren looked thoughtful. "What you fear you can't do, you have done," he said. "The only difference is, it's a baby that needs your support, protection, and care."

Desdemona imagined herself pregnant and frowned a bit. "I'm not ready, Lo," she said.

"Understood."

She gave him a disbelieving look. "Really? You *understand*?" she asked.

"Okay. No, I don't understand, but I respect your choice," he said.

They fell silent. She studied his profile as he continued to stare off into the unlit fireplace. "Anything else you want to know?" she asked.

"The boutique—"

"Is legitimate . . . *now*," she stressed. "Has been since before I traveled the world for a year."

"If MQ didn't write the book and Garrett didn't tip off the police out of revenge, you went all that time without an arrest?" he asked, eyeing her in disbelief. "You're a criminal mastermind."

"I'm not proud of that, but in Nevada and many countries, prostitution *is* legal," she said. "And in my opinion should be decriminalized in the cases of two consenting adults choosing to provide or purchase a service. Also, decriminalization would mean an ability to regulate for better treatment of women and the exclusion of minors."

"I guess now I know why you ended things with me that time we debated prostitution," he said with a tinge of sarcasm in his tone.

"I will say that you helped me see some correlation between the porn industry and sex work with sex trafficking," she admitted. "But ultimately, it comes down to no one should feel inspired by anything to kidnap, rape, and then force women of any age to sell their bodies. That level of corruption isn't brought on solely by influences."

"This will lead to an argument," he said, rising to walk over to the window and look down at the street.

"It doesn't have to," she said. "I have a unique perspective on this topic we keep bumping heads about. I think you should respect my point of view."

He remained silent.

Desdemona crossed her legs and leaned back a bit against the sofa cushions. "I'm curious. Who is worse to you? A woman out enjoying the night and has a one-night stand for fun *or* the woman who did the same and charged money for it?"

He looked over at her with his mouth open to answer, but Desdemona held up her hand.

"The correct answer is neither because both should be able to do what they want with their body whether anyone agrees or not," she answered. "A woman has a right to be sexual *and* transactional."

He eyed her with those deep-set ebony eyes. "I doubt we will agree on this. Not now. Rain check?" he asked.

Why would you need a rain check if we're done being a couple?

Hope sprang to life.

"You want me to trust you. Right?" Desdemona asked as she stood up. "Come with me."

She headed out of the living room and down the hall to reach the owner's suite. His steps echoed behind her. When they reached the walk-in closet, she moved to her safe and unlocked it before facing him. "I'm a little worked up from everything—including our talk—so I'm gonna hit the gym," she said. "Inside this safe are things that are very important to me. Things I have never shared with *anyone* before."

The large sum of cash, her diaries from the days just after her father died up until she became a madam, and the fake credentials giving her a new identity.

Desdemona eased past him and grabbed a pair of sneakers to pull on before removing her crossbody. As she left him behind, it was a show of control not to turn back, slam the safe closed, and lock it.

Would he look inside?

Would taking the money tempt him?

Would the journal entries shock him?

She didn't know.

In the gym, she ran at full speed on the treadmill as she looked out at the city in the wee hours of the morning. She felt a bit anxious at the day's events, victorious at handling her blackmailer, frustrated at her exposure, apprehensive over being charged, worried about selecting a major, and filled with an innate fear that she made a mistake in trusting Loren with her truth.

She picked up the pace, grateful that she was alone in the gym without anyone to judge her. She kept going until her sneakered feet beat against the treadmill. Her heart pounded and sweat coated her body.

What have I done? What am I doing?

She pressed the keypad to slow the machine down to a brisk walk.

I told the truth. I needed to tell the truth. The secrecy was a burden.

Desdemona slowed to a stop and stretched her limbs before sitting down on the treadmill and using a hand towel to pat the sweat from her face and neck. She continued to release breaths through pursed lips with closed eyes.

With each passing moment, she realized on the other side of her fear was a lightness. A relief.

She looked out the window. In the distance, the sun was just beginning to break the darkness. A new day. Another chance to get it right. And for every life, there was a blessing of tens of thousands of new days. Opportunities.

An emerald-green butterfly landed on the window.

"Who are you, Desdemona?"

Resilient.

As she stared at the butterfly against the backdrop of the rising sun, she smiled and felt hopeful.

Whatever happened—come what may—she would get to the other side and move on. Like she had so many times before.

From arrest. Jail. Even heartbreak.

She rose and left the gym, tossing the towel into the frosted-glass receptacle by the door. She paused in the open doorway and looked back, remembering she was in the gym when she first learned of MQ's autobiography.

She'd gone to hell and back in the interim between then and now.

Four months ago.

Somehow, in the midst of it, she had found more of herself—even the one willing to defend a woman's right to be whatever she chose. As she left the gym and rode the elevator back up to her floor, she thought of how standing up for her opinion—her point of view—felt good. Empowering.

Was I right? I don't know. But it's how I feel. Still, I'm open to being taught differently. To grow and see things differently. To learn.

When Desdemona opened the door to the condo, she found Loren sitting by the unlit fireplace, deep in thought.

But still here.

And then she noticed her diaries stacked on the corner of the end table. There was a moment of unease. They were her private thoughts, but she *had* offered them to him.

But for what in return?

His understanding? Approval? Love?

"I didn't read them," he said as she claimed the club chair on the other side of the fireplace. He pushed the stacks toward her. "I wanted to, but I didn't."

"Why?" she asked, although she was happy to still have her privacy.

"You shared a lot with me, probably more than I wanted to know," he said, locking eyes with her. "And definitely more than you wanted to share."

"I don't know, Lo, I feel different for having told the truth. Like it, love it, or hate it, it's what happened. It's what I did. It's what was done to me. And all of that has shaped who I am today. And I am really beginning to know me and like me. And forgive me."

He leaned back in the chair and bent one leg to settle its ankle atop his knee.

"Can you do the same?" Desdemona asked.

"I love you," Loren said, his tone deep and meaningful.

"And I love you. But do you forgive me?" she insisted.

"For?" he asked.

"Selling myself. Helping others sell themselves. Not being sure about wanting children," she listed, ticking each one off on a finger. "Not telling you the truth."

"I'm trying to understand you," Loren said.

"But do you *forgive* me?" she pressed on.

He wiped his mouth with one of his hands. "I'm trying," he admitted. "Do you forgive me?"

She made a face. "For?" she shot back at him.

"Leaving."

"Are you coming back?" Desdemona asked.

He looked brooding but offered no answer.

"I won't beg you and the offer is not open-ended, Loren," she told him with direct eye contact as she ignored the excitement she felt at his gaze on her.

He rose from the club chair and headed over to the kitchen, then paused halfway there to look back at her. "May I?" he asked with his hand in that direction.

"Sarcasm doesn't suit you, Lo," she said.

He chuckled before continuing on his journey, soon returning with two bowls of fruit and glasses of orange juice. "I think I have something I need to reveal," he said as he handed over her portion of the makeshift breakfast before reclaiming his seat.

She slid a chunk of mango into her mouth as she watched him. The juice of the fruit burst in her mouth and trickled down her throat.

"My parents are unconventional. My father is reserved and my mother is a free spirit," he began before taking a deep sip of the juice. "But when I left for college and moved on campus, my mother told my father she needed her own place. She no longer wanted to share a living space with my father—her husband—of twenty-five years at the time."

His frown portrayed his disagreement with that.

Desdemona hid her surprise at his revelation. To her, his parents seemed so in love.

"She moved into the second-floor apartment, relegated my father to the basement apartment, and they shared the first floor as communal space," he continued. "I saw first-

hand how that demand hurt my dad. My mother owned the
house before they met. So he felt he had no choice."

"Are they still *together*?" she asked, unable to deny her
curiosity.

Loren held up both of his large hands. "Listen, all I know
is, when I visit, we all chill on the first floor. I have no clue
what goes on between them when I leave."

"Why didn't you tell me?" she asked. "It's not that bad,
Loren."

"I was embarrassed for my dad," he explained, picking
around in the mixed fruit in the bowl. "And I was determined never to allow something similar to happen to me."

"'It's a sorry rabbit that ain't got but one hole,'" she said,
remembering him saying that when she first discovered he
had kept his apartment.

"Exactly," he said sardonically.

Desdemona considered her next words carefully before
sharing them. "Perfection is hard to obtain or maintain, Lo,"
she said. "Let me offer you some advice, same way you
offered me some during the days you were my tutor. In your
twenties—"

Loren suddenly looked annoyed. He hated a reminder of
their age difference.

She smiled. "Let me finish," she said.

He splayed his hands. "Okay," he conceded.

"In your twenties," she repeated, "you see the world in
black and white. Marriage looks this way. A career should be
this or that way. Right is right and wrong is wrong. Right?
But then you get older. You live. You learn."

He eyed her with disbelief in his eyes.

"All of the dictates on what the perfect life should look
like change—especially with age, wisdom, and a desire not
to live by the rules if it means sacrificing your peace and your
happiness," she said, rising to move over to stoop beside

where he sat. "I think you're still a little idealistic, Lo. You see the world very simply when it's anything but that. Your parents' marriage may not look like Aunt Viv and Uncle Phil from *The Fresh Prince of Bel-Air*, but the key components are there, and that's love and respect. It's what I've seen when I have been in their company."

Loren shifted in his seat. "Idealistic?" he asked before picking up a strawberry to chew.

"And a little judgmental because of it," she added, the words rushed and almost running together.

"Are you serious?" he asked, sitting up straight to look down at her upturned face.

"Yes. Yes. *Yes*," she stressed. "As are most millennials."

"*You're* a millennial," he volleyed back.

"With a Gen X mindset, though," she added as she reached to clutch one of his hands with both of hers.

He chuckled and stroked the top of her hand with his thumb. "Listen, I should have let you know that keeping that apartment wasn't just about me and you," he said. "My parents' marriage played a huge role. I should have explained that."

"Cool," she said.

"But you're even richer than I thought," he said. "Just how much loot is in that safe, Desi?"

"A million," she mumbled before rising to smooth up her ponytail as she turned to walk away.

He caught one of her wrists in his hand. "Why?" he asked. "That's insane, to just be sitting around with a million damn dollars in a *safe*!"

"I have money in the bank too," she added. "And a couple of offshore accounts."

Loren jumped to his feet. "What!" he exclaimed with an incredulous expression. "I guess you're all ready to go off and live as Janet Anders, huh?"

"I could have. I thought about it, but I didn't. I'm *here*," she said, gripping his upper arms. "And I could be in Bali."

"Bali! Who are you?" he shouted animatedly.

"Desi," she said, with a simplicity meant to calm him. "Just Desi. *Still*."

It worked.

Loren released a long, drawn-out exhale as the tension released from his frame. "Yoooo," he said, looking up at the towering ceilings. "This is a lot. It's a lot."

That exposed his neck, and she licked her lips as she hungered to rise up on her toes to lick his throat, the way she knew he liked.

"Hell, right now we don't know if old boy done offed his damn self," he said, walking away from her to splay his arms wide. "With his crazy ass. And...and...and isn't that the dude off that weird conservative news show?"

She nodded.

Loren threw up his hands as he turned to face the windows. "Aw *hell* no," he said with emphasis.

She winced and hung her head but cut her eyes up to watch him pacing. He turned to walk across the living room and down the hall to the office. After a few moments, he returned with a lit, pre-rolled blunt. Pinching it between his fingers, he offered it to her. She shook her head. He continued over to the window to open it before leaning against the frame to exhale a smooth, thick silver stream of smoke.

Desdemona carried her glass of orange juice into the kitchen to add prosecco from a bottle she had in the fridge. "Fuck it," she muttered into the glass before taking a deep sip as she crossed the space to join him at the window.

Loren looked down at her through the haze before taking the glass from her and sipping from it.

"You do know smoking weed breaks from your persona

of educated professor, talented writer, and all-around Goody-Two-shoes," she teased.

He handed her back the glass and took a toke. "I'm not as idealistic as you think," he said while holding the smoke in his lungs.

She arched a brow and took another sip of her drink.

"Answer me this," he requested before turning his head to shoot the smoke out the open window. "It never crossed your brilliant mind to use all this money you sitting on to use a surrogate to birth our baby, or a nanny to help raise our baby?"

Our baby?

"Um, *I* would birth a baby if I'm able—"

He raised both brows. "Word! You would?" he asked.

This Negro.

"*No,* what I meant was *if* I wanted to have a baby, I would birth it if I could. *If* I wanted to have children," she said.

He gave her a sly grin before he took another toke. "And raising one? Where are you on that?" he asked with a playful side-eye.

"And forgiving me?" she asked, circling back to her earlier question. "Where are you on that?"

He bit back a smile. "My heart has. It's my head that's holding back," he said.

"No need to ask which one," she said dryly, hating the memory of his dick going soft.

"It's a *lot* to process," he stressed as an excuse.

"But you're worried about babies when that requires sex, Dr. Loren Marc Palmer," she said gently, as if explaining something to a child.

"Damn. My whole name," he said.

They shared a long look. The weed smoke floated around them.

Desdemona didn't smoke, but she found him sexy as hell when he did. His energy changed. His eyes lowered. His boldness increased. And when they had sex while he was blazed, he lasted even longer.

Oh, it's a definite vibe.

Her bud throbbed to life with pleas of its own.

Lick me.

Bite me.

Fuck me.

Desdemona pressed a hand to her belly as she turned away from the temptation he was not willing to satiate. She finished her mimosa before reaching in her crossbody bag for her phone. It was a little after six a.m. She already had missed calls from Jynn and Antoine.

She called Jynn as she sat down on the sofa. It rang just once.

"How's the patient?" Jynn said.

"Up and about," Desdemona said. "Thanks for getting me a doctor."

"No problem. He owes me a favor or two—and don't ask what for," Jynn said with a suggestive hint.

"Okay, I won't," she said, looking over at Loren, now leaning against the windowsill looking over at her.

His eyes were hot.

What does that matter if his dick won't get hard for me?

Still flustered by him, she cleared her throat and shifted her eyes away.

"You able to talk shop?" Jynn asked.

"Absolutely."

"The stunt your stepmother and *Celebrity Spotlight* pulled yesterday just upped your price—if you wanted one," she said. "I lost my shit when I found out you called in, but it might have worked out for the best. Public opinion is shifting in your favor even more than before. In fact, a prominent liberal feminist is doing an op-ed on the legalization of sex work and requested a quote. We declined of course, but it's gaining traction."

Desdemona said nothing at that but smirked a bit, thinking of voicing her same opinion to Loren on the subject just a short while ago.

"So I checked, and the statute of limitations has expired for pursuing criminal charges against your stepmother and the attorney for your father's estate," Jynn explained. "Unfortunately, by revealing on air that you had knowledge of the fraud at fifteen, that started the clock. It's six years in New York or two years from the date you became aware."

Desdemona nodded.

"But if you're insistent, there might be a way to petition the court to have the statute time extended. Question is, do you want to pursue this?" Jynn asked.

Zena in jail would *be satisfying.*

Even her stepmother's attempt to be messy and cruel had propelled Desdemona forward a bit. Into her truth.

No weapons formed against me shall prosper.

"Let me think about it," she said. "A lawsuit might just keep the bullshit going."

"Does she have money for you to be able to recoup from her?" Jynn asked.

Desdemona frowned. "Hell no. She lives in a house not big as my kitchen and nowhere near as nice. Trust, she is living in her own little personal hell," she said.

"Then *that* may be her punishment."

True.

"But what I can do is leverage her fear of prosecution against her and offer not to pursue it if she signs an NDA," Jynn offered.

"Let's do that, then. That's good enough. Just to keep my name out of her sour ass mouth," she said.

"What's the name of the attorney? His ass needs to be disbarred and I *will* see to that," she said.

"Hervey Grantham."

The line went quiet for a moment.

Desdemona looked over at Loren. His intense ebony eyes were still shielded a bit by the thick haze of smoke as he watched her every move.

"Are you serious?" Jynn asked, her astonishment very clear.

"Yes. Why?" she asked.

"I interned at his law firm when I was law school. He was my mentor. *Wow,*" the attorney said, drawing it out.

Desdemona tensed. "It's true. He was my father's friend and—"

"And Zena's lover," Jynn added.

"Yes," Desdemona stressed.

The attorney fell silent.

"It's *true,* Jynn."

"I believe you. My silence is me being highly disgusted and disappointed," the attorney said.

"So, will you still pursue it?" she asked.

"He's dead. He died of a heart attack late last year," Jynn explained. "I'm texting you some proof."

When the message arrived, Desdemona opened the article about the death of the prominent attorney.

Dead indeed.

"Desi, can I call you back?" Jynn asked, clear sorrow in her voice.

"Jynn—"

"I'm not gone lie. This one fucked me up. He was everything to me, or at least I thought he was. Listen, I'll call you back," she said.

The line ended.

"Desi."

She looked over to find Loren undressing with the blunt pressed between his lips. Her mouth fell open a bit as she eyed him. With every reveal of his body as he peeled away clothing, her desire rose. The defined, tattooed arms. His rock-hard abs. Every inch of his dick, which was deeper chocolate than his medium brown complexion. It swung as he moved, touching each thigh.

Lord.

Soon he was there, grabbing her wrist and pulling her to her feet to swiftly undress her. "I need to shower, Lo," she said, feeling her excitement build as he dropped the rest of the blunt into her empty glass.

He was on a mission. His intensity was turning her on. Point blank period.

"Fuck that," he said, nudging her back down on the sofa as he knelt between her legs and pressed his face to her intimacy to smell her with his eyes on her face.

He stroked her with two fingers.

She gasped and arched her back as he strummed her clit.

When he sucked her juices from his fingers, she felt her eyes warm over. "Lo," she whispered.

"Fresh as ever," he said with a lick of his lips.

"Don't start something you won't finish, Lo," she said as he bent to press kisses and take soft bites of her thighs.

"The weed won't let me give a fuck," he said.

She stiffened.

Wait. What?

He shifted up to press kisses to her belly before continuing to suckle one of her nipples into his mouth and circling the taut nipple with his tongue. It caused her to ache between her thighs as she arched her back and flung her head back with a cry of passion, seemingly pulled from deep within her.

He moved to the other. Much of the same. Deliciously. Shivers racked her body and her heart pounded in sync with the pulsing of her clit. She was too far lost inside their fiery chemistry and desire to deny him. Or herself.

Loren pressed her legs wide open with each of his hands until his arms were straight. "Damn," he swore as he looked down at her pussy.

Desdemona reached behind her head to grip the edge of the sofa as he let a bit of spit drizzle down onto her core before he used his hips to guide his hard, curved length inside of her. Slowly. Deliberately so. Her walls gripped him tightly, seeming to form to his shape as he filled her with every thick inch. His balls were tight with his arousal and she felt them bang against her asshole as he thrust his dick inside her. Picking up speed. Fast and hard. Deep and strong.

"Lo," she gasped, reaching out to press her fingertips to his abdomen to keep him from thrusting so ferociously.

He circled his hips, causing his rod to hit the sides of her.

"Ah!" she cried out in pleasure, rotating her hips to match his rhythm.

"Desi," he moaned with his head already tilted back.

Desdemona wiggled her legs to free them of his grasp. She snapped her legs closed and crossed her ankles before sitting them on one of his shoulders. She raised her buttocks and used her inner strength to roll her hips.

"Shit," Loren swore.

She felt his dick get even harder.

Next, she pressed her bare feet to his chest and pushed to make room for her to rise. "Sit down," she ordered him.

He did, spreading his arms wide along the back of the sofa, his dick saluting her and still glistening wet from her juices. She squatted above his lap before reaching behind herself to guide his dick inside her as she circled her hips with each inch she slid down on.

Loren's mouth shaped into an "O" and his legs shot out straight as he gripped the sofa in his fists.

And she rode him, pulling every sexual weapon from her

arsenal, determined to fuck his head up. She knew from his moans, whimpers, cries, and roars that she'd succeeded before she even picked up a furious pace that left them both sweaty and shivering until they cried out together as they touched the white-hot bliss at the same time.

Loren wrapped his arms around her waist and pressed his face to her cleavage as he filled her with his seed with each burst of his climax.

Desdemona stroked his hair and pressed kisses to his temple as she slowly worked her body to drain him of every drop until his dick was weak and spent.

But in the heated moments following their climax, as she waited for the pace of her clit and heart to slow down, she felt sadness creep in through the haze. Loren hadn't looked her in the face during their sex play. Not once.

Like he can't stand the sight of me.

She winced at that and closed her eyes even as he continued to hold her tight.

"The weed won't let me give a fuck."

Things *still* were not the same and, perhaps, never would be.

Chapter Fourteen

Tuesday, May 18

"Who are you, Desdemona?" Finally, I know the answer. I found me. I know exactly who I am.

Desdemona gave the test one last run-through before she turned it over on the desk and rose to her feet. She looked around the room to find all the other students were already finished and gone.

"Oh my," she sighed.

"I hope you did well, Ms. Dean," her psychology professor, Dr. Foster, said from where he stood behind a glass podium.

"I think so," she said, picking up her keys and bag. "It was the wise tortoise who won the race over the speedy hare."

The tall, solid man with full silver hair and beard chuckled. "True indeed," he said, removing his spectacles to slide them into the front pocket of his tweed blazer. "Good luck with *everything*, Ms. Dean."

"Thank you," she said as he began to walk around the room to collect all the test papers.

Was he speaking of the ongoing police investigation or just her classes?

Who knew?

She just took the well wishes in stride.

Desdemona left the room and walked down the hall, the steps, and then out the front doors of the building into the late spring sun.

It was the last week of final exams and the campus was already beginning to look less populated as students began to pack up and return home. Tomorrow her freshman year would officially be complete with her last exam—in history. Her break would be small. She was heading right into the summer session and had plans to take courses during the winter session as well. She was determined to graduate in three years and not four.

If I'm not in jail.

The investigation was still ongoing, but thankfully, with time, the hoopla about her every movement had died down. Her name was barely mentioned on *Celebrity Spotlight* after the backlash. She didn't even need Yusef's services anymore.

So far, every blockade she put in place to protect herself from arrest was holding the line and she still had a couple of tricks up her sleeve that she could only hope would work in an absolute worst-case scenario. But nothing was ever guaranteed.

Desdemona crossed the campus and entered the building where Loren's office was located on the first floor. It was small but neat and filled with books. When she reached it, she found him staring out the window, deep in thought.

As always.

He looked so good with his hair braided straight back, emphasizing his dark eyes and warriorlike cheekbones. He wore a dark blue shirt that complemented his complexion well. Although the man looked good in everything.

As always.

She leaned in the frame, wondering just how long it would take for him to notice her. And when that time went on far too long, she finally stepped into the room with a shake of her head. She cleared her throat.

He looked up and gave her a smile that made her heart skip. "How did it go?" he asked.

She moved around the desk to give him a slow, deep kiss that ended with a moan from them both. "I think I did good," she said, using her thumb to wipe away her sheer pink gloss from his mouth.

Loren reached around to lightly slap her bottom in the sundress she wore. "Good job," he told her.

She looked past him to the framed photo on his desk next to his computer. It was of them and his parents in their Brooklyn backyard during some lazy Sunday afternoon. The sun had been high and the mood chill.

She had yet to see them since she and Loren reconciled.

"Just one more to go," Desdemona said, giving his face a caress before moving back around the desk to claim the lone seat for a guest.

"You wanna head straight home to study or go have dinner first?" he asked, his eyes on her.

"We can just cook something or order takeout," she said, shifting her gaze away from him.

"We *can* be seen together outside of this campus and the condo," he said.

She licked her lips. "Until the investigation is closed—"

"Babe," he said, with a smile. "I know you don't want my name caught up in it. I know. But fuck it. We gotta live. We gotta enjoy life like we used to. Now, we just go from here to home like we're hiding or married to other people and cheating."

She gave him an impish look. "I'm not trying to hide you from the world. I'm hiding the world from you," she quipped.

He chuckled. "Okay, *Drake*," he drawled, leaning back in his seat.

They shared a laugh.

"Listen, you say you're okay with everything, but please know I am very aware that you have to get high to fuck me," she told him.

He looked surprised and then contrite. "You caught that, huh?" he asked.

"Yes. Absolutely," she said with a knowing look as she pointed at him, playfully accusing.

He gave her a sheepish look. "All I know is not being with you bothers me just as much as your past," he admitted. "When we broke up—"

"*You* left me—" she asserted with a slight tilt of her head to the side.

"Because *you* lied to me—" he countered, copying her move.

"While *you* had a whole secret apartment," she shot back.

Loren smiled and tried to wipe it away with his hand. And failed. "Tit for tat off the table," he said. "When we were *not together*—how about that?—I was miserable. Just now, my first sight of you in that doorway made me excited like I hadn't seen you in years, when we saw each other just this morning."

"Oh. The sight of me, huh?" she asked.

"Yes," he answered.

"Then look at me when we're making love," she said.

Loren gave her a slow nod. "You don't miss nothing, huh?"

"No-*thing*," she stressed.

"Okay. Okay. Bet," he said, clapping his large hands. "I'm struggling."

"Still?" she asked.

"Still," he confirmed with another nod. "No kids. Your past. Our secrets. It's still fucking with me. I'm human. I'm working on it."

"But you can't erase the past," she said, leaning forward to press the splayed tips of her fingers atop his desk to move from one spot to another. "You have to accept it or move on."

"I know," he admitted. "I *know*."

Desdemona sat back in her chair and crossed her legs. "I wonder if we're really any further along than when you first found out?" she asked. "The only thing added back is the sex—incredible though it may be."

Loren sat up straighter and held up both hands. "Not true. *I'm* back," he said, pressing one hand to his chest. "I'm there. I'm in it. Not knowing for sure if we'll ever have kids. Not knowing if you'll have to do a bid. Not knowing if I will ever be able to erase the image of you and…and… and…"

He let his words fade with a heavy breath.

"True," she conceded.

"Above all, I hate what was done to you. I hate the hurt you went through. I hate that shit still makes you cry. I hate I can't fix that part. I can't erase it any more than I can forget *anything else* about it."

She chuckled. "Anything else, huh?" she asked. "You mean, me sleeping with other men for money?"

"Whoa!" Loren exclaimed, his face incredulous and then pained. "Like *that*?"

"Like *that*," she asserted with a head movement. "Let's call a thing a thing and get at it."

"Yo! You wildin' right now," he said, leaning back in his chair with wide eyes.

She bit back a smile. She loved the guy. He was charismatic. "What?" she asked with an unbothered air.

"Desi," he said, as if pleading.

"But let me ask because I'm curious. Is the pussy not good enough? Like worn out? No bottom? No walls? Not tight? Not deep enough? *Too* deep?" she asked. "What?"

"No!" Loren barked with a loud clap of his hands. "Pussy good. Pussy *damn* good."

"Okay. Do you feel someone else had a bigger or better dick?" she asked. "What's your insecurity rooted in?"

Loren jumped to his feet. "Insecurity! What the fuck is going on right now, Desi?" he asked with a comical expression.

"I'm trying to get at the root of your problem so you can stop making me feel like you picked me up out the fucking trash, cleaned me off but I'm still filthy, and you're trying your best to see my worth through the dirt," she explained with a scrunched-up face. "Like fuck that, Lo. You're still judging me. Low-key. *Very* low-key. But *yes*."

"No," he said, before reclaiming his seat.

"Yes."

"Nah."

"Yes, mo-ther-fuck-er."

He bit back a smile. "Man, I love your ass," he said.

"I love you too," she said.

"Can we get something to eat?" he asked, rising to his feet again and opening a drawer to remove his beloved leather book bag.

"Fine, but we're not done with this conversation," she said, rising as well.

"I know," he said, sounding dejected about it.

She leaned back a bit as she eyed him. "Really?" she asked with a mock attitude.

Loren pressed a kiss to her cheek as he steered her out of the office so he could close and lock the door. "I wanted to celebrate something," he said as they took the elevator downstairs and crossed the polished floors of the lobby to leave the building.

Desdemona glanced over at him and then paused at the sly grin he wore. She grabbed his arm. "What? What's the good news? What happened?" she asked excitedly.

"I got the agent I wanted and she's excited about the book," he said. "Like, really excited."

"Loren," she sighed softly with happiness as she stepped in front of him and pressed her hands to both sides of his face. "Baby, that's *amazing.*"

He somehow managed to look both proud and sheepish. "I want to celebrate," he said. "Can we?"

She hated the instant feeling of discomfort. "And if you're linked to me?" she asked.

"I'm not worried about that," he assured her. "My issues about your past are my own, not the influence of other people or fear of what someone else would think. That I don't give a fuck about it. Trust me."

And she did.

"Where you wanna go?" she asked, relenting on her stance against it.

"Somewhere with champagne," he said as she eased one arm around his and continued their walk to the employee parking lot under the late afternoon sun.

"I know just the place," she said, thinking of the restaurant in Tribeca that was a converted carriage house with good food, great drinks, and a great vibe.

They reached his Tahoe.

"If I can live with this car, you have got to get over my past," she said dryly as he held the passenger door for her to sit inside.

"Not equitable," he told her before closing the door and coming around the rear to eventually slide onto the driver's seat.

Desdemona turned the radio on and frowned at the sound of the news station playing. "You would listen to this in the car," she said.

"Knowledge is power," he said as he started the car and soon reversed out of the spot in the crowded parking lot.

"In other news tonight, the death of Conservative pundit and businessman Hunter Garrett—"

Desdemona froze in place on her seat to eye the radio.

"—has been confirmed. Garrett, who was officially charged with insider trading, tax evasion, and fraud several months ago, was reportedly in talks to turn states evidence against several coconspirators in exchange for a lighter sentence."

Desdemona looked over at Loren. He was looking over the rims of his spectacles and frowning as he eyed the radio as well—looking comically older than his mid-twenties.

"His body was discovered in a vehicle registered to him and parked on the street in an affluent Manhattan neighborhood. All indications are that his death was due in part to an accidental overdose. There is reporting there were drugs and drug paraphernalia discovered with the body. We'll continue to update this tragic story as details come in."

Loren reached and turned the volume down. "He went through with it, huh?" he asked.

Desdemona gave him a solemn nod, not sure of what she felt about Hunter's death. No more than she had about Majig's overdose. Both deaths freed her. Hunter was yet another man who had sought to control her—his method was blackmail—and now his death meant her secrets died along with him.

Still, she took no joy in his or Majig's death.

"Could be someone helped him along with it because he was about to snitch," she thought aloud.

She and Loren shared a look.

"Not my dog nor my fight," she said, even as she was plagued by images of him sitting in a car getting high until he died.

"That's it?"

Desdemona glanced over at him. "What's that?" she asked.

He looked incredulous. "A man you knew killed himself. He's dead. The same man you threatened—"

"*And* you gave him a quick two-piece," she added.

"Right," Loren slowly conceded. "You find out he's dead and it rolls off your back like water?"

She frowned. "No, it did not. But I'm not letting it control my day. His death will not stop my test tomorrow. Or my goal of graduating college," she explained. "Do I wish he made another choice? Yes. But was it his life and his choice? Yes. It's okay for me to make peace with that, especially since another choice was to get me caught up in a police investigation that *still* might land me in jail."

"That's true," he accepted. "It's all been just wild as hell."

"Also true," she said.

They rode in silence as Loren drove them off campus and through the busy streets.

Bzzzzzz. Bzzzzzz. Bzzzzzz.

Her phone was now off of permanent "do not disturb" status. She dug it out of her bag. "It's Jynn," she said.

Loren slowed the vehicle to a stop at a red light. "Wait. What if the dude did turn over the evidence on you, knowing he was going to off himself?" he asked.

"He wouldn't. Would he?" Desdemona asked as she let the phone continue to vibrate.

Bzzzzzz. Bzzzzzz. Bzzzzzz.

"I don't know that guy," Loren said. "But the man I saw about to bite a damn bullet had nothing to lose. Not one *fuck* to give."

The call went to voice mail.

Desdemona waited and then checked it, putting the phone on speakerphone.

"Desi, hey. Spoke to Detective Wilson. Call me ASAP."
Beep.

"Well, that told me nothing," Desdemona said, closing the inbox and setting her phone on her lap.

"Or everything," Loren added.

"The writer in you with the alternate plot lines is wearing me out, Lo," she said, with an eye roll.

"Call her," he said, making a right and smoothly steering the large SUV into a parking spot on a side street.

"Not yet," Desdemona said. "I need to think."

"About?" he asked.

"You don't want to know," she admitted, casting her eyes out the passenger window to watch a couple walking up the street together.

"About?" he asked again.

"Whether to treat this whole situation like spades and play the Big Joker," she said.

She glanced over at him at his silence and was startled by his confused expression. "You *do* play spades?" she asked. "Or is your Black Card up for revoking?"

He looked insulted. "I'm confused by what you have up your sleeve, not how to run a Boston on whoever you team up with to play me," he said.

"Okay. Spades game on deck as soon as we make sure my ass is not headed up the river," she said.

"And what's your trump card?" he asked.

She shook her head denying him.

"One of your—"

"Consorts," she smoothly added before he could use a more vulgar term.

Loren put the car in Park as he sat quietly with his jawline rigid.

Gone was their playful banter from earlier.

"I may have held out long enough, Loren," she explained. "You wanted the truth. The truth is, were it not for me having to use business numbers to reach these people, because I destroyed the prepaid phones I assigned them all, I would have handled this a long time ago. *That's* the truth."

"And if he wanted something in return?" Loren asked. "Then what?"

Desdemona frowned. "Something like what?" she asked, her voice low and giving clear warning that he needed to tread lightly.

Loren twisted his mouth as he began to lightly tap his knuckles against the steering wheel. "Ass," he said.

Clearly, he took no heed.

"Take me home," she said.

He glanced over at her. "What about celebrating?" he asked.

"Grow the fuck up, Loren," she snapped.

He frowned. "I'm a grown-ass man," he retorted.

"Then pick a side. You want to accuse me of cheating and still toast your good news with me?" she asked. "Make it make fucking sense."

"So, you just want me to be fine with you reaching out to a man who paid to screw you—"

"Or screw one of the paramours who worked for me," she added.

Loren used both hands to grip the steering wheel. "You have all these fancy terms that don't change the act," he scoffed.

Desdemona opened her phone and began to swipe through Instagram as a diversion from the annoyance he was building in her.

"How do I know you're done with—?"

"Sex work?" she asked as she double-tapped a photo of a funny meme.

"Desi," he said.

She ignored him. "Take me home, please, and then maybe you should stay at your place," she suggested with a sly side-eye look at his profile. "You still have it. *Right?*"

Loren shifted in his seat to eye her with his disbelief highlighted by the streetlight on the corner. "Good thing too. *Right?*" he countered with sarcasm.

She said nothing, even as anger and hurt caused pain to radiate across her chest.

He pulled out of the parking space and they rode to Desdemona's building in silence.

"Your pride would rather I go to jail than exchange a favor for continued silence from yet another consort who doesn't want me to reveal a secret," she said, hating the need to explain even *that* much. "I swore I would never do something like that. Never. But to save me? Damn right it's an *option*, Lo."

"Call your lawyer back," was all he said.

Desdemona was tired of the fear. It was fleeting but still troubling. "I'm not going to jail to prove to you that I can be trusted by not calling on someone who can help me," she said before calling Jynn back and placing the phone to her ear.

Loren remained silent.

"Hey, Jynn," Desdemona said when the attorney answered.

"It's over, Desi. Finally, it's over," Jynn said with obvious relief.

Desdemona's entire body went weak and she dropped the hand with the phone in it to her lap as she closed her eyes. She had a thought and jerked the phone back up to her ear. "Wait. The investigation, right?" she asked Jynn with a raised brow, needing clarity.

"Yes. The investigation is officially closed. It's over," Jynn said.

Desdemona closed her eyes again and took the deepest breath she could before she released it slowly. Relief, gratitude—and a bit of moxie at her safeguards working— flooded her. *Thank you, God,* she mouthed.

She felt like weeping but fought it. Life had been pure hell. Finally, there would be a break in the clouds to let the sun shine down on her.

"Listen, I'm on my way to court. We'll do drinks soon to celebrate," Jynn said.

"Wait!" Desdemona shouted before the busy attorney could end the call. "The boutique? Can I let it go now?"

"Absolutely. That and the bail money you had set aside with me. I need to get back to you. I gotta go. And hey, *congratulations*," she said with warmth.

"Thank you. Thanks so much for everything," Desdemona said before ending the call.

She dropped the phone into the bag sitting by her feet.

"Desi. What? Tell me," Loren implored.

"The investigation is closed," she said, leaning back in her seat and setting her head on the headrest.

Loren leaned over to press a kiss to temple, cheek, and the pounding pulse below her ear. "Good, baby. It's over," he moaned in a deep voice near her ear.

She looked to see they were sitting outside the condo building.

Home. Well, my home.

"Loren, I'm not forcing this thing between us anymore," she said. "My past is a problem for you, and although I get it, I won't be tortured by it."

He turned in his seat, with his back to the door, to eye her.

She did the same in her seat as she continued. "You are the first man I chose to give my body. For five years I was celibate until I met you, Lo. Five years. And then I *chose* you. Now you have my heart, which gives you the power to destroy me—something I have never given anyone in my life. You know it all. No secrets. Something else I've never done in my life. What *more* do you want from me?" she asked, with her eyes locked on his as she set boundaries. "Because I don't have anything more to give. You have no idea how hard all of that was for me. My whole life has been protecting myself from hurt, from lies, and from jail. And I put all that aside to have you, so I don't have anything else to give you, Lo. *Nothing*."

His eyes studied her face.

Their silence was broken up by the sounds of cars whizzing past and horns being laid on.

"You have a choice to make—once and for all," Desdemona said, feeling strengthened with every passing moment. "If you're sure you want to share this life with me—as is—then let's celebrate both our big wins tonight. You have to decide to move forward with me or linger in the past... alone."

With that, and one last look at him, she picked up her bag and opened the car door. She fought like hell not to stop, not to beg, and not to break as she left the car. She took a moment to stand in the sunshine beaming down as fast walking pedestrians passed her. She smiled a bit when a blue butterfly fluttered about her before landing on her arm. She felt such peace and joy as she raised her arm to study the beautiful insect.

It too had been transformed.

Change is good.

Even if it means giving someone you loved the freedom to make changes of their own.

The butterfly rose and briefly touched her cheek—like a kiss—before flying away.

Without looking back to see if Loren followed, she crossed the sidewalk and entered her building, leaving him to his choice.

Come what may.

Desdemona stopped in the middle of the empty showroom. She smiled a little at the sunlight streaming through the window onto the floor. She took a few steps to stand in the light and enjoyed the warmth of it.

The song "Better Days" by LeAndria Johnson came to mind.

"Bet-ter days are co-ming," she sang, loud, off-key, without a care about it.

And she believed it. And nothing—or no one—would keep that from being her reality.

With the police investigation officially closed last week, Desdemona had immediately made moves to close the online boutique and showroom. It was her last tie to her past and had never been a true passion.

Time to let it go.

For a moment she had considered reaching out to Patrice, offering her the boutique, but she refrained. Her days of setting herself on fire to keep others warm were over. With time—and with the help of her psychology class—she had discovered that she had come to resent the help she offered people because she did it out of obligation and a savior complex.

And so she threw one hell of a closeout sale before shutting down the website and fulfilled all pending orders. She donated the remaining inventory to a nonprofit as a tax write-off and paid the hefty cost to get out of the last three months of her lease on the showroom.

It truly is over now.

Just like her relationship with Loren.

He had not come upstairs that night and they hadn't spoken since. She was cool with her decision and his. It was time to focus on her goals. Herself. Her happiness.

Life goes on.

She pulled her phone from the pocket of the tailored crimson pantsuit she wore. She dialed a number. Her Big Joker.

"Hello," a deep male voice said.

"It's great having friends in high places, Judge Young,"

she said as she looked down at herself and used her nails to flick away a small piece of lint.

Her former client chuckled. "Light work," he said.

"Thank you," she told him.

His blocking the warrant to search her home had saved her. She always had a backup plan for the backup plan of the backup plan.

Fuck with me.

"Still all done with the business?" he asked, clearly wanting another taste of Angel.

"Yes," she stressed. "For good."

She thought about Loren and his belief she would return a favor with sex.

He didn't even know me.

"Too bad," Judge Young said. "You take care, Angel."

"I will, Harrison," she said before ending the call.

Desdemona took one last look around the showroom before she walked to the door and picked up her red crocodile leather tote from the floor. She left the showroom and locked it securely, pressing her hand to the door for a few moments before walking away to conquer whatever life *tried* to throw at her next.

Epilogue

Two years later

"Professor Ophelia."

The woman looked up at the sound of her name. "Desdemona," she said with warmth before rising from her seat in all-white clothing with bold turquoise jewelry to wave her in. "College graduate!"

Desdemona entered the office with the scent of cocoa butter and a vintage perfume in the air. "Yes. All done," she said, setting her book bag on the floor before taking a seat. "Today was my last final."

The professor pressed her palms together and nodded with bright eyes and a toothy smile. "Watching your journey and being even a little part of it has been a joy...Madam X," she said with a playful wink.

Desdemona's mouth opened in shock.

Dr. Ophelia clapped her hands and laughed. "Of course I knew. I have a television," she said. "But you needed a safe place to fall and not be judged. It was my honor to be that for you. And now you don't need it anymore. I am proud of you, Little Butterfly."

Desdemona dropped her head. So overcome.

"The day Professor Palmer and I were exiting the library with those other professors, we were leaving a meeting about whether to expel you," her adviser explained as she rose and came around the desk to press a strong hand to Desdemona's shoulder. "Your young man fought like hell for you in that meeting. For his Desi, as he slipped and called you."

Desdemona looked up. "I didn't know," she admitted as her heart hammered.

"He never said?" the professor asked.

Desdemona shook her head.

"Even more commendable of him, then," Dr. Ophelia said.

Oh, Lo.

And she had been so angry at him for ignoring her that day.

"I am glad you found a way to accept who you are without shame and allow it to help shape the woman you are becoming," the older woman said, pressing a palm to her mentee's cheek. "And the journey never ends. I am *still* growing and changing."

Desdemona had earned her bachelor's degree in Women, Gender, and Sexuality studies, having stuck to her goal of graduating after just three years of hard work. Over the last two years she had become a staunch advocate of victims of sex trafficking and planned to pursue her master's degree in gender studies. Soon any charges of her promoting prostitution would be beyond the statute of limitations—in New York, at least—and she was considering speaking more about her past of being a sex worker and moving beyond it.

I'm still not ready yet, though.

She licked the dryness from her lips and looked down at the newest tattoo on her other inner wrist. *Independence*, she mouthed.

Desdemona felt she could trust the woman. "The secret is out—not confirmed—but out. There is truth in claiming every part of my life—good and bad. The Madam X exposure ultimately propelled me forward," she admitted.

"Who are *you*, Desdemona?" the professor asked. Softly.

"Free," she answered.

Dr. Ophelia softly applauded her.

Desdemona steered her Maserati through the busy New York streets toward home. "Hey, Siri," she said. "Call Melissa."

The phone rang twice.

"Desi Des. What's going on, college graduate?" the woman asked in an animated voice.

It made her smile.

After the investigation closed and most people forgot about Desdemona Dean, she had finally reached out to her friend and reconnected with her. Melissa had been forgiving. Thankfully so.

"I have two tickets for you and the hubby to come to the ceremony," Desdemona said. "Can y'all make it?"

"Benjie and I will be there," her friend assured her.

"Good. I'll drop them off at your house tomorrow," she said as she turned a corner—slowing down to allow a group of teenagers to cross safely before accelerating forward.

"See you then," Melissa said.

Friends were important—especially those who pretended the hoopla of Madam X never even existed.

And those who knew it was real but still reached out to offer support in the midst of the storm. Desdemona smiled at the weekend she shared in Atlanta with Denzin as she dialed his number. It barely rang once.

"Hey, stranger!" Denzin said, his deep voice filled with his pleasure.

"Me? You're the one traveling the world and connecting with your higher self," she said.

"And it's amazing, Desi," he assured her. "I am ready for everything the universe has for me."

Close to two years ago, Denzin moved to Bali and began his spiritual journey—complete with celibacy to help maintain his focus. While she had planned to move to the country to flee a possible arrest, he had journeyed there to free himself of the trappings keeping him from learning his purpose in life.

"I love this for you," she told him.

"And I love you, Desi. Always," he promised. "Whether we see each other again or not."

"Same, my friend. *Please* believe that," she assured him, feeling blessed for remaining cool with this man who once yearned to be her lover but had become an even better friend despite the distance between them.

With Denzin, she could give her past some honest reflection and even laugh about some of it.

"No plans to come back to the States?" she asked.

"Nah. Not right now," Denzin said without hesitation.

"And what about falling in love?"

He chuckled. "It will find me once I finish finding myself."

Deep shit.

With reluctance, they ended the call. They didn't speak often, but each time they did, it was with a kinship they both needed. Desdemona turned another corner to slow down as she reached the entrance for the underground parking garage of her building. As she pulled into her spot, she eyed the empty space next to her. She grabbed her bag and climbed from the vehicle to swiftly walk over to the elevator. She paused to see the same pervert she had to tase on the elevator years ago. She'd seen him in passing, but it was their first time in an elevator alone.

I don't have my Taser.

"Good afternoon," he said with a polite nod as he avoided her eyes.

In shame.

And possibly fear, after those wattages I shot into him the last time.

When the elevator doors opened, she hesitated to get on with him.

"You go ahead," he said, taking a step back. "I'll catch the next one."

Desdemona gave him a stare that warned of a beatdown if he stepped on, caring nothing about his contrite nature. She got on and turned. The doors began to close, but she stopped them with a hand to the edge of one and eyed him. "The same respect you're giving me now I deserved when you thought I was a prostitute. Stop relegating women to levels based on your misogyny and treat us *all* with respect," she told him, her voice hard and unrelenting.

He nodded and lowered his head.

She let the doors close.

Desdemona ran her nails through her auburn blunt bob.

Ding.

She pulled her phone from the side pocket of her tote to open the text. "Antoine?" she said with a raised brow that softened to see he sent a photo of himself with his wife of a year, Astrid, and their newly born twin boys.

"'Thank you for setting me free,'" she read the message aloud.

She didn't bother to respond. She hadn't heard from him since he gave her the tip on Hunter. They had both moved on. She was happy for him.

The elevator slid to a stop and she stepped off with long

strides to reach her condo. As soon as she unlocked the door and entered, the sounds of Chopin's 'Opus 55, No. 1' played. She smiled. Her love for the music would never cease.

Desdemona began to undress and move across the living room to the piano, now positioned in front of the windows, with Loren gently stroking the keys. He looked up at her through his stylish glasses and gave her a wolfish smile as he continued to play as he eyed her nudity.

Ever his seductress, she straddled his lap, facing him as he continued to strike the keys. Face-to-face, they kissed. Slowly. Passionately.

For the last year, his mother, Belle, had taught him to play the piece just for her. And with each day he was better and better—like *anything* he set his mind to.

Including loving me.

After three months apart, he had called her. He wanted to come home. He was sure of that and was willing to give up his studio apartment and his hang-ups with her past.

"The new book hit the *New York Times* today," he told her, his words whispering against her lips.

"Just like the first," she reminded him as she raised his shirt to massage the defined muscles of his lower back. "Let's see. My upcoming graduation. A new, heavily awarded, best-selling book for you. And a baby for us."

The piano playing ended with abruptness.

"What?" Loren asked, his eyes missing no nuance of her face.

She smiled. "Three months," she confirmed.

He looked down at her still-flat belly and pressed his palm to it. The heat of his touch felt delicious.

When he looked up at her, his eyes were brimming with emotion. "All good?" he asked.

Her smile and happiness were pure and genuine. "All *good*," she assured him.

A year of therapy with Dr. Townsend—formerly known as Destiny, when she worked for Mademoiselle while attending college—had worked wonders on her healing, making motherhood a desire for her.

With a ravenous smile, Loren reached behind her to close the lid of the piano before he pressed his hands to her waist and lifted her with ease to sit her atop it. She raised a brow and slowly spread her legs before he licked his lips and lowered his head to feast upon her. Desdemona tilted her head back, dug her fingers into his wild curls, and looked up to the ceiling, happier than she *ever* dreamed she could be.

Visit our website at
KensingtonBooks.com
to sign up for our newsletters, read
more from your favorite authors, see
books by series, view reading group
guides, and more!

BOOK CLUB
BETWEEN THE CHAPTERS

Become a Part of Our
Between the Chapters Book Club
Community and Join the Conversation

Betweenthechapters.net